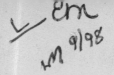

"Cowboy, you could be dangerous,"

Lauren whispered.

Still breathing rapidly, John unclasped her arms from around his neck and pressed her hands flat against his chest. His heartbeat raced beneath her trembling fingers. In a voice unsteady with passion he replied, "I tried to warn you earlier."

"I should have listened. I...we have to stop. This isn't the time or place for..."

He clinched her hand tighter. "For what?"

She couldn't very well say "making love," since love had nothing to do with the lust she was feeling. Somehow, though, it seemed more than just physical desire....

Dear Reader,

I'm not going to waste any time before I give you the good news: This month begins with a book I know you've all been waiting for. *Nighthawk* is the latest in Rachel Lee's ultrapopular CONARD COUNTY miniseries. Craig Nighthawk has never quite overcome the stigma of the false accusations that have dogged his steps, and now he might not live to get the chance. Because in setting himself up as reclusive Esther Jackson's protector—and lover—he's putting himself right in harm's way.

Amnesia is the theme of Linda Randall Wisdom's *In Memory's Shadow*. Sometimes you *can* go home again—if you're willing to face the danger. Luckily for Keely Harper, Sam Barkley comes as part of the package. Two more favorite authors are back—Doreen Roberts with the suspenseful *Every Waking Moment,* and Kay David with *And Daddy Makes Three,* a book to touch your heart. And welcome a couple of new names, too. Though each has written elsewhere, Maggie Simpson and Wendy Haley make their Intimate Moments debuts with *McCain's Memories* (oh, those cowboys!) and *Gabriel Is No Angel* (expect to laugh), respectively.

So that's it for this time around, but be sure to come back next month for more of the best romance reading around, right here in Silhouette Intimate Moments.

Yours,

Leslie Wainger
Senior Editor and Editorial Coordinator

Please address questions and book requests to:
Silhouette Reader Service
U.S.: 3010 Walden Ave., P.O. Box 1325, Buffalo, NY 14269
Canadian: P.O. Box 609, Fort Erie, Ont. L2A 5X3

SILHOUETTE BOOKS

ISBN 0-373-07785-8

McCAIN'S MEMORIES

McCAIN'S MEMORIES

MAGGIE SIMPSON

Silhouette®

INTIMATE™ MOMENTS®

Published by Silhouette Books

America's Publisher of Contemporary Romance

MAGGIE SIMPSON

is the pseudonym for the writing team of Saundra Pool and Margaret Masten. The authors, who live within blocks of one another in their Texas town, also work together at a local school. They are thrilled to be contributing to Silhouette Books.

You can write to them in care of Silhouette Books, 300 East 42nd Street, New York, NY 10017.

To our family and friends, who encouraged us not to give up our dream.

Prologue

As if apologizing for the heat of the impending day, cool moonlight bathed the rugged mountain peaks and cast soft shadows across the lone rider threading his way through the scrub of the Chihuahuan desert. The cowboy stopped when he came to a small stream, dismounted, and after glancing over his shoulder, slapped the lathered flanks of his horse, sending him north. Being afoot in this desolate area was a chance he had to take. His only hope of survival depended on his pursuer following the tracks of the horse instead of him.

Trying to maintain his balance on the pale limestone rocks littering the normally dry riverbed, he waded through a stream that had formed after a rare thunderstorm. He was tired and hot despite the chilly night air waltzing with the mesquite and tamarisk on the bank. The seductive tree limbs swayed to a phantom one-two-three beat as if pleading with him to join them in one last dance. The promise of comfort and peace almost overcame his need to survive. Death would be a sweet mistress, sweeter than anything he'd seen in a long time. All he had to do was give up and let gravity pull him to the ground. When he felt his knees weaken, he caught himself. He was losing his mind. The loss of blood had caused him to imagine things.

Licking his parched lips, the cowboy carefully fingered the encrusted mass of hair covering his left temple. His hat was long gone. He'd given up trying to remember what had happened to it. And the bleeding had stopped hours ago, but the throbbing pain still made coherent thought difficult.

Desperate to rest, but knowing dawn would break in a few hours, he knelt down and splashed his face with the cool rainwater trickling its way to the Rio Grande. He tore away part of his shirt and soaked it so he would have something to hold against his burning forehead, then he took one last handful of water and sipped it like fine wine. Soon, in the heat of the day, there would be no more water. The last of even this precious trickle would evaporate.

His unsteady gait caused him to slip as he climbed to the opposite bank. He prayed his boot prints trudging up the sand wouldn't be noticed. Not that it really mattered anymore. Wounded, without water or somewhere to go for help, he wouldn't last long in the desert. Standing erect, he scanned the limestone cliffs towering in front of him, looking for a hiding place. A place to die, where neither his pursuer nor the vultures lurking in the crevices overhead could get him. Some fifty yards away, a ledge jutted from the cliff face. There, hidden by the brush, he could lie down and rest. Slowly he made his way through the rough growth stabbing his legs. The rocks clawed at his hands as he pulled himself upward one inch at a time, one hand above the other. It took the last of his energy to drag himself up on the narrow flat rock. He rolled onto his back and took several deep breaths before he noticed that the spindly branches of a small tree guarded an opening in the limestone. A cave.

Maybe there was a God, he thought, crawling into the dark interior of the cavern. Maybe he wasn't meant to die, after all.

Chapter 1

Lauren Hamilton sat up a little taller in the saddle and took a deep breath of the crisp morning air. It felt wonderful to be back home for Thanksgiving, even if it was only for a long weekend. This morning, miles from any other habitation, the world seemed simpler somehow, and purer, a long way from the petty crimes of Sierra, Texas, where she lived and worked.

She tugged the khaki jacket tighter around her chest when a breeze rose to meet her as she descended the winding trail among rocks and scraggly wildflowers to the canyon bottom. Skirting a needle-tipped agave nestled beneath a ponderosa pine, she eased up on the reins and allowed Doc to pick his way between large boulders and ill-placed trees as she surveyed the majestic cliffs towering above her. Her fingers itched to get out her camera and take advantage of the unusual light filtering into the canyon, the resulting shadows.

It had been years since she had visited this remote area of the family ranch, but it still inspired the same awe that it had when she was a child. Her own small house in Sierra was only hours away in reality, but eternities away in feeling. Diablo Canyon was still completely untouched by the civilized world.

Pebbles dislodged by the hooves of her horse rattled down the path, creating the only sound besides the whisper of the wind through the tall cottonwoods that lined a nearly dry streambed. Coming to a small pool that remained after last night's thunderstorm, she stopped to water Doc.

Swinging from the saddle, she hopped to the ground and tossed the reins into the scrawny grass that lined the bank. Doc would drink and graze close by while she worked. She patted his flanks, then untied the saddlebags, pulled them down from behind the cantle and rummaged through them in search of her 35 mm camera. Photography was her hobby, her escape when the world of briefs, depositions and courtrooms began to close in. But in the past six years, while she struggled to make a go of the small law firm she shared with Robert Jordan, there had not been enough time to pursue this interest. Now, for a few precious hours, she was going to indulge herself.

She hung the camera strap around her neck and adjusted the new telephoto lens she'd bought just for this weekend. Looking through the viewfinder, she scanned the line where variegated cliffs rising from the canyon floor met the brilliant blue of the southwestern sky. Detecting the slightest movement, she focused on what she hoped was the fleeting image of a mountain lion and snapped the shutter just as she heard a loud pop, followed by what sounded like thunder reverberating off the canyon walls. Nearby, Doc threw his head up, searching for the source of the unfamiliar noise.

Though Lauren hadn't heard it since hunting with her father and brother as a teenager, she recognized the sound of a rifle shot. Who would be hunting on her father's ranch? Poachers? She froze, listening for anything that would help her locate their position. Nothing. But the silence made her uneasy. She wasn't given to fearful hysterics. She was too professional for that, but something was very wrong. Like Doc, she raised her head, trying to catch a scent, a feeling on the morning air.

The smell of danger was almost tangible. Perhaps it was the odor of gunpowder, but she was too far away from the source for that. Watching the rim of the canyon, she slowly began to ease backward, searching with an outstretched hand for the safety of the boulders and brush that lined the arroyo. When a second shot rang out, this time ricocheting off a nearby rock, her terrified horse bolted and took off up the canyon. Damn! Now she was stranded—with someone shooting at her!

Adrenaline raced through Lauren's blood, while her gaze flew back and forth from the canyon rim, where the shots came from, to the rump of her galloping horse. The horse would return to the ranch headquarters and her brother, Ted, would come looking for her.

She just hoped it wouldn't be too late. Grabbing her pack and instinctively protecting the camera around her neck, she dived for cover just as a third shot knocked leaves from the tree where she had been standing. Now she was certain. Someone was deliberately shooting at her!

Crouched behind a large boulder, she waited and tried to calm her pounding heart. She had to think, to figure a way to get out of there. Who would shoot at her? No one but her father and brother even knew she was riding to the canyon. This all had to be a mistake. When the person above realized he was shooting at the wrong thing, namely her, he would leave. But even as she rationalized, she sensed the danger stronger than before.

Then she heard rocks above her rolling to the canyon floor, as if someone was knocking them loose in a frantic scramble down the cliff face. The person was coming after her!

Afraid to rise up and look to see who might be searching for her, she took a deep breath. She had to think of a way out, a way to escape from the mad person she could hear thrashing through the brush along the trail that would eventually lead to her hiding spot. Never in her life had she been this scared. Focused on surviving, she gazed upward at the towering cliffs for anything, anything at all to aid her escape.

Then she remembered a cave. A cave where, as teenagers, she and Ted had explored dark recesses and discovered Indian artifacts. She could hide there if she could slip through the rocks and brush without being seen. A sense of hope washed over her.

The sounds of her pursuer came closer. He—for some reason she assumed it was a man—was making no effort to mask his movements. It was as if he knew she was defenseless. Frantic, she picked her way around the base of the cliff until she thought she was out of his line of sight. Then, fighting the absolute terror that threatened to paralyze her, she clutched her saddlebags in one hand, steadied the camera swinging on the cord around her neck with the other hand and dashed toward the cave. Seconds could mean the difference between safety and death, but she had to try to protect her food and water supply in case she was stranded for a long time. And the camera held the only possible evidence of who her pursuer was. A person who, through his rifle telescope, had spotted her taking his photograph and tried to either frighten her away or kill her.

When John McCain heard the report of a rifle echo off the cliffs, he bolted upright and grabbed for the gun on his hip. It wasn't there. Damnation! He groped around on the cold stone floor, but his fingers contacted only a few loose rocks. Then he remembered that his six-shooter had been taken away from him in San Elizario just before he'd been locked in a tiny room with the other prisoners.

He shook his throbbing head, trying to clear the grogginess that engulfed him. Certain he'd slept for quite a while, he had to pause a moment before he remembered where he was and what had woken him. A second, then a third gunshot left no doubt. He cursed Cardis, thinking the man must have found his tracks and was signaling his vigilantes to come get the gringo. And there he sat, defenseless. How he hated the feeling of being at someone else's mercy.

Determined not to await his fate like a caged animal, John edged toward the mouth of the cave to get a better view of the canyon below, so he could make plans to escape, to lay low or to kill his pursuer. When he bumped against a rock projecting from the low ceiling, pain radiated through his temple, where a bullet had grazed him. He shook his head, trying to clear up the dizziness. Memories of the firing squad assailed him, but he couldn't dwell on that. Not now.

Swallowing back nausea, he crawled toward the shaft of light penetrating the small cave. He hoped to find the threat lurking below before it found him, but large cottonwoods and mesquite trees shielded most of the canyon floor from his view. The deep shadows of early morning made things hard to see, but he thought he saw a deer dart from behind a large boulder to the rocks directly below him. The deer must have been spooked by the gunshots, too.

When he realized it was a man in a dun-colored shirt and dark hat heading for the cave, John retreated into the blackness to hide and wait. There was no place left to go. But he wasn't dying without a fight. He'd be damned if he wouldn't take at least one man with him.

He didn't have to wait long before a slight figure reached the opening of the cave, a shaft of light bathing its silhouette in a golden halo. It appeared to be a young lad not much over five feet tall—too short to be Cardis, but possibly one of his men. Soundlessly, with the grace of a predatory animal, John rose and crept forward. He wanted the element of surprise.

The boy paused to catch his breath and to peer out at the canyon, as if he expected to see something or someone following him. Then, apparently satisfied, he removed a strap from around his neck and laid a bundle on a rock ledge just inside the cave entrance. The lack of light prevented John from seeing the boy's features, but there was enough to outline his slight shape. John watched him hug his arms to his chest to quell the sudden trembling that shook his body. The kid was scared, but soon seemed to gain his composure and turned to enter the darkness.

When the youngster walked past his hiding spot, John grabbed him from behind and hauled him back against his chest before realizing his mistake. It wasn't a lad at all, but a woman. A small woman with soft breasts he could feel against the muscles of his arm. A woman who smelled of some exotic flowers. What was she doing out here?

The woman twisted and kicked to free herself from his embrace, causing her hat to topple off and her hair to brush against John's chin. Immediately the scent of flowers intensified. He fought the protective feelings the feminine scent evoked. And rightly so, because just as he was considering treating her like a lady, she delivered a swift hard kick to his shin and opened her mouth to let out a howl. She was as strong as her hair was soft, he thought, muffling the sound of her scream with his hand and bending close to her ear. Her warm, moist breath spewed over his fingers as she fought for control.

"Be quiet and hold still." His voice didn't sound like his own, but it had been days since he had spoken. He was hoarse and his throat was so dry it cracked.

Instead of obeying, the woman thrust an elbow hard into his lower abdomen and tried to push away. He caught his breath in pain. Hell! She could pack quite a punch for someone so small. He clenched her tighter until he again became aware of her softness against him. If only he felt better he could have appreciated the fact that he held a woman, but now he ached all over, and to top it off, they were both in danger. He didn't want to hurt her, so he had to make her understand. "I said shut up or you'll get us both killed."

When she stopped thrashing around, he took it as a good sign and continued, "Now, what are you doing way out here?"

At first the woman didn't answer, then he felt some of the resistance in her muscles relax. But he didn't loosen his grip. He didn't want to be punched again.

She took a breath and with a slight quiver whispered, "I was…"

When he leaned closer to hear better, he felt the smooth skin of her cheek for the first time, and again he was reminded he held a woman. How long had it been? Years? He couldn't remember.

She continued, a little stronger this time, "I was…riding when someone took some shots at me."

Her voice was husky with fear, but it was the shock of her perfect English, rather than the expected Spanish accent, that caused him to loosen his hold. What was a white woman doing out here in this West Texas desert? The handful of Anglo women in the region, all wives of successful El Paso businessmen, never went anywhere alone. Not only was this one out alone, but she was dressed like a man. Why? He'd find out later, but at the moment it was more important to determine whether she had been followed. "Did they see where you went?"

"I don't think so," she said, shaking her head against him, her hair brushing his cheek. "And I only spotted one man."

That she'd seen only one man worried McCain. It meant that the men riding with Cardis could be anywhere—waiting. "What happened to your horse?"

The woman seemed to be calmer as she answered, "He bolted and ran when the shots were fired."

John didn't know if he should believe her or not, but he really had no other choice at the moment. "Where will he go?"

"Back to the barn." She said it matter-of-factly, but John knew there wasn't a ranch house within a day's ride.

He played along with her. "How far is that?"

"An hour or two, depending...."

He felt her shrug against his chest. She sounded so honest, but there was no way what she said could be true. There was no type of shelter so close by. He wanted to turn her around to face him, though he couldn't read her eyes in the total blackness.

If what she said was true, someone would come looking for her in four or five hours, and he, Captain John McCain, would be discovered, wounded, cowering in a cave. But no, she had to be lying.

No one was going to come. Still, he felt vulnerable. They had to get away from the front of the cave. As he took a step, his boot bumped against a bundle the woman had dropped on the floor when he grabbed her. He held on to her upper arm while he bent to pick it up. His groping hand contacted what he immediately recognized as leather saddlebags. Maybe they held food and water. His stomach rumbled at the thought.

When he straightened up, a wave of dizziness washed over him and he clung to her to keep from falling. His fingers dug into her flesh as he steadied himself. "Come on. Let's go back a ways. We don't want to make ourselves sittin' ducks up here."

Thrusting her before him so she couldn't possibly see him, he turned toward the darkened interior of the cave. The blackness folded around them. When he stopped and looked back at the light, he felt her shiver, perhaps because of the chill in the air, but probably due to her fear, a fear he could feel. A fear he shared.

When they were far enough into the cave that he would have time to react if someone entered, he stopped. The woman stumbled against his side before she caught herself and tried to pull away. Not again, he thought. He really didn't have the strength to fight her if she put up a struggle. But maybe she hadn't realized how weak he was. He tightened his grip, hoping to bluff her into submission. Though her bones were small, she didn't feel fragile. She felt dainty and feminine, but not weak. He knew that from experience.

He wondered what she looked like. Was she pretty? What color was her hair? Her eyes? If he was a betting man, he'd bet she was a real looker.... He brushed the thought from his mind. Hell, the last thing he needed was a female to mess things up right now. His life was at stake.

He didn't know how long he had been unconscious earlier, but it seemed like it had been days since he'd taken a drink from the shallow creek. His throat ached. He pressed the soft leather of her saddlebags against her arm. "Water. Do you have some water in here?"

"I don't remember." The woman didn't move. She stood absolutely still, as if wanting to try his patience. And she was succeeding.

Disgusted, he said, "Why don't you check?" He didn't want her pulling a knife or gun on him, so he maintained his hold on her arm while she fumbled around in the saddlebags.

He hadn't realized he had been holding his breath until she pulled out an object and said, "Here."

"You open it," he said, determined to keep at least one hand free if she should try anything. Hiding his desperate need for a drink, he willed himself to stand still while the squeak of the metal cap being slowly turned echoed off the cave walls. Finally, she handed him an open canteen.

The musty smell of damp earth teased his nostrils as he

took the canteen in his free hand and raised it to his cracked lips. At first he allowed the liquid to trickle slowly down his throat, then he began to drink deeply, relishing the cold, life-giving fluid.

Feeling almost human again, he reluctantly handed the canteen back to her. "Much obliged."

"Think nothing of it."

Though she'd said only four sarcasm-laced words, they were spoken with a slow drawl that reminded him of the Southern women he'd grown up with. It was a voice that wrapped itself around a person, seductive in its naiveté. He was still bewildered by her presence here. With less than a hundred white people in the whole territory and only a few of them women, he was confused that she would be in this rugged and remote area.

After returning the canteen to her pack, she asked, "What are you going to do now? We can't just—" The distant sound of tumbling rocks interrupted her. "Listen."

He strained to hear. As the noise grew louder, he felt the woman edge closer to him, as if asking him to protect her from the person outside. He doubted she was even aware that his fingers had grown slack in their hold, and the only thing keeping her near him was her own free will. He pressed a finger to her lips to keep her silent.

"Stay where you are," he whispered, "while I go see who it is."

She pulled out of his loose grip. "No way. I'm going, too." Although her voice was a whisper, it radiated strength. And stubbornness.

He caught her to him and bent close to her ear. "If you want to get killed, go right ahead. I'll be right behind you, though, so don't do anything stupid. If you so much as make a sound, just one peep, I'll kill you. Do you understand?" It was a bluff. He wouldn't kill her, but she didn't know that. He felt her nod her head against his shoulder, indicating she understood him.

Not at all trusting the woman to remain quiet, he tightened his grip on her arm as a warning before he released her and crept toward the mouth of the cave. The blazing sun was just rising above the canyon rim, illuminating everything in the canyon one inch at a time. But even with its help, he couldn't see who had dislodged the rocks. Crouched at the side of the entrance, with his back to the wall so the woman couldn't jump him from behind, he waited until he saw a man crossing to the other side of the canyon. When he was satisfied the figure was moving away from the cave, he rejoined the woman in the dark recesses. Maybe they were safe for a while.

"Was it him? The man who shot at me?" she asked, her voice barely a whisper.

"I don't know for sure who shot at you, but this was likely the same man, and he's headed away from us, going farther up the canyon."

"Who do you think it is?"

"I have no idea." It wasn't really a lie. John hadn't recognized anything about the figure.

"I don't believe you," she challenged, her voice slightly stronger. "You were expecting someone, weren't you?"

John felt around in the darkness until his hand brushed the woman's shoulder to reassure her—and restrain her if he was forced to. He still didn't trust her not to run at the first real opportunity. Just because she had remained quiet once didn't mean she was on his side in this.

He felt her stiffen as he ran his hand down her arm, seeking her hand. When he closed his fingers around her cold ones and pulled her closer to him, the breath she had been holding escaped against his chest and she wilted slightly. He couldn't tell whether it was from relief or from fear, but her unconscious response made him feel guilty. He didn't really want to frighten her. He just wanted her to keep quiet. "I'm not sure I know who it is. I thought I did, but I don't understand it myself." Cardis wouldn't operate the way this man had. Cardis would have come charging down the canyon with a whole posse of Mexicans.

"What's there to understand?" Her voice pleaded with him to explain what was happening.

He shrugged. There was no way he could explain that her very presence, a female where there weren't supposed to be females, made him unsure of himself, of Cardis, of the whole god-awful situation.

She repeated her earlier question. "What are you going to do?"

"I'm going to sit right here and wait." Until he figured out if she'd been seen entering the cave, or if she'd been sent to the cave, or if the man outside was truly leaving, there was nothing else he could do. Besides, he was so weak it was an effort to remain standing.

"Wait for what?"

Her repetitive questions were beginning to tire him. "To make sure the man who shot at you leaves."

"I still don't understand why he shot at me."

"Well, at the moment, lady, I can't help you solve that riddle." He didn't tell her that Cardis had shot at him, too—from a firing squad. John wanted to ask her some questions to learn if there was a connection, but a sudden wave of dizziness, from hunger or loss of blood, left him feeling light-headed. He didn't know how much longer he could stand upright without assistance, so, setting aside his need for answers, he felt for the cave wall with his free hand and slowly levered his body to the floor. "Lady, I need some rest in the worst way. Why don't you lie down here beside me?"

She hesitated as if weighing her options before she tried to pull away. "No."

He squeezed his fingers around her hand. "Come on, I don't have time for games. Look. What I said about killing you before, that was just to get you to be quiet. I can't risk you giving away my hiding place if you try to leave." He tugged her downward until she stumbled and almost fell to the floor.

He caught her to keep her from hitting the rock, and for a split second her slight weight pressed along his body before she pulled back and rested on her heels. She appeared to ignore the fact that he had pulled her down on top of him. Maybe she wasn't as aware of him as he was of her.

In a voice that seemed to reflect a sudden insight, she said, "That man is after you, not me, isn't he?"

"It looks to me like he's after both of us," he told her, settling back against the cold wall.

The woman sitting unwillingly by his side asked insistently, "Who are you?"

"We'll both be a lot safer it you don't know." It sounded trite, but it was true. He was sure there was a price on his head, because Cardis's pride wouldn't allow Ranger John McCain to live. If this woman really didn't know who he was, he sure wasn't going to tell her and endanger her further.

"What have you done that you can't tell me who you are?"

He knew by the tone of her voice she was beginning to think he was an escaped convict. In a way she was right. He'd just let her think that, he decided, and maybe she would be scared of him and not give him any more trouble. Playing on her growing doubts, he growled, "You sure ask a lot of questions that are none of your business."

At her silence, he edged into a prone position and pulled her against his side to restrain her. He had to keep her close in case she tried to get away while he slept, but he hadn't counted on the way her body would feel pressed to his. Even in his beleaguered state, he was very aware of the warm curves against his arm, of the loose tendrils of hair spilling across his shoulder, and her scent. Oh, the glorious scent of a woman—the blend of flowers and clean skin and just a hint of musk that stirred his half-dead senses as he began to slip into unconsiousness.

Her sudden squirming, as if to get away, had him instantly alert. "Listen, lady. I'm not going to hurt you, so be still. I have to get some rest," he told her harshly.

In a surprising display of submission, the woman obeyed him, and after some time, his body started to relax, only to be jarred again as she began shifting as if trying to get comfortable on the hard floor. He was never going to rest if she kept this up.

"Here, put your head on my shoulder." He let go of her hand and tried to slide his arm under her, at the same time knowing it was a mistake to hold her closer. "I'll never get to sleep with you squirming around." Another wave of chills crept over him. One minute he was hot, the next cold. "Besides, we'll both be warmer."

"No, I—"

"Just do it, lady, so I can go to sleep," he commanded, his voice filled with exasperation. She raised her head slightly to allow him to slide his arm beneath her. He pulled her to him, cradling her head in the indention of his shoulder, then, as the warmth of her body settled along his side, he sighed.

It was the first comfort he'd felt in...he had no idea how long. He drew her close and, giving up his fragile hold on consciousness, drifted off to sleep.

John tightened his embrace on the woman he held in his arms as visions of a massacre danced gruesomely in his head. He was the last Texas Ranger standing on the dusty street in San Elizario after his compadres had been felled one at a time by the firing squad. He twisted and turned as he struggled in his sleep, then a scream ripped from his body.

"Atkinson!"

Chapter 2

Startled by the man's cry, Lauren opened her eyes abruptly. In the total darkness she couldn't see a thing. She tried to move but was effectively pinned by someone's arm. Where was she? Who held her? Then she remembered the sniper from the crest above, her mad scramble to the cave, then a new terror—this man who held her like a lover. She felt his warmth pressed along her breasts, stomach and thighs. While she slept she had rolled onto her side, facing him. Now her head rested comfortably in the muscled indention below his shoulder and she could feel his heartbeat under her cheek. In her partially awakened state the whole thing felt so natural and right, but as she gained more consciousness, reality began to soak in.

Was she crazy? How could she have gone to sleep in the arms of a stranger—a man she had never met and had yet to see? The only explanation was that she was exhausted from long hours at work. Last night at the ranch she had been so keyed up she'd been running on excess adrenaline and hadn't slept well. Fatigue and the stress of her recent misadventure must have finally claimed her, and she had virtually passed out in this cowboy's arms.

No matter how good his arm felt around her, she had to remind herself she was a captive. He hadn't hurt her, if you didn't count the tender flesh of her underarm, where his fingers had dug into her. Tomorrow she would have bruises. If she lived to see tomorrow.

Though he'd threatened her, she didn't really believe he meant to kill her. There was something about his manner, his voice, that was reassuring despite his words. When he'd grabbed her and hauled her against him she'd been terrified, but that had faded into an uneasy awareness as he demanded a drink, then rest.

His arm tightened, drawing her closer, and his even breath became shorter and faster as every muscle pressed along her side tensed. She froze. Was he awake? Having a nightmare?

A moan escaped his clenched lips, then from an unconscious hell he groaned, "Don't shoot! My God, Atkinson! No!"

The words seemed to have been wrenched from his very soul and Lauren lay still waiting for more. But the man grew still. Who was Atkinson? Who was shooting? Nothing made sense. She waited until she felt the tension leave the man's body before she stirred, trying to relieve the pressure of the rock floor on her hipbone.

Her movements made her more conscious of the fact that she was lying next to a living man. A man who was definitely running from something—someone. Was he a criminal? Her logical brain said yes. Her instinctive side refused to believe he was bad.

But if he wasn't a criminal, then who was he? Why was he hiding in a mountain cave? She put her hand on his left shoulder to wake him from his nightmare, but when he said nothing more, she thought better of it and decided to let him sleep.

As long as he was asleep, he couldn't stop her when she tried to escape. And she had to try. The man who shot at her might come back when he realized he'd lost her trail.

She wondered what time it was. She couldn't tell how long she had slept. Would Ted be looking for her yet? Her left arm was pinned against the man at her side, so she couldn't check her watch.

Surely Doc had gotten back to the ranch by now and alerted everyone. She knew her father would be very alarmed when he saw the riderless horse. He tended to be very protective when it came to his little girl, and though he was proud of her accomplishments, he still didn't understand her need to succeed and stand on her own. Several times lately, he'd hinted that he would like to see her married. Unless she got out of this cave that wasn't likely to happen.

But her brother or father might not come for a while. She had no way of knowing if they'd learned she was in trouble. And she couldn't just sit and wait. To wait like a helpless female for someone to come to her rescue wasn't her nature. She'd always been a person of action.

Maybe she could get away from her captor while he slept. Keeping her torso still, she carefully inched her legs back, putting a narrow space between them and the man's warm body. But when she began to ease her hips away, he wrapped his arm tighter around her and pulled her closer, until she was almost on top of him. It was difficult to ignore the contours of hard muscle that didn't give against her softer flesh. The man was built like a well-trained athlete.

She lay quietly until his breathing became deeper and more regular, then she tried moving backward again. His embrace immediately tightened. That wasn't going to work, so she decided to try something different. She wondered if he had a weapon. That knowledge might determine her next move. Carefully, she fingered the duster under her cheek. The coat felt expensive. It would be a luxury for most ranch hands she knew. A couple of neighboring ranches had been sold in the years since she had left home to attend college and open her practice. She had never met the new owners but wondered if this man could be one of them.

But what was he doing out here? She doubted that he'd come hoping to photograph a mountain lion like she had. No, she reasoned, whoever had shot at her had tried to kill this man, too. Otherwise, why would he be groaning, "Don't shoot"?

When she'd questioned the cowboy, he hadn't been co-operative, and she doubted he was going to be any different when he woke. So anything she learned about him was going to have to be from her own initiative.

His voice had been deep and had a mature quality. She couldn't put her finger on why, but there was something about his manner that made her think of a time gone by. Of a desperado.

She knew he was tall, because when he'd jerked her against him, his belt buckle had dug into her back, and the top of her head hadn't reached his chin until he'd leaned down.

If she moved, she was afraid he would waken, but by being careful, maybe she could find out enough about him to identify him later. Raising her hand, she lightly searched for the curve of his upper lip. The bristly hair growing there caused her to pause. A mustache.

Touching him in this intimate way was having more of an effect on her than she had expected. She realized her fingers practically shook where his breath warmed them. The urge to withdraw her hand and cram it into her jeans pocket was strong. But if she did that she might never know what he looked like.

When he didn't move, she drew her fingertips up and across hard cheekbones until she felt the soft caress of thick lashes. Carefully, she circled the delicate skin below his closed lid. Tiny creases radiated from the corners of his eye, she noticed. He wasn't a young man, but he wasn't old, either. He was a man in his prime.

His flesh burned with fever under her fingers. Was he ill? She hoped he wasn't seriously injured or sick.

He'd seemed faint earlier, but it hadn't made him too weak to manhandle her. His fingers around her wrists had been as effective as a pair of steel handcuffs.

She continued moving her fingers down the ridge of his jaw. He would be a handsome man in the light, she felt sure. The muscles of his face were tense, as if he had been clenching his teeth. Even in sleep he didn't allow himself to totally relax.

The short stubble that covered the lower part of his face felt like coarse sandpaper, evidence that he hadn't shaved that morning. Her fingers brushed against the straight hair growing above his collar. It felt clean when she rolled it between her fingertips, so he must have recently bathed. He couldn't have been in the desert for more than a day or two.

Moving her hands carefully to keep from waking him, she continued her exploration. She found the collar of his shirt unbuttoned and was not surprised to feel damp, curly hair in the open neck. She guessed his shirt hid a chest covered with wiry hair.

Unsolicited, a thought crept into her mind—about how many other women had lain beside him and felt the heat from his skin against their own flesh after they had made love. Maybe that was why he continued to sleep so soundly. Maybe he was used to sleeping with a woman wrapped in his arms. Maybe he was married.

His breathing was still regular and he hadn't moved, so she became bolder and more careless in her search. She had to get this over with. She didn't want to be affected by touching him. She didn't want to think of him as an attractive, desirable man. She had to remember he was her captor, and probably a common criminal, as well.

His chest felt hard and muscled beneath the broadcloth of his shirt. But she'd already known that. Whatever else he was, he was definitely a fine male specimen. But finding out what he looked like wasn't her only goal. She needed to find out if he was armed.

Running her fingers under the open front of his duster, she discovered a pocket, which held a pen. Nothing there to give her any clue to his identity. Then her fingers brushed against something hard over his left breast.

A gun. Maybe, just maybe, she could get it and make her escape. Surely he wouldn't be foolish enough to call her bluff if she had a gun pointed at him. If so, she didn't know what she would do. She knew how to use a gun—most ranch girls did—but that didn't mean she could use it against another human. She prayed he wouldn't try to stop her. The thought of injuring him made her sick. All she wanted to do was get away.

Her hand stilled as she listened for any sign that he might be waking. When he didn't move, she easily flipped the snap on his holster. The resulting pop seemed to echo loudly in the cave, though she knew it had been barely perceptible. Again she paused and waited, then, holding her breath, she tried to slowly ease the gun out of his shoulder holster.

With lightning speed, the man grabbed her hand in a crushing vise. "What are you doing?" His voice was cold and deadly, daring her to lie.

Lauren gasped in surprise and pain. The fingers around her wrist were so tight they prevented the flow of blood. A tinge of fear began to creep up her spine as he swung around hard against her, causing him to sprawl practically on top of her. She felt the belt buckle pressed into her stomach and the rough ridge of his zipper against the tender inside of her leg. The explosive nature of her predicament began to sink in. She was totally at his mercy.

He lowered his mouth until she could feel his lips brush

the crest of her ear. His breath was warm and ragged as he practically spat at her, "I asked what you were doing."

Determined not to show her fear, Lauren cleared her throat and tried to push him away. She didn't want to feel his body over hers. "I—I was checking you out. You wouldn't tell me anything about yourself so I resorted to learning something about you my way."

"Running your hands over me isn't going to answer the kinds of questions you want answered." The scorn in his voice didn't conceal the sexual innuendo.

She ignored the undertones. "It's a little too dark for me to run my eyes over you," she retorted, frightened that he would be angry, but not at all embarrassed by her bold search. She had to be bold if she intended to survive this ordeal. "How long have you been awake?"

"For a while." He seemed to relax a little.

The thought of him lying there awake while she ran her hands over him *did* embarrass her. "You could have said something."

"I didn't want to."

She thought she detected a hint of humor in his voice, as if he was enjoying her discomfort. She didn't like being at a disadvantage. In this situation she had to accept that physically she had no choice, but verbally she could hold her own. So she decided to steer the conversation away from the personal. "It wasn't very smart of you to leave your gun where I could easily get to it."

"My gun?" He released her hand and reached for the gun, as if he'd forgotten about it.

"Yes, your gun." Now she had a chance to scoot out from under him and she took it, but she didn't move away because she knew he would immediately grab her.

She could hear him awkwardly fumble with the holster and weapon, but he didn't say a word.

"I wouldn't have shot you, you know," she said. The words just slipped out. For some reason she wanted him to know she hadn't meant to hurt him. "I just wanted to get out of here."

"Not yet." His own words weren't threatening. In fact, they sounded more like a promise he'd deliver on later.

She knew he would let her go as soon as he thought it was safe. As soon as the sniper was gone. She suddenly remembered the name he'd called out in his sleep. "Who's Atkinson?"

The cowboy tensed against her side and he seemed to choose his words carefully before he spoke. "How do you know about him?"

She had surprised him, she could tell. "You called out his name in your sleep."

"Did I say anything else?" His tone was cautious and worried.

Lauren decided honesty might be the best way to get the cowboy to tell her what was going on. "A little. You said something about not shooting after you called out Atkinson's name."

The man beside her let out a deep breath. "He was just a guy I used to work with."

"Is he the one trying to kill you?"

"No." He stirred restlessly, as if answering her questions made him uncomfortable.

She wanted to reassure him so he wouldn't clam up again. "I didn't think so. Did someone shoot at him, too?"

His voice was barely a whisper. "Yes."

Whatever he was remembering, it must have been painful, she thought. Yet she couldn't stop herself from asking more questions, even if they did cause him pain. Maybe she would find out something that would help her—them— get away. "Was it the same man who shot at me?"

"That I don't know."

"You don't know?" Her voice was gentle as she probed. "Or you won't tell me?"

Lauren felt him shrug and knew that he wasn't going to answer. She had to accept that for now.

Time dragged slowly by, and she became more and more conscious of his arm wrapped around her and his body pressed against her. She could almost feel the tension and anger leave him, as if he were willing it through some type of meditation. Not only did he have a strong body, but apparently he had a strong mind.

When it became almost unbearable to remain still, she made a request. "Do you think I could sit up now? This floor is getting hard." While it was true that the floor was uncomfortable, she was hoping a change of position would mean he need not hold her so closely.

"Sure." He pulled her with him as he struggled into a sitting position against the wall.

So much for putting distance between them. "Thanks."

Silence again. He seemed content to dwell on his own thoughts, but the silence and waiting were driving her crazy. "If you won't tell me who you are, would you at least tell me what you look like so I can imagine you when I talk to you?"

He shifted, bringing his face closer to the top of her head, where she could feel his warm breath in her hair. His voice was devoid of all anger when he spoke. "Umm, let's see. I'd say I'm pretty ordinary. I have two hands, two feet, two eyes...."

"So do most people." Lauren groaned aloud in mock frustration. She, too, could pretend that only a short while ago she hadn't been debating whether she could pull a trigger if he tried to stop her escape.

He loosened his hold on her slightly and laughed.

His laugh was a deep, hearty chuckle—one that made her feel comfortable and made her think she'd have liked this man, had they met under different circumstances. "You seem to feel better now," she said to him.

"The sleep helped. Thanks for letting me rest."

She was amazed at his words of thanks. One minute he threatened to kill her and the next he was being considerate. She realized with certainty that this man was not going to hurt her, that he was who he said he was. Call it a gut feeling or woman's intuition, she knew she was safe. "You're welcome. Now, are you going to tell me what you look like?"

"What do you want to know?" His hand slid down her arm, but this time it didn't feel restraining, but more like a caress. Or was her mind playing tricks?

She didn't stop to think about it. She wanted to take advantage of his open invitation to question him. "What color is your hair?"

"How about blond?"

She shook her head in disbelief. She knew he'd lie to protect his identity. He would be a fool not to. "I noticed your hair is thick around the bottom, but I'll bet it's thin on top."

"Why do you say that?"

"Your voice." She found its gravelly tones intriguing. "I'd say you were in your forties, maybe older."

"You're good, but you're wrong."

"I don't think so." He'd lie about his age, too.

As though he could read her mind, he asked, "Why would I lie?"

"You're afraid I'll be able to describe you when I get out of here, so the more false information you feed me the more incorrect my description."

"I don't have any reason to fear you describing me," he said, but his words didn't ring true.

"Okay, then, let me feel." Before he could stop her, she reached up and fingered the thick locks of hair falling over his forehead, then she quickly withdrew her hand. There was something different about touching him while he was awake—when she knew he was awake. Something much more disturbing.

"Satisfied?" he asked softly, almost tenderly. "Now, ma'am, since you got to feel of me, it's my turn."

Lauren tried to pull away, but his arm held her tightly against him. She took a deep breath and tried to swallow the lump in her throat. Despite the utter foolishness of it, she wanted to know how his touch would feel when he wasn't just trying to restrain her. She was unable to move when his hand brushed her neck ever so slightly as he searched for her hair. It was so fleeting she wasn't sure she hadn't dreamed it. Then she felt the gentle tug as his fingers closed around the loose tendrils of hair hanging down her neck.

For a couple of seconds he paused, seeming to enjoy the texture of her hair as he rolled it between his thumb and index finger. Then he cleared his throat and asked, "What color's your hair? You had on a hat when you came in the cave, so I couldn't see it."

The feel of his fingers against her hair was almost hypnotic. She had to force herself to respond, and then she didn't have the will to lie. "Blond."

"I bet it's beautiful."

The compliment touched her very soul. Somewhere in the back of her mind came the thought that she should stop him, but she had neither the strength nor the desire to do so. She wanted him to let her hair down. She wanted him to continue touching her.

Her breath caught in her throat and her pulse quickened in anticipation as he shifted to reach her better and began to gently work the pins out of her French roll. The weight of her long blond hair caused it to cascade to her shoulders when he released the last pin. Never before had she been so aware of how sensual it felt against her neck. He continued to thread its length through his fingers as he combed loose strands away from her face and gently tucked them behind her ear. She couldn't have moved if she'd wanted to.

His fingers were slightly unsteady, and she knew that he, too, was affected by what was happening. Then, as if coming to his own senses, he let the silky strands slide through his fingers and fall to graze her cheek. "What are you really doing out here?" he asked.

The magical spell broken, she pushed against his side to put some space between them. This time he allowed her to move so only their hands were linked. Though his touch was light, she knew if she pulled farther away his grasp would tighten and he would restrain her. He was going to give her only so much freedom. But the space allowed her to gain control of her breathing and some semblance of reality.

He said, "I asked you a question."

"I told you. I was out riding when someone took a shot at me." She shuddered, remembering the fear she'd felt when she'd realized the man on the cliff was trying to hit her. "I'd gotten off my horse to take a photograph of what I hoped was a mountain lion, but it turned out to be a man with a rifle. I hid in here and that's all I know."

"You take photographs?" he asked. "Like Mathew Brady?"

Lauren frowned. Why would he refer to Mathew Brady, who'd been dead for the last century? Was the cowboy a history buff? "Not exactly like Brady. I've got a 35 millimeter with a zoom lens. Photography's a hobby, a diversion from my job."

"Let me get this straight. You take photographs, and you have a job?"

"You're right on both counts. I'm an attorney."

"A female attorney?" His voice was filled with skepticism.

"Yes, in Sierra, and don't make it sound so objectionable. It's an honorable profession." She hoped the cowboy wasn't someone who harbored a grudge because he thought he'd been wronged by a lawyer sometime in his past. If that was the case, she'd just made a mistake by telling him what she did for a living. "I'm taking a break this weekend to visit my dad here on the ranch."

The cowboy shifted and sat up straighter. His voice full of certainty, he said, "There's only one attorney for a hundred miles around here, and he's a man."

This time his words confused Lauren, making her wish she could see his face to determine if he was teasing her or if he truly believed what he was saying. "Cowboy, I don't know where you've been or what you've been doing, but West Texas is full of attorneys and quite a few of them are women."

She felt the man's growing tension as he increased the pressure on her fingers. "You said your dad has a ranch nearby?" He asked the question as if he didn't believe her.

"Yes, I did. It's been in the family since 1895." Her ancestors had been some of the early pioneers in the area.

The man sat silently for several seconds before he spoke. This time his words were direct, more like he was interrogating her than having a conversation. "What's today?"

"Saturday."

"No. The date."

"The twenty-fifth."

"No, the full date."

"November 25."

"The year, dammit."

Confused, Lauren told him.

The man slumped against the cave wall and murmured in a low voice that she had to strain to hear, "That can't be right."

Lauren was discomfited by the man's response. He hadn't known what year it was. She'd been so sure earlier that he'd been in recent contact with civilization. His clothes weren't dirty or ragged. He'd bathed, shaved and even wore aftershave. But still he'd been upset to hear what year it was. "How long have you been out here?"

When he didn't answer, she recalled how hot his face had felt against her cool hand. Maybe he was ill and couldn't remember. "Are you sick?"

"I...I don't know. Just a little groggy, I guess. I'll be okay in a few minutes."

"I hope so. You seem confused." The man worried her. There was something wrong with him, but she couldn't tell whether it was brought on by his physical condition or not. If he was truly ill she couldn't just go off and leave him out here. He might die. "Are you sure you're okay?" she asked, squeezing his fingers.

"I think so," he said, then lapsed into silence as if he needed time to process what she had told him.

The rocks beneath her were getting harder by the minute, so to ease her aching bottom, Lauren shifted sideways. The cowboy jerked when she accidentally bumped his head. "Oh, I'm sorry. You *are* hurt, aren't you?"

"No." His voice was laced with pain.

She knew he wasn't telling the truth. But his response was just like a man, she thought, thinking of her father and brother. "Yes you are, or you wouldn't have groaned." She ran her hand across his forehead and felt beads of perspiration.

When he didn't make a move to stop her, she continued searching until she felt the congealed mass of blood at his temple. It could have been caused by any of a number of things. But for some reason she knew what had hit the man. "You're wounded. Did the guy outside shoot you?"

"Something like that." He flinched as she fingered the wound.

It wasn't very deep, but she was sure it hurt, and because he was already running a fever, she suspected it was getting infected. "Why didn't you go to a hospital?" She asked the question, though she knew the answer.

"I didn't have that option."

"I see. Because there wasn't one close by or because you couldn't risk being caught?"

"A little of both."

He seemed to have relented and given her an honest answer. Maybe he was beginning to trust her. But his answer had lent credence to her suspicion—that he was involved in something illegal. That still wasn't reason to leave him wounded out in the desert. "You have some fever, so the wound may already be infected. I've got a first-aid kit. I'll see what I can do. Do you have a flashlight or anything that will give off a little light?"

"Uh, no, I don't reckon."

"Will you move to the mouth of the cave, then?"

"How many times do I have to tell you that you don't need to see me or know anything about me, lady?"

"Okay. We'll do it your way. In the dark. But if I hurt you, it's your fault." She cursed the blackness as she felt around for the saddlebags she had dumped carelessly on the floor when he'd tugged her down beside him.

Finally, she found the first-aid kit. "Hold out your hand." Dropping two aspirin in his open palm, she said, "Swallow these. Here's the canteen if you need a drink to wash them down."

"What are they?" the man asked, skepticism in his voice.

"Aspirin for your fever."

"*Aspirin.*" He repeated the word as though it were new to his tongue.

She listened as the man gulped the water. "Okay, let's see what we can do about that head wound. This may hurt," she said. His cheek quivered at her tentative touch as she searched for the wound. His flesh was smooth and too warm.

She wrapped dampened gauze around her fingers and carefully dabbed the wounded area, trying to clean it, then she applied a generous amount of cream to what felt like a shallow gash. The darkness and her own agitation made her fumble as she tried to cover the wound with a simple pad. When he gasped, she hurriedly withdrew her hand and asked, ''Am I hurting you?''

''No.'' She could hear the tension in his voice as he added, ''Go on, finish up.''

Quickly she secured the bandage. ''That'll make it a little more comfortable,'' she whispered, ''but at the first chance, you had better see a doctor.'' Her fingers lingered at the side of his head. Against her better judgment, she wanted to continue touching him, to brush the hair from his forehead.

''Much obliged for the doctoring and the advice.'' His voice was low and strained, but he seemed to have regained some of his earlier strength.

''You're quite welcome,'' she said, wondering at his use of an expression she associated with her grandfather. She traced his eyebrows lightly with her fingertips. ''What color are your eyes?''

''Red! Lady, do you realize the situation you're in? You're in the middle of nowhere with a man you know nothing about and you're acting like a—a barroom strumpet.'' He rolled over, effectively pinning her beneath him. ''I could kill you, compromise you or whatever I want, and you can't keep your hands to yourself!''

Chapter 3

John didn't know what had made him react so violently to her touch or to say such a crude thing. He just knew he had to put an end to her gentle caress. Her touch ignited feelings he didn't want or need to feel. No woman had ever driven him crazy by just lightly grazing his face. But this one did, and he hadn't even gotten a good look at her.

He didn't have to see her to know she was a threat to his well-being. She'd doctored his wound, all the while thinking he was a criminal. She'd been nice to him, but he didn't want her to be nice to him. When she was nice, he liked her, and he didn't want to like her. He wanted to keep her at a distance so he could be rational. The logical side of him said her story was a lie—it had to be a lie. Women weren't attorneys. Her family couldn't own a ranch here. They weren't a hundred and some odd years in the future.

So why did his heart tell him she was good and kind and truthful? The memory of her running her hands over him while he pretended to sleep caused even his wounded body to respond. As if she understood the direction his thoughts were taking, he felt her squirm to push him off, but he kept his weight resting along her length.

She gasped, "I was tending your wound, not copping a feel. You're not going to hurt me or you'd have already done it, so quit threatening me."

Her indignant tone renewed his efforts to put emotional distance between them. John laughed, trying his best to make it sound just a tad wicked. "I didn't feel up to it a little bit ago, but now that I feel better—who knows what I might do."

Apparently considering his words, she tensed, but didn't move or make a sound for a couple of seconds. She must have decided he was bluffing because she retorted, "I've been told I'm a pretty good judge of character. And I think your rattle is worse than your bite."

"I could be a good character or I could be dangerous as all get-out." He raised himself up on one elbow, taking his weight off her body, allowing her freedom to move. He hoped she wasn't foolish enough to touch other men the way she had him. They probably wouldn't act like gentlemen. Not that the way his body felt right now was all that harmless, but he did have the fortitude to control it. "Now, I'm going to give you some advice, lady. Don't trust everybody. For all you know, I could be a serpent talking."

Even though she could have moved, she didn't. "Are you saying you're a snake?"

"No, ma'am, I'm not. But I may be a bit like Adam in the garden who ate the forbidden fruit. You're awfully tempting." He buried one hand in her hair, then brought it up to his nostrils and breathed deeply. That scent again. He knew he would remember it forever. As illogical and as wrong as it was, he still felt the stirring in his loins. He had to make her reject him. He didn't have the strength to stop if she encouraged him, so he tried again. "And I don't have anything better to do right now than..."

"Than what? Pluck me from a tree?"

He liked her spirit. She wasn't easy to intimidate. He'd have to try harder if he was going to make her cower. But he wasn't sure that was what he wanted. In fact, he was enjoying their verbal sparring. He lowered his head close to her ear to make the next words sound even more boastful. "I think I can guarantee you'd enjoy—"

"You're a little too confident for my taste." She pushed his head away and tried to wiggle out from under his body.

Releasing her hair, he rolled off of her and shifted back to a sitting position against the wall. He decided the best thing to do was to change tactics. He'd keep his hands to himself while they talked. "Displaying confidence is a mark of honor. Anything less is cowardice. You should know that you never let your opponent think otherwise."

Without so much as brushing against him, she scooted up to lean against the wall in turn. "Now we're opponents? I thought we were on the same side. Us against him."

He could still feel her body heat, though she was inches away. "Maybe that's what you want me to think. You could have planned all this." Even as he said the words he didn't really believe them. More than anything he wanted to hear her deny that she was one of Cardis's pawns.

"Wait a minute. You think I planned to be shot at and to meet you in this cave?"

"Could be." On second thought, Cardis might be using her to lure him out into the open, where he could be captured.

"Get real. I'd have certainly chosen a more comfortable place. Besides, what would I gain?"

He didn't have that part figured out. Actually, he didn't have anything about her figured out. "That's what I want to know. What *are* you doing out here?"

"I've already told you." She enunciated each word slowly, as though she was talking to a child. "I was on an early morning ride when someone took a shot at me. It doesn't take a genius to try to hide from bullets, so I hid here."

"You don't have to be sarcastic, but for your sake, I hope your story's true." If it wasn't, they were both going to be in a lot of trouble. He wasn't going to allow Cardis to take him without a fight. And now that John had discovered he had a gun, though he didn't know how he'd gotten it, the confrontation was likely to be deadly.

"It's definitely true. But why would it matter if it wasn't?"

"If the right people thought you could lead them to me, you could be in danger even after you leave here." He forgot his decision to keep his hands to himself as he fumbled in the darkness for her hand. Upon finding it, he tightened his fingers around hers. "And if you're working for them..." He left the obvious unsaid.

"It would help a lot if I knew who the so-called 'right people' are. What have you done?"

"My job." There was no way he could explain everything that had happened to him during the past few days. And it was better she didn't know. The details were too sordid. "That's all I'm going to tell you."

"I've leveled with you, cowboy, and wish you would with me." Her tone pleaded with him. For some reason it was important to her for him to trust her. "I wish you believed me."

He thought about what she'd said, then reluctantly admitted, "For some strange reason, I do." He squeezed her hand tighter. "I don't know why, but I do."

Lauren understood what he was saying, because for totally illogical reasons, she, too, trusted him. Still, she wanted to know why he was being so secretive. As an attorney, she'd been taught to continue asking questions. Sometimes, like water eroding rocks, constant questioning produced answers. "Please, tell me what's going on. Maybe I can help."

"No, I think you'll be safer not knowing anything."

Disappointed at his response, but at the same time feeling special because he wanted to keep her safe, she sighed and leaned back. "Are you feeling better? You were burning up with fever earlier."

"The nap and water helped, and the...aspirin. I'm much obliged to you."

"Obliged enough to tell me your name?"

"No, not that much. It wouldn't be wise for me to tell you, just as it wouldn't be wise for you to tell me yours, and I've already explained why."

Lauren shivered, as much from the knowledge that they couldn't even exchange the common pleasantries of names, as from a sudden chill that seemed to permeate the dark cave.

When the cowboy gently disengaged his fingers from hers and pulled away, she was disappointed. The disappointment was replaced with relief and a certain excitement as he put his arm around her shoulder and, without saying a word, pulled her closer against his warm body. Resting her head on his chest, she could hear his heartbeat and feel his ribs move with each breath. The intimacy was unsettling. She wanted to snuggle closer, to wrap her arm around his waist, and at the same time she wanted to jump up and run, to get as far away from this sensual man as she could.

She shifted in an attempt to erase the disturbing thoughts from her mind. He didn't move when her head bumped the gun holster, but earlier, when she'd discovered it, he'd acted surprised as well as angry. Had he forgotten about it? She asked, "Why are you carrying a gun?"

"Most people carry one for safety or for food. Guns are necessary out here."

In a sense, that was true. A lot of people carried a weapon when in the wilderness alone. But she knew he wasn't referring to safety from four-legged, wild animals.

"Then why haven't you used it to get away from here? You could shoot that man out there."

The cowboy took his time before he finally provided a clipped answer. "I've got a pistol. He's got a rifle. No match."

She had to agree. In his weakened condition, he would have been foolhardy to go up against a man with a high-powered rifle. The cowboy's fever might have gone down, but she figured he was still weak. If only there was something she could do. "If you'll just tell me who's after you, maybe I can help. After all, I'm an attorney and the law's designed to protect people."

The cowboy grunted. "Look, lady, I told you. I'm not involving you in this any more than you already are." Continuing to cradle her in his arms, he stroked her hair, curling small strands around his calloused fingers. "But since you claim to be an attorney, tell me about your work."

"I don't just *claim* to be an attorney, I am one." If she concentrated on his words she could ignore his hand, the way it stroked the hair away from her face, the way it made her feel—all confused.

"I beg your pardon, ma'am, for using the wrong word."

"Apology accepted." Lauren explained her usual day to cover her growing physical awareness of her companion. "I joined a one-man firm in a small town when I got out of school. I work from seven to seven. Then I go home, too drained to have much of a social life. Sometimes I bring work home with me or I watch a little television." As she heard the words she realized how sterile and boring her life sounded.

"Television?" he asked, stumbling over the word.

"I like to catch the evening news. Why? Are you one of those people who think it's a waste of time?"

"I wouldn't know."

"You don't watch TV?"

"No, I don't reckon."

"Maybe you're smarter than most of the population." She wondered if he was some eccentric hermit who had come to West Texas to escape civilization. When he didn't respond, she continued, more to fill the empty space with noise than to impart any great information. "Usually I take files and my supper to bed and read until I fall asleep."

"It's a mite hard reading at night, isn't it?"

"Not at all." Lauren twisted, trying in vain to see the man in the blackness. He had strange responses to everything she said. "You sound like my grandmother, who always told me it would hurt my eyesight."

"I sorta object to being compared to someone's grandmother."

Lauren smiled at the feigned hurt in his voice. He was about as unlike someone's grandmother as one could get, something that was becoming harder to ignore the longer they were together. "I didn't mean..."

"I know." This time his voice was low and seductive. "Are eating and reading all you do in bed?"

The question was arousing rather than insulting. Lately, sleep had been about all she'd done in bed, but after a day in a cave with this stranger who radiated masculinity, she was beginning to wish otherwise.

She swallowed the lump that formed in her throat. "Are you asking if I share my bed with someone?"

"Do you?" Winding his fingers in her hair, he drew her face upward.

She couldn't move. Excitement pitted her stomach, daring her to forge ahead. "I'll tell you...if you'll tell me what I want to know."

"No deal, lady." His breath mingled with hers. "I just want to know if you're married."

"Oh." Hardly able to breathe, much less talk, she answered, "No, I'm not married." All thoughts of what she had wanted to know were forgotten. He was going to kiss her. She could feel the tension in his muscles as he pulled her to him, expertly searching for her mouth in the darkness. His hand cupped her chin, giving him better access to her waiting lips. With practiced skill he teased her top lip, all the while giving her an opportunity to pull away if she chose.

Abandoning all common sense, she chose to remain still. She wanted him to kiss her. She wanted it more than anything. His mustache brushed the sensitive skin around her mouth as he continued his exploration of her bottom lip. She knew nothing about this man, but his arms and his lips felt so natural. She cautiously returned his kiss, memorizing the taste and feel of him. Later in her lonely bed she would remember the stranger's kiss and the longing he'd awakened.

His lips moved gently over hers. They teased and played with her until she ached. Tightening his hold on her trembling form, he eased open her lips, igniting a fire she hadn't expected. Her body responded with a flood of desire. Suddenly, she wanted more than his teasing. Every part of her begged for the passion promised by his lips.

She moaned softly as she wound her arms tighter around his neck. Encouraging him further, she parted her lips to accept his exploring tongue. She was melting. The outside world with its gunman no longer existed. Only this man's touch, his kiss, his smell and the darkness around them were real. The kiss seemed to go on forever, or perhaps time stopped—she wasn't sure.

When both of them were breathless, he left her lips and feathered kisses across her cheeks and down her neck. She tilted her head back to offer him better access to the tender flesh there, almost pleading with him to continue. He seemed to understand, because his hand at her back forced her tighter against him and he lowered his head to kiss and nip at the hollow of her throat. She couldn't restrain the groan that escaped her parted lips.

When he raised his head she realized his breathing was

as ragged as her own, and she was sure if she'd been able to see his eyes they would have burned with the hunger she felt. He was as moved by what was happening between them as she. All it would take was a touch from her and he would make love to her there on the floor of the cave. He didn't have to say anything. She just knew.

She whispered her thoughts aloud. "Cowboy, you could be dangerous."

Still breathing rapidly, he unclasped her arms from around his neck and pressed her hands flat against his chest. His heartbeat raced beneath her trembling fingers. In a voice unsteady with passion he replied, "I tried to warn you earlier."

"I should've listened. I...we have to stop. This isn't the time or place for..." Lauren wasn't sure how to finish her sentence.

He clinched her hands tighter. "This isn't the time or the place for what?"

She couldn't very well say "making love," since love had nothing to do with the lust she was feeling. Somehow, though, it seemed more than just physical desire. But she couldn't say that to a man she'd never even seen, so she whispered, "For getting carried away."

He loosened his hold as if he, too, had regrets. "I wish it *was* the time and place, but you're right. We need all our senses to watch for our friend out there."

Relieved and disappointed that he'd complied with her request, Lauren wondered who posed the most peril to her well-being—the gunman or the cowboy? "Do you really think the man will come back?"

"I know a little about character, too, and that man doesn't give up easily."

"You still won't tell me who he is?"

"Don't you ever quit, lady?"

"No, cowboy. I don't give up easily, either." Fighting

for control, she pushed away from him and into a sitting position.

"Then let's change the subject."

"What do you want to talk about?" It didn't matter what they discussed because she couldn't think straight. His kiss had seen to that. And it wasn't just the kiss. Her response confused her. How could she, an intelligent, mature woman, be so attracted to a man she knew nothing about?

"You choose," he said.

She was saved from making a decision when his stomach rumbled and she realized he probably hadn't eaten in a while. He'd been thirsty when she'd entered the cave, but he hadn't said anything about food. She'd brought provisions for the day and had more than enough for two. "Would you like something to eat?"

"Yes, ma'am. I'd be mighty grateful for anything you've got."

"How about a ham sandwich?" Thankful for something to get her mind off his kisses, she dug in her saddlebags and, after locating a sandwich, handed it to him.

The crackle of plastic wrap echoed in the still blackness as he folded back the wrapping from the thick slices of homemade bread. As she listened to the cowboy take bite after bite, she wondered how long it had been since he'd eaten. While she appreciated a healthy appetite, the man was wolfing down the food.

He stopped eating when he seemed to notice his rudeness. "I'm sorry. You want a bite?"

"No, I have another one."

"This is really good grub. How many of these did you bring?"

"Two." She unwrapped the remaining sandwich. "I only want half of this one. Would you care for the other half?"

"How come you have two if you only want a nibble?"

She heard the distrust in his voice. "I wasn't meeting

anyone, if that's what you're thinking. Our housekeeper, Maria, insists that I be prepared for the day.'' Lauren unwrapped the sandwich and handed the cowboy half.

He resumed eating, but more slowly. ''How long were you planning on riding?''

''It depended how long it took to get the photographs I wanted. I planned to be home by dark.'' She squinted at her watch, and in the dark she made out the tiny green phosphorescent dots. ''The sun will be going down pretty soon. It's after five.''

He stopped eating. ''How can you tell in here?''

When she tilted her wrist toward him, he reached across and fingered the dial, though he seemed to avoid touching her again. ''Quite a timepiece you've got there,''. he muttered.

The crackling of plastic and sounds of chewing took the place of conversation as the two finished their meal, lost in their own worlds. Lauren wondered if the cowboy was reliving the kiss in his mind, too, or if he was more concerned about their plight. She also wondered why no one had come to find her. Maybe Doc hadn't made it back, or maybe something else had gone wrong.

The cowboy's polite cough interrupted her thoughts. ''Uh...would you happen to have some more water?'' he asked.

''Yes.'' She pressed the canteen against his arm. When his hand closed over hers, she almost dropped the precious water.

After he finished drinking, he said, ''If I ever have to hide out again, I hope it's with you. You're pretty handy to have around.''

With a tinge of hope, Lauren asked, ''How will you find me?''

''I can always look in caves.'' He set the canteen down and leaned back against the rock.

''Cowboy?'' The word was almost an endearment as it

rolled from her lips. "That man can't wander around out there forever. You said he was heading up the canyon earlier. He's probably gone by now. You could come back to the ranch with me—no strings attached." If the cowboy was in legal trouble she'd take care of him. Maria, the Hamiltons' housekeeper, who loved keeping secrets, would help her nurse him back to health. No one else would ever need to know of his presence.

"No, I can't risk your getting hurt."

"I'll be fine. You can stay at the ranch—"

"No," he interrupted. "Even though I'm pretty sure the man is gone, there's an outside chance he could be hiding farther up the canyon, waiting. I don't think he'll try to harm you again if he doesn't connect the two of us. He probably mistook you for me earlier."

"I can't just leave you here. Not in your condition. What will you do after I'm gone?"

"I'll wait."

"Then what?"

"You don't listen well. Drop it or we don't talk." He mitigated his harsh words by finding her hand in the darkness and giving it a squeeze. "How big do you think this cave is?"

His dismissal hurt, but she followed his lead. "The best I remember, this cave's not all that big, only twenty yards or so deep."

"You've been here before?"

"Lots of times. These cliffs are dotted with small caves, but this one is special. I started using it as a place to escape to and dream of wild adventures when I was about thirteen. If we had a lantern, I'd show you the Indian markings on the wall over there. The Apache roamed this area for years until the Comanche and cavalry ran them off."

Lauren paused in her story, remembering how grown-up and adventurous she'd always felt in this cave, never suspecting that one day—today—she'd have a real adventure.

"But the most interesting story about this cave is that a Texas Ranger died here sometime in the late 1800s. His remains are buried on our ranch."

Chapter 4

The cowboy's voice was low and strained when he asked, "You say a Texas Ranger died in this cave. What, ah, what was his name?"

Lauren answered, "I don't recall anyone ever saying, and I'm not sure he really was a ranger."

"Then what makes you think he was?"

"Because that's what I was told as a little girl, and I believed every word of it." Lauren smiled as she remembered her adolescent fantasies. The mystery of the man's death, alone and unknown, had always been part of the allure that drew her to the cave. Still, when she'd been in the cave before, she'd had the security of a flashlight or lantern for company. Now she had no light, only this stranger beside her for protection.

Her voice softened as she recalled the tale. "An old-timer told my grandfather the story of the ranger, and Grandad loved repeating it."

The cowboy shifted as if he was uncomfortable. "What happened?"

"The old-timer said a skeleton was found here about the turn of the century, and he always speculated that the guy was involved in the Salt Wars."

"Salt Wars?"

Lauren noticed his words were low and forced. "Yes, back in 1877. I guess calling it a war is stretching the use of the word a bit, but two opposing groups were trying to gain control of the Guadalupe salt flats. It's a long story."

The cowboy coughed, then shifted positions again, his movements echoing through the cave. "Well, since, uh, we're stuck here, why don't you go on and tell me? It'll help pass the time."

"Sure. Let me think. It's been a long time since I've thought about it." Lauren leaned back and tried to reclaim the feelings she'd had as a little girl sitting on her grandad's lap, listening to a legend from the old days. "I remember how Grandad always prefaced the tale by saying that someday he was going to research it. But he never got the chance. Anyway, the people who found the skeleton presumed it was a ranger's body because pieces of blue wool uniform and some brass buttons were found with it. And since a ranger had disappeared in this area about thirty years before the bones were found, it was a likely solution."

Suddenly, a loud screech came from the mouth of the cave, causing them both to freeze until they simultaneously realized it was a large bird that had chosen a rock near the opening as a vantage point. When it dived back into the canyon, Lauren heard the cowboy take a ragged breath and she released her own. Seeking comfort, she scooted closer until their arms were pressed together and she could feel his clenched muscles through the cloth of his coat. She realized he had been as startled by the sudden sound as she had. Neither spoke for several seconds.

When they both were breathing normally again, he said, "You were saying?"

Lauren continued, "Grandad said that for hundreds of years, everyone—Spanish, Mexican, Anglo, Indian, it didn't matter who—shared the salt from the beds. It was more precious than gold before iceboxes came along.

"After Texas joined up with the Union, there was a judge—I think his name was Charles Howard, but don't hold me to that. Anyway, he saw the salt as a way to get rich and decided to charge people for what they were used to getting free. To say the least, the locals took offense in a big way. After a few people had been killed, the governor sent four rangers—like they were a garrison of troops—to protect Howard."

Lauren hesitated, trying to recall the rest of the story. "I don't remember exactly what happened next, but somehow the rangers ended up facing a firing squad in San Elizario. A man named Attson...Atkin...something that started with an *A,* was the first one shot. Grandad always made it sound so gruesome."

She felt the cowboy tremble against her arm. What had she said? He'd become agitated when she'd mentioned the man's name. The name that was so similar to the one the cowboy had cried out. She rotated so she was facing him, though she couldn't make out more than a slightly darker shadow against the stone wall. She wanted desperately to see his face, to see into his eyes when she asked, "Isn't that like the name you mentioned in your sleep?"

He stiffened. "Umm. It's probably just a coincidence."

Lauren wasn't so sure. She didn't believe in the supernatural, but there was something about the cowboy's uneasiness and all of the "coincidences" that made her want to run out into the sunlight and let it wash away the eerie feelings.

At her silence the cowboy prodded, "What happened then?"

"The only other thing I remember hearing is that by some quirk of fate, one of the rangers escaped. Grandad said he apparently got as far as this cave before he died of dehydration or exhaustion—or maybe a gunshot wound." Her feeling of melancholy intensified. "Being out here all alone sounds like a frightening way to die, doesn't it?"

The cowboy was silent, as if thinking about what she'd said. Finally, he spoke, but his voice was tight with controlled emotion. "Yes, yes it does."

"When I was a little girl I felt sorry for him, so I put wildflowers on his grave because I thought there was no one to care about him. His family didn't even know where he had died." Lauren recalled the many times she had wondered about the mystery that lay beneath the grave marked by a mound of smooth river rocks. "Funny, but I haven't thought about him, or any of this, in a long time. I expect it's an interesting story. There have to be some records about him somewhere." She'd never considered the real individual as much as she'd fabricated romantic yarns about him. Now, she wanted to know who the man was.

The cowboy gently withdrew his hand from hers. Then she heard the sound of his palm rubbing his forehead.

"Are you okay?" she asked. Was his head hurting or had her story upset him? She'd always found the story romantic and a bit sad rather than upsetting.

His voice was stronger when he spoke, as if he'd mentally gotten control of what was bothering him. "I'm fine. I just don't exactly cotton to being in a cave where someone hid out and then died. It packs a little too much irony to suit me." Suddenly, he stiffened. "Listen. Do you hear anything?"

"It's probably the vulture returning."

"No. It's the sound of hooves. Someone's coming."

Lauren strained her ears until she heard the faint sound of a horse neighing in the distance, then the faint sound of a voice. She sat up straighter, trying to make out the words.

The cowboy stood slowly, drawing her up to stand next

to him. His fingers tightened around her wrist when the second call echoed off the cliffs.

The voice from outside hollered, "Lauren!"

"That's my brother, Ted." She started to walk toward the opening, but the cowboy held her back.

"You sure that's your brother?" he asked, his words barely above a whisper.

"Of course. I've listened to his voice arguing with me all my life. My horse must have made it home, so Ted came looking for me. He'll never let me live down having to be rescued."

The cowboy tightened his grip until she was worried that he wasn't going to let her leave. Then she realized that he was concerned she would give him away. She longed to reassure him, to caress the tense muscles until they relaxed. "It's okay, I won't tell anyone where you are."

"I'd appreciate it if you didn't." He sighed and then, when the clattering of horse hooves on the rocks grew louder, leaned close to her ear. "Now let's get your pack together so you can get going."

She raised her hand and gently touched his cheek. "Won't you come with me?" She knew the answer before she felt the slight shake of his head as his warm lips kissed her fingertips. She ached for those lips on hers again. This might be her only opportunity. "Well, cowboy, I guess this is goodbye, then."

Sliding her hand behind his neck, she pulled his head down as she stood up on her tiptoes. She felt him hesitate before his lips met hers in a tender kiss. She arched against him when he ran his hands down her shoulders to the small of her back. The musky male scent of his skin filled her nostrils, and the silky weight of his hair teased her fingers. She yielded further when his large hands encircled her waist, pressing her into direct contact with his lean, taut body. In her desperation to take more than memories with her back to the real world, she deepened the kiss, taking all he could offer in the few seconds that were left to them.

As Ted's calls became louder and closer, the cowboy stepped back, releasing her. She would have fallen if he hadn't steadied her shoulders before he bent down to pick up her saddlebags.

"Go," he commanded as he thrust the pack into her hands.

She handed the canteen back to him. "You keep it. There's a little water left." Leaving the cowboy alone troubled her. Wanting to do as much as she could to help him, she fumbled around in the pack for a moment. "Here's a candy bar in case you get hungry," she said, tucking it into his shirt pocket. "And you might need the first-aid kit, too."

His voice reflected an uncertain independence. "Again, I'm obliged to you. Now go before I change my mind."

With all the dignity she could muster, Lauren walked toward the dimly lit entrance, which promised safety. Yet the security and safety she wanted was staying behind. At the mouth of the cave she picked up her camera, stuck it in the saddlebags and put on her hat. Turning toward the darkness that sheltered the stranger, she said, regret tinging every word, "Goodbye, cowboy. Take care."

She barely heard his whispered reply, "Another time, lady. Another time."

Keeping to the brush to conceal the location of the cave from anyone who might be watching, she forced herself to pay attention to the dangerous descent. What she really wanted was to run back to the cave and beg the man to come with her. Lost in her thoughts, she scarcely noticed the thorns of the mesquite tearing at her skin and clothing.

Willing himself not to follow the woman, John moved closer to the front of the cave and crouched in the early evening shadows. He could see her mount a horse in the

distance and ride away, side by side with the man she had
called Ted.

Before she turned the bend in the canyon, she twisted in
the saddle as though she wanted one last look at the cliff
face. He knew she was searching for a glimpse of him.
After she disappeared from view, he edged back into the
cave and slumped against the wall. The fever and hunger
were gone, only to have the void they left filled with confusion.

Now he could think about his predicament without the
distraction of her soft skin and seductive voice. Memories
boiled in his mind, bumping each other aside until he had
trouble focusing on anything.

He knew he was a Texas Ranger, a fact that his wife,
Annie, had hated when she was alive. His sister was caring
for his small son back in San Antonio, and as soon as the
dispute about the salt beds was settled, he'd planned to get
back to him. But the lady had said it was more than a
hundred years later, in which case the dispute would be
settled and he'd be dead. But the Good Lord knew he was
in too much misery to be dead.

Her claim was too far-fetched to be anything besides
ridiculous. It was 1877, and he was alive, nursing a throbbing headache. Someone else's bones were buried on her
dad's ranch. If she'd told the truth, that is. Cardis could
have sent her with some cockeyed story, to lead him astray.

John knew the idea of her working for Cardis was lu-
dicrous when he thought about it. Those things the lady
mentioned, like women lawyers and a passel of people living around here, couldn't be true in 1877. Why, he doubted
if five hundred people lived between San Antonio and El
Paso.

Yet he knew things weren't as his good sense supposed.
After all, he'd examined the watch on her wrist, and it
wasn't like anything he'd ever seen.

"The remains are buried on our ranch," she'd said. Were

the remains his body? Or was all of this just a nightmare and he would wake up soon?

He ran his fingers over his hair and face. Although they felt familiar, something was different. His hair was shorter and his beard was replaced with stubble. Fingering his mustache, he was chagrined to realize the end curls were gone. In their place was a dandy's trimmed mustache.

Stepping out of the cave into the glow of the setting sun, he turned his hands over and over, studying them. They weren't his. The nails were well cared for, while his own would have been encrusted with blood and dirt. And the tip of his middle finger, the one he'd severed in a knife fight when he was a kid, had mysteriously grown back.

The standard-issue, loose wool trousers he'd been wearing when he'd entered the cave had been replaced with tight, softer trousers of a fabric he couldn't identify. The scratchy wool shirt was gone. With rising confusion, he stroked the oilskin of the duster, so similar to those worn by drovers. Where had it come from?

And the gun? He hadn't had a gun to fight Cardis. He frowned as he slid his fingers over its smooth, cold surface. Hell, he'd never seen a gun like this.

And Cardis? Who was the rifleman outside the cave earlier if it wasn't Cardis? Who was out to kill him? Looking at a body he didn't really recognize, John had to face the most frightening question. Who was he?

"Oh, God," he cried in a genuine plea for intervention, "what's happened to me?"

Leaving the cowboy alone in his confused state troubled Lauren. Yet, as she had dozens of times in her practice, she had acted on instinct, wanting to believe he was on the right side of the law and needed time to escape. She felt a moment of doubt when she recalled his erratic memory, his elusiveness.

"Okay, sis," Ted asked as they wound their way out of

the canyon, "what happened to you? I thought Dad was going to have a heart attack when your horse came in without you."

Lauren glanced at her younger brother. "I nearly had one myself."

Ted cocked an eyebrow. "Say what?"

"You won't believe what happened to me."

Fixing her with a sibling's knowing eye, he said, "Give me a try."

She looked at the lengthening shadows, knowing it would be dark by the time she and Ted got home. "You won't tell Dad what I'm going to tell you, will you? He doesn't need the worry."

"It depends on what you tell me." Reacting to the look she gave him, he amended his response. "You've got my word. Cross my heart." He made the sign they'd used since childhood to show their sincerity at keeping secrets.

Lauren related the events of the day, leaving out the stranger in the cave and what he'd done to her heart. Acting against her professional training and plain old common sense, she found she just couldn't place him in jeopardy.

Ted emitted a low whistle when Lauren finished telling him about the danger she'd been in. "Where did you say you were when you were shot at?" After she told him, he responded, "I'll go back tomorrow when the light's better and have a look around to see if I can find anything. A cartridge or footprints. Something."

"I doubt you'll find anything, but it'll be worth a look."

"You do think you got the guy's picture?"

"I pushed the shutter, but I can't swear I caught his image. And I'm just assuming it was a man. Another thing, Ted—I'd rather that no one saw me take the film in to be developed. You know how word gets around in a small town. Aren't you going to El Paso Monday?"

"I'll be leaving before your feet hit the floor."

Lauren made a face at her brother. "That'll be a first."

"You want me to take the film in and have it processed for you or not, big sister?"

"Would you, please?"

"Sure, but it may take a couple of days."

"That's okay. Just so I get it fairly soon. Ted, this had to be a case of mistaken identity." Realizing her near gaffe, she tried to cover. "I mean that it just doesn't make sense for anyone to be shooting at me."

"You haven't been dealing with any scum lately, have you?"

Lauren emitted an unladylike snort.

"Well, good gosh a'mighty, sis. That's not a dumb question, because you *were* shot at." Ted shook his head at the thought. "And whether the shot was meant for you or someone else, you've got to call the sheriff."

"I will as soon as we get back to the ranch." Suddenly, she was eager to get home, and the closer she and Ted got to the house, the more unbelievable the whole day became. She'd been shot at and, rather than flee when she'd had the opportunity, had found comfort in the arms of a stranger. Arms whose warmth countered the coldness of the cave. In his embrace, she'd felt strangely safe.

She reined in her horse, shifted in the saddle and turned to look over her shoulder. The mouth of the distant canyon was a black, jagged rip torn in purple cliffs obscuring the setting sun. The cowboy was going to be hard to forget. What was he doing now? Would he try to get out of the canyon? Where would he go?

With the confidence of a child knowing her prayers would be answered, she prayed for the cowboy's safety. She wanted him to get away from whoever was after him. Even if it was the law.

She and her brother had no more than reached the edge of the corral when their father rushed out to meet them. "Thank God you're both all right," Jack Hamilton said. "I called the sheriff's office and told him that we might need his help finding you, Lauren. Know what he said?''

Before she could answer, he continued, "Van Rooten said there's been a murder. A guy named Saul Rodriquez was shot last night just a few miles from Diablo Canyon.''

Chapter 5

Wednesday afternoon, Lauren hurried into her office, slung her briefcase in an armchair and picked up the messages Lyna had piled neatly on top of the desk. Holding the telephone to her ear with her shoulder, Lauren began to return calls as she leafed through the stack. The third note said, "Robert wants to see you. Pronto!"

She'd been in district court for the past two and a half days and hadn't gotten a chance to tell him about her weekend. Lauren wondered if Vera, the dispatcher at the sheriff's department, had told her husband about Lauren being shot at. Then her husband had told the gang at the coffee shop, including Robert Jordan, and now Robert wanted to hear the details. This was life in a small town, Lauren thought, hanging up the phone and starting down the hall.

Over three days had passed since her experience in the cave, but it seemed like only hours. The memory of the cowboy's scent, his touch and his kiss was still so fresh.

She rapped softly on the senior partner's open door before entering the room. "Lyna said you wanted to see me?"

"Sure do. I've been waiting for you to get back. Come on in and have a seat, Lauren." Robert gestured toward a chair.

She sat down across from his desk as he reached for an antacid bottle. "Something interesting may have come up." He popped one of the white tablets into his mouth and dropped an extra one in his shirt pocket. "Something very interesting."

Lauren waited as he mulled over his words. After practicing law for thirty years, Robert Jordan wasn't excited by very much. This must be pretty good. And from the way he was acting, he didn't know about her experience. So her guess must have been wrong. Sheriff Van Rooten must not have told his deputies or even Vera, because the news would have been all over Sierra by now. That puzzled her. Why would the sheriff be hiding the fact that she had been shot at?

Scratching his shoulder, Robert asked, "Have you heard anything about the McCain arrest?"

"I imagine everyone in West Texas has heard about it after this morning's big splash on the front page of the newspaper." Jonathan McCain, the son of one of El Paso's most prominent businessmen, had been arrested for the murder of Saul Rodriquez, the murder that had worried her since her father had made the announcement this past weekend.

After learning about Rodriquez, Lauren figured that what had happened to her in the canyon was in some way tied to his murder. There just weren't many men walking around with rifles, shooting at people. Robert might be of some help filling in the missing pieces before she told him her story.

He got up and began pacing the floor. "With that headline, I reckon so. His father, J.C., is a friend of mine. He and his daughter, Helena, came by here this morning. They want me to defend him. But J.C. doesn't want his son to know that he's footing the bill. He's afraid Jonathan would refuse our help.''

Lauren hadn't foreseen this turn of events—Jordan and Hamilton representing the man who might have shot at her. She had to tell Robert about her weekend. She twisted in her chair to follow Robert's movements. ''Why? It seems to me that he needs all the help he can get.''

''I expect you're right, but J.C. insisted that he be kept out of the picture. There was some kind of falling-out between them a long time ago, before I met the family. He doesn't think his son would accept his help now.'' Robert walked over and stared out the window at the distant mountains.

''You can't get by without telling a client why you're defending him. What about the contract for legal representation?'' She didn't like the idea of manipulating a client, even for a good purpose.

''His sister went to see him and told him that she's making the arrangements.'' Jordan turned and looked at Lauren as though he'd answered any ethical qualms she was having. ''Which she is. It seems that she and Jonathan have kept in touch through the years, and he trusts her. J.C.'s just picking up the tab.'' Robert paused a moment and massaged his fingers before continuing. ''I went to see Jonathan McCain a little bit ago myself and he signed the contract.''

''What did you find out?'' Knowing the first impression of a person was often telling, Lauren was interested in his opinion. Robert was good at sizing up a client.

''Not a blessed thing. The man hardly said a word. Then he said he didn't even know a Saul Rodriquez, much less shoot him.'' Robert rubbed his balding pate. ''The body was found near your dad's place, wasn't it?''

''About ten miles away, on a ranch called the Bar M. The land was sold back in May, and neither Dad nor Ted have met the new owner. Which, according to the paper, was Jonathan McCain.''

"Apparently there was a reason he didn't want to socialize with the neighbors." Robert grunted. "The sheriff said he kind of stumbled on the murder. According to him, he'd gone out Friday night to see his friend Saul. Said that Saul, who was working out at McCain's, was expecting him. When he got there, there was no sign of Saul, so Chester thought he ought to look around a bit. He headed toward one of the barns near McCain's airstrip and saw what he thought was a body, rushed over and found Saul, dead. About that time a shot rang out, throwing up dust close to his heels. Chester said he didn't need a second invitation to vacate the premises, so he hightailed it across the desert with McCain hot on his tracks. Our client supposedly fired several more shots at him. Chester hid out until the next afternoon. That's why he didn't report Saul's murder until then."

What Lauren heard crashed headfirst into her weekend escapade, intertwining the cowboy, the murder and the man who'd shot at her. Surely Chester had made the same connection after she'd called him and reported being shot at, but he hadn't even tried to get back in touch with her. Maybe he was so caught up in the case that it had slipped his mind? If McCain was the man who had shot at her—if he was the murderer—then how did the cowboy fit into this? Could the cowboy be McCain? But as quickly as she considered the idea, she discounted it. The cowboy had been hiding, not hunting. None of it made any sense.

She forced herself to listen without interrupting as Robert continued, "The media's made a big to-do about McCain being able to evade capture for three days. The way I see it, though, if he traveled by night and hid by day, it wouldn't have been easy to catch him. The desert's pretty big. I think he was probably on his way to Mexico since he was captured only a few miles from the border."

He paused and came around the desk to face her. "Anyway, the reason I asked you in here was to see if you would go to the arraignment with me tomorrow. It'll only take a few minutes. On the surface, the D.A. should have a turn-key conviction. That means I've got to look a little deeper than the prosecution.''

"I think I can clear my calendar, but…'' Lauren had to tell him about being shot at.

"Great. I know what you're thinking.'' He wagged a finger at her and said, "It has nothing to do with Jonathan being the son of an old friend. Anyway, I'll be the attorney of record, but I'd like your input. Maybe you can help me spot a weakness in their case. I have a gut feeling that there's more here than meets the eye.'' The old leather chair squeaked when he sat back down and pulled a sheaf of papers in front of him.

"That's what I'm trying to tell you.'' Lauren leaned forward. "I may know what your gut feeling is based on. I was riding in a canyon on Daddy's ranch when…''

The phone rang.

Robert picked up the receiver, listened for a second then said, "Transfer it.'' Then he turned to Lauren. "It's a guy I've been trying to get to return my call for a week so I need to get this. I'll come to your office as soon as I finish here.''

That evening, while Ted stood looking over her shoulder, Lauren looked at the photograph she'd taken in the canyon as she told him about Robert asking her to go to the McCain arraignment.

Ted asked, "What did he say when you told him that McCain could have been the guy who shot at you?''

"I never got the chance to tell him the whole story. He was called out of the office and never got back to me. I've left a message to call me on his answering machine at home. But, this photograph may free or convict McCain.'' She held the photo to the light and tilted it this way and that, trying to see more clearly, hoping to find a clue that would identify the person standing on the rim of the canyon.

"Can you make anything out?" Ted asked after he, too, had studied the print.

"No. The person was too far away for me to get a good shot, even with my new lens." Disappointed, Lauren slid the print between two cookbooks. "I'll take the negative to another lab in El Paso. I know a guy there who uses a computer to enlarge and enhance grainy images."

Ted picked up his hat. "Well, sis, I can't do any more here, so I think I'll hit the road. I'd like to get back to the ranch before too late."

"Thanks for everything."

He paused with his hand on the doorknob. "You gonna be all right here by yourself?"

"I've lived by myself for almost ten years. I'll be fine."

"Yeah, but people weren't shoot'n at you."

Lauren laughed and closed the door behind him. It was nice to know she had family that cared about her and would come through when she needed them.

Thinking about the firm's new client and the caring family he obviously had, she picked up the file Lyna had given her and headed toward her bedroom. Midway through the living room she stopped beside an overstuffed chair and stared at the photo hanging above the fireplace. It had been taken years ago. The mauve, melons and soft blues of the sunrise in Diablo Canyon echoed around the room, pulling it together in peace and harmony. But that wasn't why she studied the photo tonight. Tonight, like every other night for the past four days, she searched the print for the faint shadow of the cave.

Her passionate response to the stranger who had hidden there haunted her. Usually she succeeded in blocking it from her memory at work, but at night the memories often kept her awake.

His faceless image intruded on her despite her efforts to

totally forget him and the cave and his kisses. Especially his kisses. Sometimes she thought it had been another woman who had behaved so irrationally.

Her own experience in the canyon—being shot at and her subsequent refuge with the cowboy in the cave—kept niggling at her. The more she thought, the more unanswered questions she had. If McCain was the man who'd fired at her, then she needed to know who two other people were and how they fit into the picture: the cowboy and the man whose name he'd cried out in his sleep—Atkinson.

The next morning, Lauren, still not having spoken to Robert, wondered if she'd be able to help defend McCain as she hurried to keep up with her partner, who was taking the courthouse steps two at a time. Halfway down the hallway of the building, her partner said, "I'm going in to talk to McCain before the hearing. Why don't you check with the D.A.'s staff to see if there's any new information? I don't want any surprises today."

Twenty minutes later, after visiting with Alex Stewart, the district attorney, and learning nothing new, Lauren entered the courtroom through double doors. It was crammed with spectators and reporters who had driven from as far away as Midland-Odessa and El Paso. Lauren was afraid this trial would be turned into a circus, with a rich man's son being in the center ring. Alex needed the publicity for reelection, the newspapers needed the increased circulation, and the television station was after the ratings. Lauren felt sorry for the absent McCains who'd told Robert their presence wouldn't be welcomed by the accused.

Through a gap in the crowd, Lauren caught a fleeting glance of Robert talking to a tall, dark-haired man who had his back turned to her. The man nodded occasionally to something that was being said. With a few deft turns, she maneuvered through the crowd until she reached the bar and got a good look at his face. Knowing the man was Jonathan McCain, Lauren couldn't keep from staring. He dominated the courtroom even though he was handcuffed and sandwiched between the bailiff and a deputy. The jail coveralls accented his height and build. In fact, he was the only man she'd ever seen who made jail clothes look good.

Making herself turn away from him, she sat down at the large oak table prepared for the defense and opened McCain's file. She wanted to scan once more the limited information.

Name:	Jonathan McCain
Age:	40
Birth date:	September 25
Parents:	J.C. and Alicia McCain, El Paso, TX
Sister:	Helena Clark, El Paso, TX
Address:	Bar M Ranch, Rio Bueno, TX
Credit:	Timely, no problem
Education:	El Paso High School and USC Berkeley
Military:	Army
Land records:	Major stockholder in Bar M Corporation 250 sections Rio Grande County
Priors:	Arrested for possession of a controlled substance at age 17. Case dismissed
Charges:	First-degree murder in the November 24 slaying of Saul Rodriquez

According to Robert's notes, Sheriff Van Rooten suspected that Jonathan McCain was involved in drug trafficking and was known to have associated with members of a Mexican drug cartel. But the sheriff hadn't included any of that information in his report. Lauren wondered why. She was eager to hear Chester's testimony.

Glancing back up, she saw that Robert was still talking

to Jonathan McCain, but their client didn't seem to be responding. She wanted to go listen to what was being said, but she realized she wasn't really Jonathan's lawyer—she was just an observer for the moment. After today, she might be a witness against him.

She shifted in her chair, uneasy at the thought. She'd been schooled to know that appearances were deceiving, and this man proved it. Jonathan McCain was just what her secretary had raved about the afternoon before—he had the kind of looks that made half the women in West Texas want to testify in his defense.

Shaking her head, Lauren resumed looking at the file. She leafed through the attachment outlining McCain's bank transactions for the past seven months. A large sum of money had been telexed from a bank in Mexico City to open the account, with other deposits following at monthly intervals.

Finished with the report, she began making notes to pursue for the defense, wondering if the deposits could be a salary, albeit a large one, rather than illegal monies. It would take finesse to find avenues in which to sabotage what seemed like a solid case for the prosecution. After all, she thought, McCain was going to be a tough client to defend—murder with testimony by no less than a county sheriff.

"Lauren?"

She jumped at the sound of Robert's voice and glanced up just as her partner continued, "Lauren Hamilton, this is Jonathan McCain."

"Hello." Lauren's greeting was lost in the noise of the courtroom. She was mesmerized by the man's green eyes as he nodded in her direction.

"Take your seats," the bailiff announced in a voice loud enough to bring the stragglers out of the hallway.

Lauren motioned for Jonathan to sit in the end chair next to her, while Robert pulled out the chair closest to the aisle and sat down with a determined look on his face. Jonathan stared straight ahead while Lauren and Robert conferred for the few minutes they had before the judge entered.

The prosecution took its place across the aisle. Lauren was reminded of people preparing to play war. Sides were chosen and all the parties were lined up in opposition. Today, representatives from the district attorney's office, bolstered by Sheriff Van Rooten sitting behind them, were nearly smirking in self-satisfaction. It was as though they had possession of the only cannon and cannonballs available and were preparing to raze their opponents. Lauren and Robert, in turn, hoped to find other weapons.

"The Honorable Judge Antonio Estrada presiding..." the bailiff announced, bringing the people in the courtroom to their feet as a short, white-haired man with piercing black eyes entered the courtroom and stepped up to the bench. Lauren had been in his court many times before. He was known to be very tough: a modern-day hanging judge with a grudge against drug offenders. Although Jonathan wasn't charged with any drug violations, hints and rumors smudged his case.

Out of the corner of her eye, she could see McCain beside her. Expressionless, he stood ramrod straight, staring ahead at the man who held his future in his hands. McCain's lips were pressed into a grim line. He reacted only slightly when a guard approached and grabbed his arm to lead him before the bench.

As he moved away, Lauren felt the cool air rush in to replace the man's warm body in the space beside her. At the bailiff's orders, she and other spectators in the courtroom sat down. To cover her nervousness, she picked up the papers lying in front of her and realigned the edges by tapping them on the tabletop.

Robert accompanied his client and the deputy to the front of the courtroom, where they were joined by Alex Stewart. Lauren watched as the four men stood motionless before the judge while the charges against Jonathan were read.

"Jonathan McCain III is being charged with the offense of first-degree murder, alleged to have been committed on or about the 24th day of November, in Rio Grande County, Texas...." Droning on, Judge Estrada's voice sounded like a computer until it finally wound down. Looking directly at the handcuffed man standing before him, he asked, "Do you understand?"

"Yes, sir," McCain answered in an emotionless tone.

At the sound of his voice, Lauren leaned forward.

"Can you afford an attorney? If not, one will be appointed for you."

"My attorney is present," Jonathan replied clearly, returning the judge's stare.

Lauren's fingers crushed the papers she was holding as she heard his voice distinctly. McCain *hadn't* shot at her, after all. He was the cowboy, the man she'd promised to protect.

Chapter 6

The handsome, clean-shaven man standing before the judge was the man Lauren had held and kissed with a hunger she'd never felt before. The man who'd brought out a wantonness she hadn't realized existed in her. But now, in the courtroom with a crowd surrounding her, she forced herself to slowly expel the breath she'd been holding and maintain a stoic appearance.

Now what was she going to do? She couldn't very well jump up and announce she'd spent the day after the murder in the defendant's arms. But she had to do something. She hoped the arraignment would be over soon. She had to talk to Robert...and to Jonathan McCain.

The judge's voice penetrated the fog that surrounded her. He was discussing bond with the two attorneys.

"Your honor, the prosecution asks that bond be denied. The defendant has ties in Mexico. We have reason to believe that he may leave the country," Alex declared.

"Judge, it's true my client once operated a business in Mexico, but so have half the businessmen in this area.

That's no reason to deny bail. Consider that Jonathan McCain has property here, and he has no prior convictions.'' Robert Jordan continued to argue with the prosecutor. Finally, Judge Estrada proclaimed the bond to be two million dollars and Jonathan to be restricted to his ranch.

Lauren shook her head. The judge had effectively given both attorneys what they were asking for. He'd granted bail, but it was so high few people could post the required $200,000 deposit. She looked at Jonathan. Outwardly, he gave no indication of the emotional turmoil he must be feeling. Instead, he stood nearly at military attention as the conditions of his bond were laid down, as though none of it touched him.

Relaxing, knowing at least part of the charges against Robert's client were unlikely, she leaned back, drinking in the cowboy's appearance. He had rich, coffee brown hair and eyes an electrifying shade of green. His hair was trimmed and his mustache gone.

The deputy clutched the accused man's upper arm and pulled him toward a heavy side door. On his way out to the hall, Jonathan paused directly in front of Lauren, his strength catching the escort off guard, causing him to stumble. She leaned forward slightly, meeting the cowboy's gaze. With a weak smile, she tried to communicate who she was and offer hope before he was led off once again.

Ignoring the D.A.'s gloating look, Lauren almost ran after Robert in excitement when the court was dismissed. She had to tell him of her startling discovery. ''Robert, you—''

''Well, that's all we can do here,'' Robert said, holding the door of a small anteroom for her. ''I'd better contact J.C. and see if he wants to arrange for bail. Two million is steep but I guess we should be thankful that it was granted at all.'' He rubbed his chin and shut the door. ''Don't you think it's a little strange that the D.A.'s office isn't pursuing the drug angle?''

Lauren tried to focus on what Robert was saying, instead

of pouring out her own news. "Maybe they think they have enough evidence to get a murder conviction, so they don't want side issues to detract from the basic case." It was the best she could do in the circumstances.

"Maybe so," Robert said, working his tongue in his cheek like a ruminating cow. "What they have's not a bit good for our client. It looks like the rifle used to kill Rodriquez belonged to Jonathan. Then, with Van Rooten seeing—"

"Hold on a minute, Robert." Without apologizing for interrupting, she hurriedly explained, "I've met our client before—but I didn't know it until I heard his voice in the courtroom. This case might not be the greased slide into a dark prison cell that Van Rooten says it is."

When Robert turned to face her with a special predatory gleam in his eye, she knew she had his full attention. Lauren nodded toward a couple of chairs. "Let's sit down. I've been trying to tell you something since yesterday afternoon." Turning to watch Robert's expression, she launched into her tale.

"The morning after Saul was killed, I went for a ride to take photographs in Diablo Canyon. It turned into a nightmare when a man with a rifle took a shot at me—three times, in fact." Lauren shivered. "My horse bolted one direction and I bolted in another. I hid in a cave, but there was already a man in there. That man wouldn't let me see his face, or tell me who he was. Robert—" Lauren leaned forward and enunciated slowly "—the man in the cave was Jonathan McCain. I recognized his voice in the courtroom."

Robert let out a low whistle.

"He was very confused about everything, brought on I think by a fever caused from a bullet wound to the head. He was hiding—I gathered from the same person who'd shot at me. He seemed genuinely afraid for his life. And he was carrying a handgun; not a rifle like Saul was shot with.'' She paused to catch her breath.

''By the time Ted found me, the man stalking me in the canyon with a rifle was gone. Oh, and I got a photograph of the man shooting at me, but the image was too small for me to make out who it was. I plan to take it to El Paso as soon as I can.''

Robert closed his slackened mouth, the corners tugging upward in a sly grin. ''Then Van Rooten...''

''Is lying about McCain tracking him through the desert Saturday morning.'' Lauren finished his sentence.

''Why?''

''Bad eyesight?'' Lauren offered.

''Mistaken identity?'' Robert's grin was growing larger.

''On the take?'' Lauren's grin matched Robert's.

''Hot dog!'' Robert slapped his thigh. ''Now we got us a fight.''

John McCain stretched out on his hard bunk and stared at the ceiling. He was convinced he was going mad. What else would account for what was going on around him? Every passing hour since his arrest had been more bizarre. When the men had found him in the desert and escorted him to what they called a helicopter, he'd instinctively climbed in and positioned himself so they could buckle a belt over him. And he hadn't been scared when they lifted off and flew through the air. It was almost as if he had done it before, but if he had, that memory was gone, too.

He'd watched the streets full of horseless carriages and bright lights through the tiny window in his jail cell. Everything was different. Nothing was familiar. But the people here knew him, including that woman who'd come to see him, claiming to be his sister. It hadn't pleased him being rude to her, but he didn't know her from Eve. Still, she'd been patient, but when she showed him some pictures of kids that she said were his nephews, he thought of his son, Thomas, wanting desperately to see him. The woman called Helena had left after she got no response from him, telling him only that she'd see to it he had a defense attorney.

Today in the courtroom he could sense that everyone— even Robert Jordan, the man who'd been hired by the woman—thought he was guilty of killing someone named Saul.

The only one who had given any indication of thinking differently had been the blond lady. Had he really seen the compassion in her blue eyes or was he grasping at straws?

He felt like he should know her, but if he'd seen her before he knew he would remember. She was one of those women who left an indelible impression. It was more than beauty. It was presence and warmth. In another situation he would have touched her just to experience the feel of her creamy skin, the softness of her hair.

She looked like he imagined the lady in the cave. She was about the right height and she was blond, just like the lady in the cave had claimed to be. Surely there couldn't be very many attorneys in West Texas that fit that description. But what was she doing with his counselor?

Sitting up on the edge of the bunk, he buried his aching head in his hands and willed himself to block out all of the rampaging, unanswerable questions that cluttered his brain. He had to concentrate on getting out of jail. He had a son in San Antonio who needed tending—if he could get back to 1877. He couldn't let himself go crazy.

The throbbing in his temples had almost abated when he heard the metal clink of a key being inserted into the lock of his cell. The sheriff spoke to someone just out of the range of John's vision. "You can talk to him in here. Not anyone else in the jail this afternoon, so you got your privacy."

A woman said, "Thanks, Chester. I appreciate your leaving your lunch to let me in."

John sat straight up when he heard her voice.

The sheriff answered her as he slid the cell door back. "Don't mind it at all, Lauren. I'm just not too comfortable leaving you in here with this murderer, so I'll leave the door to the hall open so I can hear you holler if you need me."

A small woman stepped into the cell. It was as if her presence brought life to the dull gray surroundings. She wore a dark blue suit jacket and a skirt that didn't quite reach her knees. John couldn't stop staring at the long expanse of bare legs—more leg than he could ever remember seeing. He doubted his deceased wife had ever shown that much flesh, even in bed.

He caught himself and slowly raised his eyes toward her face. God! He hoped it was the lady. He needed her. When finally his gaze locked with hers, he knew. A look of recognition shone from her eyes. And memories. She, too, was remembering the passion that had flared between them.

He stood and took a step forward. He wanted to gather her into his arms and hold her tight, to draw strength from her. But something in the way she quickly veiled her emotion-filled eyes stopped him. In a low voice he spoke. "Hello, lady."

"Hello, cowboy." She stood a couple of feet away, looking up at him, waiting. A stray tendril of long blond hair had escaped from the neat chignon she wore and now hung down the side of her face.

He couldn't prevent himself from reaching out and touching it. He'd meant to brush it behind her ear, but he didn't want to let go. It felt right to thread its silky length between his fingers just as he had before. Sliding his hand behind her neck, he urged her nearer, close enough that he could smell the exotic perfume she wore. In this awful nightmare he was living, she was his only point of light. Even at the worst times during the past few days, when he'd thought all was lost, he would concentrate on her and he would feel better. Now she was standing only inches from him. She had come to help him. He knew that without being told.

He wanted to kiss her, but again her eyes warned him away, so he took a deep breath. "Is it too trite to say you're a sight for sore eyes?"

"No, not at all."

"I guess I was a little preoccupied in the courtroom, so I missed your name."

"I'm Lauren. Lauren Hamilton. I'm with the law firm representing you."

"So this is a business visit." Disappointment washed over him.

"Yes and no. Business is the only reason I could get in to see you, but..."

He smiled and caressed the back of her neck. "I'm glad you came."

"Jonathan..."

"John," he corrected.

"Okay. Jon." She stepped back slightly and he dropped his hand. "We need to talk quietly in case..." She nodded toward the open door.

"Sure." John understood what she meant. For days now, he'd been afraid to talk. Now he had the lady to reach out to.

"What did you do after I left the cave?" she asked.

"I watched you and your brother leave the canyon." He licked his lips as a vision of the woman's silhouette retreating from him flashed through his mind. He remembered wishing he'd gotten a better look at her to have something to cling to, something besides the memory of the softness of her body and the strength of her will. He'd always been of the opinion that a woman would be too fragile to survive in harsh territory, but apparently the lady didn't know it. She had not only survived, but like the delicate rose on the prickly pear cactus, exhibited tenderness and strength. The memory had kept him going during his ordeal in the desert.

"I took you at your word, lady—that you wouldn't tell anyone where I was. Still, I realized it was dangerous for me to stay in the cave. So after a couple of hours, when it was good and dark, I headed toward the river."

"You were weak when I left you. You had one candy bar and a canteen half-filled with water. How did you think you could make it to Mexico?"

"I had to try. I thought if I followed the creek through the canyon and headed south, I had to find the Rio Grande. Then I could follow it to a settlement. I was able to refill the canteen, so the water lasted a couple of days. I hid during the days and walked by moonlight."

"That's what Robert guessed you'd done," Lauren said, glancing toward the hallway. "But it was so cold, Jon. It's a wonder you're not sick."

"I suppose." John frowned, unsure he wasn't sick. If you could call losing his mind being sick. All the time he'd staggered through the desert, he'd felt Cardis was hunting him. But it wasn't Cardis who'd found him. It was someone in a contraption called a helicopter. It was someone who showed him it wasn't 1877. He'd seen no need to resist. Not with a half-empty gun. Not if females were lawyers and machines flew.

Not if he wasn't even sure who he was.

He was yanked back to the present when the lady began speaking again.

"Robert said he talked to you, but you wouldn't tell him anything. If you want him—us—to help you, you're going to have to tell us what happened."

"I told him what I know. I don't remember anything about a Saul or a ranch that I'm supposed to own." He'd always dreamed of owning a ranch, but he'd considered it beyond his wages as a Texas Ranger.

Her brow furrowed into tiny lines as she studied him.

"You were confused in the cave, too. Do you think it's because of the head wound that you can't recall anything else?"

"I honestly don't know." He gingerly touched the wound that snaked through his hair. It was just a dull ache now. He remembered more than he was willing to tell her right now. She wouldn't want to help defend him if she thought he was crazy.

She sighed. "We need to get a doctor to check you out. You may have amnesia."

"I've already seen a doctor." The man had seemed nice enough, but John hadn't told the doctor about his confusion. He just couldn't blurt out that he was from the past.

"And?"

"He said I don't have pneumonia. There wasn't anything else I could tell him." When John saw a shadow of disbelief cross her face, he added, "Trust me again for a while. Okay?"

"You have my word. Jon, even if you can't remember what happened, I do have some good news. You're going to have to be patient and not say anything to anyone else until we get this thing figured out. Promise?"

"I don't have much choice, do I?" he asked, looking down at her. Somehow her presence reassured him and helped him relax.

She smiled and shook her head. "Not really, unless you want to rot here."

"Then I promise."

"I thought you'd see it my way. First, Jon, I may be your alibi. Plus, we may have a lead with a photo I took of the man who shot at me."

Voices drifted into the cell from the outer office. Lauren began talking hastily. "It sounds like Robert got away from the reporters, so he'll be here shortly. Is there anything else you need to tell me before he comes in?"

John wished he could tell her something, but nothing

made sense. He closed his eyes, trying to draw on a memory that would clarify what had happened to him, but his last recollection was still that of Cardis and the firing squad. Of 1877, not the present. "Wish I could, but I really can't."

In a soft voice she reassured him. "That's okay. It'll come. Robert will see about arranging bail."

John snorted. "I don't think he needs to bother. No one I know can come up with two million dollars." Hell, he doubted there was that much money in Texas. No, if this lady's hopeful attitude didn't pan out, he was going to be in this tiny jail cell until he either broke out, which looked unlikely, or was hanged for murder.

She reached out and touched his arm. The contact was light but encouraging. "It's just a percentage of the set bail. Besides, if anyone can, Robert will get you out of here."

The sound of a man's footsteps and voice bounced off the metal alley between the cells as he neared. "Lauren, you there?"

"Yes, in here, Robert," she answered, stepping back from John.

"I finally got away from those barracudas." Robert stopped at the jail cell. "You remember anything yet, McCain?"

John shook his head.

"Hell, boy, you're going to be hard to defend."

In spite of himself, John couldn't help liking the older man. But he still couldn't tell him anything.

Robert kept talking. "Has the sheriff been in to see you? Maybe to talk you into confessing?"

John tilted his head sideways. "Yes. Three or four times a day he's dropped by, but not for a confession. He just stares at me sometimes, and other times he asks a lot of questions—just like you. And I can't answer those, either."

"I'm a little worried about his intentions," Lauren said in a lowered voice, glancing up to make sure no one else was in hearing distance. "I know Chester lied about hiding from you last Saturday. But we don't know if he killed Saul or if someone else did, or what other lies have been told. So while you're in here, Jon, watch your step.''

"Great." John offered a grim smile. He'd been jailed by a man who was lying about him. A man who could kill him.

"Has he acted like he knows you?" Lauren asked.

"No, and I haven't gotten the idea he's out to make me his new friend.'' The fact was, the sheriff's attitude was downright hostile. John figured that was natural. What Lauren had said shed a new light on it.

Robert eyed Jonathan's head. "Chester said Dr. Olguin's been in to see you. By any chance did you mention to him that you've lost your memory?''

"Hell, no. I don't want them to think I'm crazy.''

"You're too late for that." Robert chuckled. "Anyone who tries to cross the desert without food is automatically considered crazy. Anyway, it's obvious you don't remember much—leastwise to Chester. Let's keep it that way. So, if you do recall something, you're to tell us. No one else, you understand? Your safety may depend on it.'' Robert turned to Lauren. "If you're done in here, we better get busy.''

John held his breath as Lauren turned to face him again. God in heaven, he wanted to be alone with her for a few more minutes. Maybe if he could kiss her, he could gain enough sustenance to endure the jail for a little longer. She could apparently tell what he was thinking because her soft pink lips parted slightly as her gaze dropped from his eyes to his lips.

"I can't stay," she whispered, backing out of the cell, "but I'll be back as soon as I can. It's your turn to trust me.'' Then she hurried after Robert.

John stood and studied her departing figure for several seconds before the sheriff arrived to lock his cell. He'd been thinking about a woman and possibly missed his only chance to escape. Then it occurred to him that the sheriff might have wanted him to try.

Again Lauren took two steps for every one of Robert's as they walked to his beat-up pickup. She felt as if she'd been hit by a Brahman bull. Only a week ago her life had been simple, busy...and boring. Now it was anything but simple and boring. All because of one man.

It had been hard to walk away from him. Despair and confusion had clouded his eyes, which had begged her to comfort him. She'd longed to put her arms around him and take away the pain. He couldn't know the willpower it had taken for her to leave him in that cell. And while she had no choice, she vowed to do what she could to get him out as soon as possible.

She wanted to focus on this one case to the exclusion of all else, yet she and Robert both had other clients who had to be dealt with. Their business hadn't come to a standstill because they were representing Jonathan McCain.

But her heart had.

She climbed into the beat-up old pickup and snagged her hose on the worn seat. "Buy a new pickup, Robert."

"Don't have time," he said. "Besides—" he patted the peeling vinyl on the dashboard "—this honey's got another hundred thousand miles on her."

Lauren rolled her eyes.

Robert ignored her expression. "What did you learn from that boy?"

"Nothing except what he did after I left the cave. He claims he can't remember anything else."

"Amnesia's a tricky thing." Robert shook his head. "He better hope his memory comes back pretty quick."

"Maybe when you call his parents you can find out something from them that will jog his memory."

"I'll do that."

"Robert, I'm a little concerned about Jonathan being out

on bail. If Van Rooten is involved, then Jonathan's not safe—in jail or out.''

"I know."

"Chester has always been a blowhard, but he's seemed to believe in the law he's been elected to uphold. How or why would he be involved?"

"I think we touched on that. If drugs are involved, then his motive has to be money. Hell, sheriffs out here work for peanuts. That would explain how he was able to get that expensive pickup he drives. Let's assume drugs are an issue. That means we've got to find out who he's working with. Small-time border smugglers or a larger group? Or is he working for himself?"

"And how is Jonathan involved? Is he involved in the smuggling, but not the murder? His bank records would support that theory." Lauren longed to know the truth about the man who'd so easily and quickly caused her heart and ethics to war with one another.

The next day, Lauren was still dwelling on the what-ifs and surely-nots as she drove Jonathan home. She adjusted her sunglasses and tried to concentrate on the long stretch of highway that led south of Sierra toward his ranch. Jon hadn't said much while she had taken care of the paperwork granting his release. He'd asked where the money had come from. When she'd told him his family, he'd looked puzzled and lapsed back into silence. From what Jon's mother had told her, if Jonathan remembered anything about his father he wouldn't have taken the money.

Glancing out of the corner of her eye, she saw only confusion in the man staring out the window, searching the countryside as if it were the first time he'd seen it. She was so used to the terrain that she hardly paid attention to it anymore, but thought it would be enlightening to see it through Jonathan's eyes. Only small rugged mountains broke the mile after mile of rolling brown grassland that stretched in all directions. The barbed-wire fences and the couple of ranch headquarters tucked away in valleys some distance from the highway were the only signs of human habitation.

"Jon, do you remember anything at all about your family?" she asked, wondering if she'd detect any hint of residual bitterness.

He shook his head and looked at her. "Why?"

"I met them yesterday afternoon." Lauren and Robert had decided to drive to El Paso after seeing Jonathan in the jail. Although the bail money was handled by wire, Lauren had other things on her agenda. She wanted to deliver the negatives to the lab, and she needed to meet Jonathan's family to see if they could help their son regain his memory. She glanced at Jonathan, seeing similarities between him and the tall man who'd greeted her the day before. Although Jon's dark hair and bronzed skin obviously came from his mother's Spanish heritage, his eyes and smile were like his Irish father's.

"And?"

"I told them you couldn't remember them."

"If these people are my parents, why haven't they been to see me?"

"That's a long story, Jon. They told me a lot of things about you. Maybe some of it will spark a memory." She reached over and covered his hand with hers. "Some of it you won't like hearing."

"I haven't liked much of anything, yet. Why should this be any different?"

"Your mother, Alicia, talked to me privately while Robert and your father, J.C., arranged for the bail money. You'll be pleased to know that she and your father believe you're innocent of murder."

Jonathan rubbed his hands over his thighs, then half lifted his fingers. "I really don't know how to react, Lauren. I don't remember anyone named Alicia or J.C."

Lauren noted the look of anguish on Jonathan's face, but knew she had to continue. "Your mother said as a youngster you were headstrong and rebellious."

Lauren could still see his mother standing in the sunroom, fingering a pot of yellow **chry**santhemums, a faraway look in her eyes. "You see," Alicia McCain had said, "Jonathan and J.C. had a frightful falling-out when Jonathan was only seventeen. During his senior year in high school, he and a couple of his friends were arrested for possession of marijuana. But through it all, Jonathan said he was innocent of the charge.

"J.C. didn't believe him even though Jon was never prosecuted. Instead, J.C. ranted and raved, and he and Jon got into fight after fight, until finally my husband told Jon to leave. At the time, I thought it was my obligation to stand by my husband." The corners of her mouth curled slightly as she sought to get Lauren to understand. "You know, the obedient wife."

"You mean you've had no contact with Jon in all these years?" Lauren had asked.

"Yes and no. He stayed in touch with Helena and we communicated that way, so I knew he owned an import-export business in Mexico before he bought the ranch. I've only seen him twice since he left for the army—both times at Helena's. He's as stubborn as his father about apologizing." Tears filled Alicia's eyes. "I told J.C. I was going to see our son now, that enough was enough. Surprisingly, he agrees and feels that in some way he's to blame for this."

Lauren hadn't known how to empathize with the McCain family, since her own parents had always been so supportive. Still, she'd listened as Alicia reminisced about Jonathan's childhood, his athletic prowess, his sense of humor.

While Lauren told Jonathan what his mother had said, she watched him for some form of recognition. She was disappointed.

"Oh, yes," she added, "your mom sent some family

pictures for you to look at and one of your old high-school yearbooks. I'll leave them with you so you can see if they help you remember.''

Jonathan nodded.

''Also, I saw an old tintype photograph of your great-great-grandfather while I was at your parents' house yesterday. The man in the picture looked exactly like you.''

Chapter 7

"Umm." Jonathan shifted uneasily in his seat. "That's not all that unusual—looking like your ancestor."

"Maybe not, but there was something else I can't describe. I got kind of a creepy feeling." As they peaked a crest in the road, Lauren noticed the thunderclouds building to the southwest. The tall white pillars towered over the distant mountains, teasing them with rain. She hoped she would be back in Sierra before any severe storms developed. It was dangerous to be caught in the desert after a downpour. Flash floods were common.

She glanced at her passenger, who seemed to have shut her out. Had discussing his family upset him? Was he recognizing the passing landscape? "Do you remember where the turnoff is?" she asked.

He shrugged. "No."

"I thought maybe seeing familiar surroundings would trigger some memory."

"I hoped it would, too, but it's still like I told you back at the jail. I don't remember a thing."

"I know you said you didn't remember owning a ranch, but I'd hoped that—"

"Then I'm sorry to disappoint you," he interjected, cutting her off. He sounded exasperated, as if he was tired of explaining the same thing over and over.

She knew he must be frustrated. "You haven't disappointed me at all, so don't worry about it." They'd passed the road to her own father's ranch a few miles back, so she realized no more than fifteen miles separated the two ranch headquarters. "Just help me watch for the next turnoff. It will take us to your place."

Lauren wasn't the only person who hoped that seeing something would jar a thought, a memory of some sort. John had hoped the same thing. Other than a few flitting flashbacks, nearly like the feeling of having a word on the tip of your tongue, he was a stranger to his surroundings. He liked the looks of the pastureland and could imagine the grass being green in the springtime. But now the dry grass blanketed the countryside, with no familiar landmarks leading to a revelation about who he was.

Finally, he gave up and leaned his head back. In just a short time, he'd already learned that a car was not only faster than a horse, but more comfortable. He tapped his fingers over the head wound, which was nearly healed, and remembered how Lauren had gently tended to his injury in the cave. Even in the dark, she'd been more careful than the doctor who'd pushed and poked and jabbed at it in the jail. The headaches weren't as frequent anymore, but the jumble of unknowns running around inside had gotten worse.

From half-closed eyes, he watched the woman who'd introduced herself as Lauren Hamilton, although to him she was still "lady." She'd said he had parents, as well as the sister who'd come to see him, but he was sure they weren't the family he remembered. Yet these relatives had been willing to put up the bail for him. For that he should be grateful. And now this beautiful lawyer, his lady, was driving him out to a ranch he supposedly owned. He hoped they still had cattle and horses on ranches nowadays. At least he knew something about those.

Lauren glanced at him. "Are you going to be okay?"

"Yes, ma'am."

"Being addressed as ma'am makes me feel old."

He opened one eye and glanced toward Lauren. Her smooth, flawless skin held only a hint of tiny laugh lines at the corners of her eyes. He was suddenly curious. "You never did tell me how old you are."

"Asking a woman her age isn't a way to impress her, but since our file revealed that you're forty, you can't say much about my being thirty."

John bit his bottom lip. "I'm forty, you say." Damn, that was right. He *was* forty. More things might be the same as he remembered. "Other than what Alicia told you, what else do you know about me?" He couldn't bring himself to say "my mother."

Lauren told him the limited information she'd been able to find out from records and from people who claimed to know him. She paused and glanced at him before she slowly added, "The sheriff said you could have been smuggling cocaine from your ranch and that Saul might have discovered what you were up to."

John knew she was watching him for a reaction, but he felt like they were talking about someone he didn't know, so it wasn't hard to appear stoic.

When he remained silent, she continued, "Chester said you probably found out Saul was going to turn you in, so you killed him."

Inwardly, John flinched. Nothing she said rang a bell with him. He wasn't exactly sure what she meant by smuggling cocaine, and he didn't know anyone named Saul. They had him mixed up with someone else. But why couldn't they see that? He wanted this straightened up. He wanted to tell her who he was—John McCain, Texas Ranger—but he didn't think she'd believe him.

She'd think he was loco, then he'd have no chance to work himself out of this mess. The only good thing he could see right now was that she'd said she didn't believe he was a murderer. When she'd told him that in the jail cell, it was like manna from heaven. "I sure don't remember killing anybody."

"Jon, has it dawned on you that Chester could have mistaken you for someone else and that the real murderer not only shot at you, but was also the person who chased Chester through the desert? Or Chester could have been the one doing the shooting. Anyway, the task at hand is to find out who the real murderer is. Any ideas?"

He couldn't say Cardis, because unless he could travel through time, too, Cardis had been dead a century or more. All John could do was sigh and answer, "No idea."

"But in the cave you seemed to be aware of some others. You just wouldn't tell me any names other than the one you blurted out in your sleep—Atkinson."

"I think I had to have been mistaken about him." Atkinson had to be dead, too. Shot in San Elizario.

"Look, I'm working with your attorney. You not only can, but you should tell me whatever you know. I won't tell anyone but Robert. It's privileged information. So whatever is bothering you, perhaps I can help you with it."

More than anything in the world, he wanted to lay his heart out, to be understood, to be helped, but his own uncertainty stopped him. "I'm not sure I can tell it straight myself. Give me a little time, and when I get it figured out, you'll be the first to know."

"Good." She slowed down as they approached a dirt turnoff with a cattle guard at the entrance. "This must be it, because the next turnoff is at least five more miles down the road. We'll just drive until we come to your mailbox."

He didn't see much point in responding to the statement.

He knew she was miffed at him because she thought he was holding out on her, and if their positions were reversed, he would be, too.

The car bumped along the dirt road, crossing a couple of dry arroyos before climbing onto a rolling, grass-covered plain that hadn't seen a cow in several years. John spotted the buildings of a ranch about the same time Lauren did.

"Looks like we found it," she said, slowing down at a mailbox that had Bar M stenciled on its side in black letters.

John sat up straighter and surveyed the land everyone said was his. It was beautiful open grassland surrounded by rugged mountains—just the type of place he'd dreamed of buying after his years with the rangers were over. A place to raise a family and enjoy living rather than just being glad to be alive for one more day. He'd had too much of the latter. And it didn't look like his luck had changed. Even though he rejoiced in being free of the jail cell, there he'd felt safer. Now there was nothing to keep whoever had been trying to kill him from trying again.

Danger was part of his job as a ranger, but he regretted dragging the woman beside him into his mess—whatever it was. When the car stopped, he instinctively reached down and smoothly unbuckled the belt before catching himself. How did he know what to do? he wondered as he climbed out and retrieved the sack of groceries she'd insisted he needed. He waited until she had come around to join him before starting up the path that led to a large stone house. A porch swing creaked as a gust of wind whipped down the long veranda stretching across the front.

"The clouds are sucking wind as they build. Looks like we may be in for some rain tonight," Lauren said.

"A rancher can always use it." He paused at the front door, feeling as if something wasn't quite right. Carefully, he depressed the latch and gave the door a shove. It flew inward. "How were we going to get in if the door had been locked?"

Lauren grinned. "I forgot to mention that one of my many talents is picking locks."

"It is?" He was momentarily startled by her words before he decided she was teasing him.

"No, but I can climb in small bathroom windows." She stepped ahead of him into a large room and looked around. "Do you recognize anything?" she asked.

He stared at the large area with its tan leather furniture placed in front of a huge stone fireplace. Built-in bookcases filled with volumes lined the back wall, and on the nearest wall, tall French windows looked out onto the long front veranda. Not exactly what he'd expected.

At first glance, the room was orderly. Then he noticed the books in the shelves were crooked and their edges weren't aligned. The sofa was shifted slightly from where it had obviously sat on the rug. "No, I don't think I've ever been here before, but it sure looks like someone else has." He used the side of his foot to push a pillow out of the way.

"Yes, it does. Probably the sheriff and his boys. He got a warrant after your arrest, and I'm sure they went through the house and outbuildings looking for any evidence."

Even though this wasn't his house, John felt violated in some way. The knowledge that someone had pawed through Jonathan McCain's possessions bothered him.

Lauren must have sensed his agitation because she touched his arm and suggested, "Let's put away the groceries, then we can look around."

They proceeded to work together in silence, putting the food away. After a few moments Lauren closed the refrigerator door and turned to face him. "Jon, even though the court ordered it, I don't think it's safe for you to stay here."

"That entered my mind, too. There's a lot of wide-open space here that makes me a good target anywhere I go."

"Don't joke. I'm serious. You need a bodyguard."

"I'm serious, too." He grinned at a sudden thought.

"Are you going to stay out here with me? *You* could be my bodyguard." He knew she wasn't as immune to him as she'd like to pretend. The way she'd kissed him in the cave and the way she was looking at him now proved that.

Lauren swallowed. "Someone has already tried to kill you. That someone may come back now that you're out of jail."

"They tried to kill you, too," he reminded her, taking a step closer. "You may not be safe, either."

"I've told you, Jon, that I was probably mistaken for you in the canyon."

He measured her with his eyes, then let his gaze rest on her bustline, remembering how the round orbs had felt pressed against him. He fought the desire he felt building inside. "Sure. That wouldn't be a stretch of the imagination at all, considering that we're almost the same size and body build."

He watched her fight the impulse to pull the edges of her rose-colored jacket over the pearl buttons peeking from the narrow opening. She won, but a flush the same shade of pink crept up her throat and settled on her cheeks.

He couldn't suppress a chuckle at her discomfort. This was the first time he'd seen her at a disadvantage since the cave. She wasn't as tough as she pretended. Beneath the businesswoman facade lay a lady that could be embarrassed. The knowledge intrigued him.

"Don't laugh. I had on a jacket—" her look dared him to make a comment "—so I really could have been mistaken for a man."

"You could be right, but that's not what I'm concerned about now. Are you offering to stay with me or not? Surely one of your duties as my attorney is to make sure I'm safe?" He closed his hands over her shoulders and gently massaged the taut muscles there, knowing what her answer was going to be.

Her voice grew huskier as he caressed her. "I am not

your attorney. My duty toward the firm extends only so far, and right now my duty is to clear you.''

"I'd like that, lady, but I also want you...."

She reached up and touched a finger to his lips. "Please don't say any more. My firm represents you and there is a fine line we can't cross now, no matter what we want."

"I see." Disappointed, he dropped his hands from her shoulders and shrugged. "Then I suggest we look around." That at least would give them something to do. And maybe he wouldn't want to take her in his arms so badly.

After they had looked through every room and discovered nothing of interest, Lauren said, "I'd like to see the rest of the buildings and the murder scene before it gets late."

He held the back door open for her, though he wasn't sure he wanted to see the murder scene.

"If you'd like," she said as they took the steps together, "I'll call my brother, Ted, to see if he can drive over to stay with you."

"Thanks, but I'll pass on the offer." He couldn't trust her brother any more than anyone else. John followed her into a building attached to the barn and drew up short when he saw her walk over to a vehicle he recognized as a car.

She patted it. "Nice car. Is this yours?" He shook his head while she tried to open the doors. "Locked. I guess the keys are in the house. We'll look when we get back."

Lauren was dismayed to find an expensive, late-model Mercedes in the garage instead of a four-wheel-drive pickup or some other rig favored by ranchers. Though she'd read the registration information in his file, it hadn't seemed real until now. She'd tried to push the sheriff's accusations of drug dealing to the back of her mind, but this caused her to doubt Jonathan, and she didn't like that. She knew deep inside that he hadn't killed Saul, but Jon didn't appear to know if he'd sold drugs. In fact, he hadn't denied what she'd repeated. Now, when she looked back at him, he appeared confused.

Trying to hide her growing uncertainty, she turned and walked toward the metal barn. She slid the large door open and paused for her eyes to adjust to the dimness. As she stepped inside she heard a *meeow* just as a small furry animal dashed against her leg. She screamed and jumped backward, bumping into Jonathan, who had followed her.

He clutched Lauren's shoulders to steady her. "I'm guessing you scared that old barn cat as much as it scared you."

"I doubt it," she said, holding her hand over her heart while she regained her breath. "I hope you don't have any more animals lurking about."

"I can't tell you if I do or not," Jonathan answered.

Lauren looked around carefully before leaving the barn and strolling to the corral. Soon she forgot the cat as she realized there hadn't been any cattle in the pens for some time. Weeds clogged the shipping chutes and alleys. Suspicions flooded through her.

When he'd asked, she had wanted to stay here with him, but she and Jonathan McCain had no future. He was now the firm's client, though she was convinced he wasn't guilty—of murder. She wasn't so sure he was innocent of flying drugs in and out of this remote Texas ranch. These empty pens attested to that. He'd supposedly been on this ranch for months. If he hadn't been raising cattle or horses, what on earth had he been doing here all that time?

It was impossible to imagine he could be part of the drug trade that corrupted society. Though she shouldn't let her personal feelings interfere with her professional judgment, that was just what she was doing. Was it because Jonathan was handsome and had an indefinable presence that set some men apart that she wanted him to be guiltless?

She felt him as he stopped beside her and rested his foot on the bottom board of the fence. He hung his arms over the top rail and said, "Doesn't look like I was much of a rancher."

As much as it hurt, Lauren had to agree. She tried to quell the sinking feeling she had in the pit of her stomach. She had tried to deny he was involved in drugs, but then remembered the large sums of money that had been telexed from Mexico. As she looked around she had to accept the possibility that he was involved in something illegal.

She noticed a long, paved surface running from north to south about a quarter of a mile from the house. The airstrip. Lauren headed there as fast as she could, hoping to leave the unpleasantness behind. Yet the closer she got to the airstrip the worse she felt.

She knew time had wiped away any traces of whatever it was she hoped to find. Still, she felt compelled to try. Reaching the edge of the smooth surface, she stopped and rested her hands on her hips as she stared at the asphalt. The wind whipped through her blond hair and muffled her words. "This is the airstrip where Saul's body was found."

Jonathan had followed her and now stood looking out across the area. She actually saw the moment when his shoulders slumped, and she wanted to reach out and comfort him.

"You *don't* remember, do you?" she asked. Beneath his dark tan, his face was pale and drawn, perhaps from exposure and lack of food while he was in the desert, she supposed. But there was something else. A thinly veiled veneer of tension and hopelessness marred his almost perfect features. He looked like a wounded warrior.

He answered her with a negative shake of his head.

While she walked up and down the strip and studied the ground, he knelt on one knee and plucked a piece of grass to roll between his fingers. He looked at the horizen, at the buildings and at the sky while apparently making his own mental search. Finally, he threw the grass down and joined Lauren. "Find anything?"

She shook her head. "The sheriff said Saul was killed on this end. I guess the light rain shower we had the morning after the shooting washed away all the tracks and any traces of blood. I didn't find anything." She tried to keep her voice professional. "I'd hoped we'd find something to help you."

"Me, too."

She saw the flash of lightning a split second before she heard the clap of thunder and felt the first drop of rain. Jonathan grabbed her wrist as he broke into a sprint, nearly dragging her back toward the house. They reached the front porch just as the shower grew heavier. The wind had picked up and the sky had grown dark in a matter of minutes. Intent on their search of the airstrip, Lauren hadn't noticed how close the storm had gotten. If she didn't want to get caught she had to leave soon.

"I'd better get on back to town before it gets really bad." She avoided looking Jonathan in the eyes because she was afraid her doubts would be there for him to see. "Will you be okay?"

"Sure."

"Well, call me if you need help." She stopped short. "Jon, you don't know how to use the telephone, do you?"

They hurried into the house and she showed him how to use the phone. "Good. Now, I've got to go." Without another word, she made a mad dash through the rain to her car. Through the windshield, she waved at Jonathan, who was standing on the veranda, hands in his pockets. The lonely image tugged at her heart as she turned the car around and sped away.

The sinking feelings she'd had when she'd seen the airstrip and realized that at least part of Van Rooten's tale could be true refused to go away. As larger and larger raindrops began to pelt the windshield, she turned on the wipers and gripped the wheel tighter. The dirt road would quickly get slick and muddy if the rain kept up.

Somehow the storm suited her mood. How could she have let herself begin to care for the firm's new client? For two miles she berated herself. She had made bad choices before in trying to save the incorrigibles in high school and college. Surely she had learned something from those experiences. Was there something wrong with her? Why was she attracted to bad boys who weren't suitable?

After she'd parted ways with yet another bad boy last year she'd said that she was turning over a new leaf and was only going to date middle-aged accountants whose wives had died and left them with two kids and a mortgage. And then Jonathan McCain showed up, and in one day in a cave, he'd stolen her heart.

By the time she started down the hill leading to a deep arroyo, she had to fight to keep control of the slipping tires. It had rained harder up in the mountains and now the once-dry bed was a roaring, swollen tempest of water and debris.

She knew better than to try to ford a running creek. And it might be hours before this one would be safe to cross. She could sleep in her car, but not only would that be uncomfortable, November nights in the desert were cold. That left going back to face Jonathan.

She turned her car around carefully and started to the ranch with a growing sense of anticipation. As stupid as it was, she wanted to spend more time with him. By the time she pulled up in front of the ranch house, the rain had begun to fall in sheets and the lightning stabbed angrily at the surrounding mountains.

Between claps of thunder and bolts of lightning, John saw low-lying lights draw close to the house. Using the lightning flashes to see by in the growing dimness, he returned to the kitchen and hunted through the drawers until he found a large butcher knife and tucked it into the top of his boot. It wouldn't be any protection against a rifle, but he'd be damned if he was going to be a sitting duck for whoever was out there.

Then he waited in one of the rooms facing the front of the house so he could see out the window. It was several minutes before one of the flashes illuminated a small woman making a dash for the house.

Lauren! Why was she back? He knew the answer immediately. The deep arroyo they'd crossed earlier had been flooded. Thank goodness she'd had the sense to come back here instead of trying to cross it, he thought, hurrying to the front door.

Just as he got there, Lauren threw open the door and dived inside. She was soaking wet. Her clothes were plastered to her body and her hair had come unwound and hung down her back in tendrils. Using both hands, she wiped the rain from her face. "Wow. This is what Dad calls a real gully washer."

"Was the arroyo already flooded?" As she nodded, he pushed the door shut behind her, then guided her into the living room. "I'll get a fire going so you can dry off."

"Thanks," she said between chattering teeth. "I see the electricity went off because of the storm."

He'd heard of electricity, but he wasn't sure what it was doing out here and why it would go off, so he nodded. He could sense her presence only a few feet behind him while he set the logs and kindling. Within minutes the flames were beginning to lick around the wood. "Now we need to get you out of those wet clothes." The thought of her naked made his gut tighten. If she insisted on maintaining their distance it was going to be a long night.

She rubbed her arms, shivering from the cold. "Do you have anything here I could put on? A robe or something?"

"I'll go check the bedrooms." He went down a hallway where he thought the bedrooms should be located and in the growing darkness searched each one until he found the one that was probably his. Hanging on a hook on the back of the closet door was a terry-cloth robe. He grabbed it and a towel he found in the bathroom and carried them back to the living room. "Here. This should work." He handed her the towel.

He knew he should leave, but he stood fascinated as she dried her hair in front of the blaze in the fireplace. The urge to touch her blond strands as he had before was overwhelming, but he resisted the need by cramming his hands in the pockets of his pants. When she finished, she tossed her head back to fling the damp locks over her shoulder.

Her movements as she silently slipped off her shoes and hung her jacket on the back of a nearby chair were so sensual he almost moaned from the sheer frustration of being so close to her and not being able to take her in his arms as he had before. What he wouldn't give for that anonymity again.

Her fingers paused at the buttons of her blouse. "Maybe I should go to the bathroom to slip out of these wet clothes."

"I, uh, no. That's not necessary. You need to stay in front of the fire." He was kind of embarrassed that she'd caught him staring. "I'll go see if I can make us some coffee." At least that would give him something to do. He couldn't shadow her all evening with his tongue hanging out like a little lapdog. He had more pride than that. But not much more, he thought, remembering how sweet she'd tasted when he'd kissed her.

Lauren toweled off her naked body and picked up the robe Jonathan had laid on the sofa. As she slipped it on, she noticed the faint smell of male musk and his cologne. Whether Jonathan remembered it or not, she knew he had worn the robe recently.

Trying to hitch the hem up so it wouldn't drag on the floor, she tied the belt and then padded barefoot to the kitchen, all the time reminding herself to suppress any feelings Jonathan might ignite.

When she stopped in the doorway, she noticed he had found an old kerosene lantern, lit it and set it on the counter beside myriad pots and canisters. The golden glow danced around the room. When he heard her come in, he turned. Confusion and anger at his own inability were written all over his face.

Despite her earlier resolution, she ached to soothe his troubled soul, so she tried to pretend she didn't notice anything wrong. "I guess since the electricity is off we can't use the coffeemaker. Maybe we can find one of those old-fashioned pots that are set on the range."

He held up a blue enamel coffee pot big enough for ten people. "I found this. Will that do?"

"Yes. Did you find the coffee?"

She took the coffee he offered and filled the pot to the midpoint with water and set it on the gas range. "Do you have another match so I can light this thing?"

He handed her a box. "These were in a drawer."

"Apparently the electricity goes off here pretty often because you seem prepared—with the lantern and all." She lit the range. "Now, let's find something to eat. Aren't you glad we got you a sack of groceries?"

"There's some more stuff in here." Jonathan opened a cabinet to reveal canned foods and an assortment of crackers.

Lauren watched him search for a saucepan to heat some soup. He really didn't seem to know where things were kept. His "amnesia" wasn't just an act. He honestly couldn't remember.

Side by side they prepared dinner. Lauren could tell Jonathan was still upset, because he didn't smile or tease her. She would have enjoyed the camaraderie that had developed while they were in the cave.

"Would you like to go back in the parlor to eat by the fire, where it will be warm?" he asked, pouring a couple of cups of coffee.

"Yes, that sounds good." Though he appeared to be in a dark mood he was still considerate of her soaking and subsequent chill. Between them they managed to carry all of the things to the living room and put them on the coffee table.

Lauren sat cross-legged, the robe tucked between her thighs. Jonathan joined her on the floor. They ate in silence, which, she reminded herself, was best because when he was being charming, he was a hard man to disregard. In fact, he was a hard man to disregard even when he was feeding himself chicken noodle soup.

When they were finished, he stacked the dishes on a corner of the table, leaned back against the overstuffed sofa and stretched his long legs out in front him. His thigh was mere inches from her knee, Lauren noted, trying to quell her physical awareness.

He ran his hand through his hair and sighed. "You said you believed me when I said I didn't kill anyone. Why would you believe that when you believe I'm guilty of smuggling?"

When he looked at her, she could see the hurt lingering in his eyes. She thought for several seconds before she answered. "Jon, I try to deal in facts, though most of the time that's impossible. I learned long ago there is no black and white, no right or wrong and no fairness where the law is concerned. Many times guilty people get off—and sometimes innocent people go to prison. I've even defended people I knew in my soul were guilty and gotten them off. But the victory was bittersweet."

She hugged her legs to her chest and continued, "When I looked at the evidence and the sheriff's testimony, I figured this was going to be one of those cases. I never doubted Robert could get you out on bail. He's the best in West Texas.

"But sitting in the courtroom listening to the charges after I knew who you were, I realized things didn't add up. The sheriff says you were tracking him the day you and I were in the cave. But I know even if I hadn't been with you, you were in no shape to be running through the desert that day. You'd been wounded. Yet in his report, the sheriff never mentioned shooting at you, and he claimed Saul didn't have a gun on him, so where did you get your gunshot wound? It also bothered me that Saul was killed with a rifle, but you had a pistol.

"Last but not least, if you had murdered a man, you wouldn't have been hiding from the sheriff. You would have been trying to kill him as he claimed. Instead you seemed to be avoiding a confrontation. The day we were together, you could have slipped up behind the man shooting at me when he started down the canyon."

"We don't know if that was the sheriff."

"You think it was someone else?"

He shrugged and turned toward her, resting his elbow on the sofa and cradling his head in his hand. "I question everything right now."

"Well, if the sheriff is to be believed, it was just you and him and the Chihuahuan desert. When I talked to him the afternoon I visited you in jail, he claimed where you'd chased him was at least eight or ten miles from Diablo Canyon, where I was." Lauren was thinking aloud now. "There are lots of things that don't add up. A lot of confused identities."

"So you're saying that the only reason you believe I didn't kill this Saul is because things don't add up?" His voice cracked.

"No. Because I was in the cave with you, and know the timing was off, and because of...other things. The state's evidence may point to you right now, but..."

He leaned forward and stroked her hair. "We both know evidence is only as good as the person presenting it. It's always colored by our own experiences, and since I don't remember mine, it's dangerous for me to accept things as they appear."

"I don't take it at face value, either. I—"

"Don't kid yourself, Lauren. You saw that strip this afternoon and you decided I was guilty of smuggling...cocaine, was it? And you got out of here as fast as you could."

Lauren knew there was some truth to his accusation. When she'd seen the car, the empty corrals and the airstrip, she'd assumed the worst. But that was all they were—assumptions. As foolish as it seemed, she still believed he was innocent. When she looked into his burning eyes, some of her faith in him must have been visible, because his fingers tightened in her hair and he expelled a deep breath.

"Didn't you?" he demanded softly.

She nodded. "But I left for another reason." She hadn't left because she'd thought he might be guilty. She'd left because she had been scared. Scared she was falling for a criminal.

When she didn't continue, he asked, "Do you want to enlighten me?"

"Not really. As you said earlier, it doesn't make any sense even to me." At the same time she feared his attraction and welcomed it. As all ability to reason fled from her, she allowed Jonathan to pull her closer.

"Would it have something to do with this?" He caressed the side of her cheek with his thumb until she felt it all the way down to her toes, which at that moment chose to wiggle of their own accord.

He smiled. "I see that it does." He drew her closer until she was almost sitting on his lap. Her robe had worked itself loose enough that where it barely clung to one shoulder he easily brushed it down her arm. "Your skin is so soft, so beautiful. Since we met, every day we've been apart, I've dreamed of doing this." He brushed her bare flesh with his lips.

Lauren moaned and leaned her head back, savoring the wonderful sensations he was arousing. Slowly, he worked his way up her neck to her waiting lips. When finally they claimed hers, she was lost. Reason, good intentions and common sense left her while his hands worshipped her face, her neck, her shoulders.

Perhaps it was the robe slipping still farther down, exposing the top of her breast, that brought her to her senses.

"I can't!" she gasped. "I can't get involved with a client."

Jonathan's voice was husky with passion. "We're already involved."

"No. Not this way. Please, please, Jon. I can't." She pulled away from him and went to stand in front of the fire.

He, too, stood. "Well, do you want the sofa or one of the beds?"

Chapter 8

Lauren twisted and turned on the sofa, trying to get comfortable. She'd been afraid to take Jonathan up on the offer of a bed, afraid of what it might lead to. A bed was too intimate. Too big. Too dangerous.

Her self-control went only so far, and already she had proven that where Jonathan McCain was concerned, she had very little. Thank God she'd had the sense to call a halt to their lovemaking before things had gotten totally out of hand.

Though he had presumably gone to his bedroom, his presence seemed to haunt the room where she lay. Sweet, peaceful sleep eluded her while a different image of Jonathan flittered through her mind every few seconds. She ran her fingers along the edge of the sofa where he had sat, where he had held her in his arms and kissed her with a passion she couldn't have imagined a month ago. Maybe she *should* have taken one of the beds. There at least she wouldn't see his face, smell his scent, hear his voice in the golden glow of the remaining flames.

Was he having as hard a time sleeping as she? Was he even now aware that only a few partitions separated them? She found comfort in the thought that he, too, yearned to fulfill what they'd started in the cave.

She hugged the Indian blanket to her breast and watched the fire die to red-hot cinders, taking with it the warmth that had flooded the room earlier. She still found it hard to believe that she was so tempted by a man she knew so little about. Maybe the elements of danger and mystery were what attracted her. Lauren drew a fingertip over her mouth, tracing Jonathan's kisses, and knew she was just as susceptible now in the wee morning hours as she had been the first day she'd met him.

Sleepless hours later in the gray dawn, she shivered. The fire in the fireplace had died long ago and a chill had settled in the room. Seeing the faintest light entering the long windows, she sat up on the edge of the sofa and listened for movement from the bedroom. Not hearing any, she picked up her still-damp clothes and quietly crept to the bathroom to dress before Jonathan got up. She ran her fingers through her hair, trying to get the tangles out, and then tried to smooth her suit into some kind of presentable appearance. Then she tiptoed back to the living room.

She'd just finished folding the blanket and hanging it over an afghan rack when Jonathan called out to her from the hallway. "You decent yet?"

"Yes, or at least as much as possible without a comb or toothbrush."

"Then I'm coming in."

Even though they hadn't actually made love, Lauren still felt some of the same morning-after awkwardness seeing him step into the open doorway of the living room.

"Good morning," she said.

Shirtless, his jeans hanging low on his hips, he watched her without saying a word. His shoulders were as wide and well muscled as she remembered, and a sprinkling of dark hair covered his torso. She swallowed. He could have put on a shirt, but somehow she knew he was aware of the effect he had on her and was reminding her of what she had turned down the night before.

"Good morning," he said.

Silently, aware she was having the same effect on him, Lauren watched him swallow. She smiled before hastily latching on to a subject that was as far away from her thoughts as she could get. She walked over and flipped on a switch and the lights blazed overhead. "The electricity's back on."

Jonathan looked slowly from the switch to the lights. "So it is," he observed noncommittally.

"How about some coffee? I need some caffeine to get started." Trying not to bump against his body, she edged past him so she could go to the kitchen.

"I could do with a cup, too." He followed her.

She added coffee to the automatic drip coffeemaker and poured water into the top. The white plastic-and-glass appliance seemed so sterile next to the old blue enamel pot with its charm and romance.

They stood in awkward silence until the coffee had finished brewing. Then, while he watched with a troubled expression on his face, she poured the steaming liquid into a couple of mugs, handed him one and leaned back against the counter. "I need to get to town before someone misses me and starts worrying."

He nodded and took a sip while cupping the warm mug in his hands. "What do I do now? I'm not very good at just sittin' around waiting."

Somehow she knew that. "Since you don't remember anything, I suggest you read everything you can get your hands on, listen to the radio and watch television." She leaned over and turned on the small set hanging above the counter. "Maybe all the stimulation will help." She straightened. "I would advise you that if you do remember anything, *don't tell anyone* before you talk to Robert or to me.''

Jonathan stared at her and slowly tapped a finger against the cup before asking, ''When are you coming back?'' The momentary longing in his eyes was quickly veiled.

''I don't know.'' She set her mug on the counter and turned back to face him. She wanted to stay, but she knew that would be folly. Never had she had a man affect her so deeply that she was willing to put her career second. Her work had been the driving force in her life. Now she wanted to protect Jonathan and offer him what little comfort she could. And she suspected that he wanted the same. The need had been written in his eyes before he had caught himself. ''I don't think it's a good idea for me to be here. It's hard to maintain a professional distance from you.''

''After last night you must know how I feel about you,'' he said slowly, ''but if you say the word, I won't insist on a response. For now.''

She ached to have him explain just how he did feel about her, but that would be tempting fate. Was he merely experiencing lust, or did he have the same overwhelming need to know her that she had to know him? She wanted to learn everything about him, from his favorite color to which side of the bed he slept on, to whether he sang in the shower. Yet she couldn't allow herself the luxury of hearing him whisper words of love and desire into her ear, because she might not be strong enough to walk away.

''What's your favorite color?'' she blurted out. That was the least personal of all the things on the tip of her tongue.

Without hesitation he answered, ''Blue. The exact color of your eyes.''

She was wrong about it not being a personal question, but she willed herself not to get sucked into the intimacy his words created. ''You didn't have to think about it, so you do remember some things.''

''Not necessarily. I could have just decided that in the

past twenty-four hours.'' He set his mug beside hers and stepped closer.

She wanted to touch the hair that grew on his chest, but instead clasped her hands together in front of her, creating a fragile barrier between them. "I thought you said you wouldn't insist if I said the word."

"But you haven't said the word."

"Jonathan, things haven't changed since last night. I can't do this. In a way, you're my client as well as Robert's and..."

"And you can't get involved." He finished the sentence for her as he backed away and ran his hands through his hair. "If I fired your partner as my counsel, then there wouldn't be anything standing in the way. Is that right?"

She turned away from him and walked to the back door. Through the windowpane the airstrip stared at her. "That depends."

"I see. I'm only fit to..." he hesitated, apparently searching for the right word "...to make love to if I'm not a drug smuggler."

"I didn't say that."

"You didn't have to. I see where you're looking. You're afraid I'm a drug smuggler, not a rancher. I can't give you any assurances because I can't remember myself."

"Although you can't remember everything right now, your basic personality is probably the same. You're kind— you tried to protect me when I was in danger." She hesitated, wanting very much to believe in his goodness, but even he couldn't provide that reassurance. "I know dealers, like anyone else, can be quite personable, but they don't protect people. They prey on other people's weaknesses."

He walked up behind her. "And you think I could have been involved in drugs. I saw it in your eyes."

Fighting the doubts that plagued her, she turned to face him. They had been over this last night. "I don't know if you were or not." She watched the muscles in his jaw tense while she tried to explain her mixed-up feelings. She, too, was troubled by her uncertainties. Finally, she waved her hand toward him. "Jonathan, I can't reconcile all of your different..." she struggled for a word "...your different sides. There's the man I've gotten to know and then there's the person you don't remember. A person who's been accused of several crimes."

"And there's the problem." John fidgeted before a wry half smile echoed his inner pain. "The sad thing is, I *could* be guilty. So recovering my memory may not be what I really want. But I do want to know something." He licked his lips and then, copying Lauren's earlier actions, looked out the window at the landing strip.

"What do you want to know, Jon?"

"About drugs. About drug smuggling. Anything you can tell me that's gone on around here." *Give me a link, build me a bridge. Help me know who I am.*

As though she was trying to decide how best to explain it, Lauren paused before saying, "Most of the contraband smuggled across the Texas-Mexico border is marijuana, but we are seeing more cocaine because it's more profitable. That's what Van Rooten suspected you were trafficking. Usually smugglers around here fly it in under radar, then they have some system in place to distribute it in El Paso or San Antonio."

"This cocaine—what does it look like and what does it do?" John knew only something of excessive value was worth smuggling. Why was cocaine in that category?

"It's a white powder and it gives the user a real high— almost euphoric—but it doesn't last long and the user wants more."

"Why would he need more?" He wondered if this drug was like alcohol. He knew several men who couldn't leave the bottle alone.

"It's psychologically addictive. It causes the brain to

play tricks on a person. The user wants or needs increasing amounts, doing about anything to get the money to buy it.''

Hearing her description of cocaine, John didn't know what to think, what to feel, what to ask. What if he'd been one of those users who'd do anything to get more? Had this deceptive white powder played with his brain? God, he hated having questions and no one to answer them.

Across the counter sat his only hope. But as much as he longed for an end to his confusion, he didn't want to endanger her. Few women had made much of an impression on him in his life. The thought startled him. Which women had impressed him? He tried to conjure up an image of his wife, his Annie, but only a faded image in a coppery lithograph appeared. A still image, nothing vibrant. Nothing like the shiny-nosed, tousle-haired woman who'd stirred his emotions and now waited patiently while he tried to deal with his inner turmoil. ''Would I be able to tell if I had used it in the past?''

''I think it depends on how long it's been since you used it.'' Her voice was low, as though she realized the concern that was building in him.

''That's not much help.''

She reached across the countertop and laid her hand on his, providing warmth where none existed. ''Jon, are you wondering if your loss of memory is due to cocaine?''

He nodded.

''I guess you could have a drug test, but—again, I'm speaking as an attorney—I don't advise it. The D.A. has decided not to pursue the drug angle. Why, I'm not sure, unless they don't think they have enough evidence to make it stick. And right now, all they've got is Van Rooten's supposed hunch, which is pretty lame. The rain wiped out all the evidence, if there ever was any. Until we get the murder charge taken care of, I don't think we need to add any fuel to the fire. They can go after capital murder and the death penalty if they can prove you killed Saul in the process of a drug deal.''

He sighed. Somewhere out there was the answer to this mix-up of identities. He just had to find it, but it looked like he'd have to wait a while longer. As a ranger, he had always been a man of action and facts. He didn't believe in spirits or ghosts or any of that newfangled science stuff that claimed a man could travel through time.

He wanted to tell Lauren that he was John McCain, not Jonathan. Not the brother of that woman Helena who'd come to see him. Not the son of whoever those people were who'd paid his bail. Not the owner of this ranch. And she'd figure he was as crazy as a pony that had eaten locoweed.

Besides, the similarity of names was too bizarre to be a coincidence. Jonathan and John McCain. Something was going on whether it was Jules Verne or demons or...no! The one thing he sensed keenly was that regardless of the time frame, *he* was a man of the law—a Texas Ranger, not a common smuggler and murderer. But he didn't know about this man named Jonathan.

While Jon was lost in his own world, Lauren looked at her watch. She wanted to talk more, but it was almost seven-thirty. ''I've got to go. Robert will have a posse out looking for me if I don't show up for work. Do you think you'll be okay here?''

''I'll be fine,'' he said. ''You just go do what you can to get this misunderstanding cleared up.''

She noted the false bravado in his voice. He was more concerned about his fate than he wanted her to know, but she answered in kind. ''It won't be long. Then you'll be a free man.''

''I have faith in you, counselor.'' He briefly brushed her cheek with the back of his fingers.

''I'll come back as soon as I have some news. Take care of yourself, and I'll call to see how you're doing.''

As she once again drove down the muddy road that led

away from Jon, she went over the same scenario she had sixteen hours earlier. How could she allow her feelings for Jonathan McCain to interfere with her professional judgment? Unfortunately, Lauren was finding it quite easy, so easy that she discovered she even had to concentrate on driving.

Only the residual effects of mud and a few puddles remained in the arroyo as a reminder of last night's treacherous flash flood. She carefully drove across the rock bottom and had started to climb the other side when she noticed tire tracks leading to the arroyo, turning around and going back toward the highway. Someone had driven out this far after the rain last night and been unable to continue on to the ranch. The thought sent a shiver down her spine.

She stopped her car and got out to study the track pattern. From the distance between tires, she guessed it was a car rather than a pickup. And the zigzag pattern was not the mark of heavy-duty tires.

Concerned that whoever it had been would come back, she called Jonathan as soon as she got to her house.

After four rings he answered. "Yes."

"Jonathan, someone came out as far as the arroyo last night but had to turn around and go back to the highway. I don't know who it was or what is going on, but please be careful. The person could return today now that it's drier."

"I will." John didn't know what was going on, either, but he'd be damned if he was just going to sit around and wait to be convicted of a murder he didn't think he'd committed. So after he hung up, he began to check things out. The five slots in the gun case were empty. He remembered Van Rooten had said that he'd confiscated four rifles from McCain's house and had recovered the fifth rifle "used in the cold-blooded murder of Saul Rodriquez" in the desert.

Wondering what else Van Rooten and the deputies had hauled out of the house, John looked around, not knowing what should or should not be there. But he did know he shouldn't stick around here. Not if someone was coming for him. So he grabbed the butcher knife and headed to the barns.

Keeping his eye out for the old tomcat that had scared Lauren the evening before, he slid open the door to the metal barn. He didn't much care for the cold, hollow feeling of the large space inside, so he closed the door and strolled to an old weathered barn. It would have looked like every other barn he'd ever seen it if hadn't been falling down. A sense of loss and sadness settled over him as he surveyed the empty hayloft and stalls.

Trying to shake his melancholy mood, he walked over to what he assumed was the bunkhouse. Three doors opened into the long adobe building. Testing the first door, John wasn't surprised to find it unlocked. He stepped inside to discover, not a shared bunk area, but instead something that was set up like an apartment. The first two rooms, covered with dust, showed no sign of recent occupation.

John remembered the sheriff saying he'd searched the place and Saul's family had come for his personal belongings, so John doubted he'd discover much in the third room, either. With trepidation, he pushed open the door, hoping that in this room he'd find something about himself by discovering something about Saul.

A few old dishes were in the cupboards and some magazines were scattered on the small wooden table. A mattress with striped ticking rested on the metal bed frame. Nothing was left to identify Saul as a person.

Disheartened, John sat down on the edge of the bed and opened the drawer of the bedside table, surprised to see a Bible. He picked up the leather volume and ran his fingers over the edges of the pages. Annie had read the Good Book every day, he remembered, but he couldn't recall the last time he'd read it. Maybe it was time.

He turned to the Psalms. ''What...?'' There in a cutout

square lay a clear bag of white powder. Was it cocaine? As he learned more and more about the man he was suppose to be, John lost some of his confidence. This bag could mean Saul and Jonathan smuggled drugs. And if they'd smuggled drugs, he might **have** killed Saul regardless of what Lauren had said.

John's throat tightened when he realized an unknown accomplice of his could have chased the sheriff through Diablo Canyon. And it could have been that same person who'd shot at Lauren. And the same person who'd tried to come out to the ranch last night.

John buried his head in his hands and considered the real possibility that he was both John and Jonathan McCain. If that was the case then the man whose body he inhabited might truly be a criminal who deserved to die for his sins. And he was falling in love with a woman who had vowed to help him. What if he was guilty? Then he would drag her down with him. He couldn't do that.

John walked out in the hills, and with the heel of his boot, dug a hole. Squatting, he dumped the contents of the bag into the hole and stirred it with a stick until the brown dirt hid any trace of white. Tearing the sack into tiny pieces, he added it to the hole, covered it and walked back to the bunkhouse to wait. He didn't know if he'd done right or not, but no one was going to catch him with anything that could cause him more grief or justify Lauren's doubts.

No one disturbed John's solitude all the rest of Saturday, and so by Sunday morning he decided Lauren had to have been mistaken about a visitor. From his hiding spot in the bunkhouse he'd seen nothing except the rolling prairie and the looming mountains.

He'd decided he wanted something to eat other than the eggs he'd made the night before and had thought about going down to the main house when he saw dust kicking up in the distance. Stepping back from the window, John watched a gray car come to a stop in front of the house. While he was too far away to recognize anyone, he could tell it wasn't Robert and it wasn't the sheriff.

Something about the way the man walked struck a chord. John closed his eyes, then looked again, but by that time, the man was out of view. If he was the person who had tried to come during the rainstorm, he wasn't secretive.

Even from this distance, John could hear the him calling out, "Jonathan, you in there?" The man circled around the house and began pounding on the back door, then went in. John licked his lips, pulled the knife out of his boot and waited.

In less than five minutes, he saw the man get back in his car and leave. Relieved but curious, John wondered what he had done inside. Since this must be the person Lauren had warned him about, he waited an hour to be sure the guy didn't come back. Then John headed down the hill to the house.

He was disappointed to find that nothing inside had been disturbed. Thinking maybe a note had been tacked to the front door, he stepped out on the porch. Again he found nothing. Maybe Lauren's fears had been exaggerated. He stared at the road and remembered her fading image. Already, he wanted her back with him.

A scraping noise around the side of the house alerted his senses. He crept across the porch and peered around the corner just as the wild tomcat made a dash back to the barn. John sighed and let out a nervous laugh, feeling foolish for having been spooked.

He squinted toward the horizon where the road vanished. No dust, no motion. Even so, John thought he ought to get back to the bunkhouse, where he had a better view of the road leading up to the main house. Whoever had been in that gray car might decide to pay another visit. Deciding to take the photographs Lauren had brought him from his par-

ents' and a little grub back with him, John stepped inside
the house again and began gathering things together.

After he'd looked around, he stuck a few magazines in
a sack with the pictures and went to the kitchen for food.
As he scrounged in the refrigerator, he heard another scraping noise on the back porch. Figuring the cat had come
back, Jonathan closed the refrigerator door and started outside. He froze when he heard a voice.

"McCain?"

"Damn!" John muttered softly, recognizing the sheriff's
voice. Where had he come from? Had he been let out a
ways back by the person in the car? Or had he come on
his own and hiked cross-country?

"You in there, boy? Get your ass out here 'cause I
wanna talk to you."

Talk, hell, John thought. If he'd ever known anything,
John knew Van Rooten didn't want to talk. If he'd wanted
to have a conversation he'd have knocked on the front door
instead of sneaking around to the back. John could see the
setting sun glint off the metal surface of a gun as the sheriff
stepped off the porch. John dropped to the floor so he
couldn't be seen if the sheriff looked through the windows.
He suspected Van Rooten planned to kill him.

"McCain. You coming out or do I have to come in and
get you?"

John looked around. His only weapon was the knife, and
it was no match for a gun. Maybe he could hide behind the
door and surprise the sheriff if he came in. Then he thought
of how it would look if he, a man out on bail for murder,
stabbed the local sheriff. Lauren wouldn't be able to do a
damn thing for him.

He had to run.

He crawled down the hallway to a bedroom, then stopped
to listen. He heard the back door burst open and footsteps
in the kitchen. John hastily pushed open a window, and

when it emitted a screeching sound, he feared Van Rooten must have heard it.

John had to get out fast. He inched the window up as quickly as he could, holding his breath, praying for silence.

He scrambled out the window and glanced around for a place to run, then took off in a crouch toward the old wooden barn. When he entered the rickety structure, he slid around the corner and leaned against the rough wall, breathing hard from the sprint and hoping he hadn't been seen.

He eyed the house through a crack in the wood and saw Van Rooten step back outside on the porch, gun drawn. Knowing he had to hide before the sheriff came looking for him, John stumbled into a stall and squeezed behind a stack of rotting lumber.

With every ounce of his energy focused on listening, John heard Van Rooten outside the barn, his footsteps a faint skitter on the hard-packed dirt. Clutching the knife tightly in one hand, John waited until the sound receded.

As the sheriff headed away from the barn, John's head began to swirl and his knees turned to rubber. Trying to restore his equilibrium, he dropped the knife and grabbed the stall railing, but the dizziness got worse. Just before he knelt on the floor, an image of Van Rooten holding a rifle flashed through his mind. The sheriff was bragging about the highfalutin people he was tied up with.

John clutched his head with both hands. He remembered Van Rooten saying, as clear as day, "I ain't got nothing to worry about because my lawyer buddy will keep me looking clean."

And then John's mind went blank as he collapsed into darkness.

Chapter 9

The ringing telephone startled Lauren. She'd spent most of Sunday working in her too-quiet office. Pulling her eyes away from her computer screen, she answered the call with her usual greeting. "Jordan and Hamilton. May I help you?"

"I certainly hope you can. This is Chester."

Lauren looked at the ceiling and forced pleasantness into her voice. "How're you doing, Sheriff?"

"This isn't exactly a social call, so I'll get right to the point. I drove out to McCain's ranch this afternoon and guess what?" Without waiting for a response, he continued, "He was nowhere to be found. Where do you reckon he went?"

"He has to be out there, Chester. Maybe he was asleep and didn't hear you." *Or most likely, he was smart enough to avoid you.*

"I don't think so, missy. I knocked, I hollered and I honked my car horn. I woke every coyote in a two-mile range, but your Mr. Jonathan McCain didn't show hide nor hair of hisself. Considering the restrictions on his bail, I'm just a *lit*tle bitty bit more than concerned.'' Chester sniffed. "You don't reckon he's skipped, do you?''

Hearing the hidden threat in Van Rooten's words, Lauren was a little concerned, too. Not that Jonathan hadn't shown his face, but that the sheriff had already paid him a visit. "No, I don't think he's skipped, Chester. But if it'll make you feel better, I'll check on him right now.''

"Good idea, little gal. I want to see your client eyeball-to-eyeball in the morning so me and the deputies can focus our attention on a few other goings-on rather than having to put out an APB on McCain again.''

After Van Rooten hung up, Lauren held the receiver like a club, relishing the thought of using it to beat the condescending chauvinism out of Chester Van Rooten. Aggravated that she'd lowered herself into having Chester-like thoughts for even a few seconds, she pulled herself together and flipped off her computer.

She was still irked that he'd dismissed her report of being shot at by saying that he'd heard through the grapevine that some guys from central Texas had been hunting that day. According to him, they'd probably mistaken her for a deer, and when she figured out their mistake, and considering it wasn't hunting season anyway, they'd hightailed from the area. While she couldn't prove it, she was sure this was another one of Chester's lies. What was he up to, anyway? Was he a participant in illegal activities or was someone buying his favor? He'd never been mistaken for a paragon of virtue, but he'd always seemed to be on the up-and-up.

She wasn't really concerned about Jonathan skipping out. After all, she herself had warned him to stay hidden after seeing the tire tracks. When she'd gotten into town yesterday she'd swung by the sheriff's office to check the tire patterns on his car. They had matched and so did the pattern on the deputy's car. And the car next to it. She figured most of the cars in town had the same prints.

Hoping Jonathan was in his house now, she tried calling him, but when there was no answer, she decided she'd better drive out. Since someone needed to know where she was going, and she figured Lyna would worry less than anyone, she called the secretary and explained the situation.

Paying no attention to the passing landscape as she sped southward, Lauren fretted about Jonathan. What if something really had happened to him? What if Van Rooten wasn't at the root of this mystery and the real villain had gone out to see Jonathan first? Could Jonathan be somewhere alone, hurt? Trapped?

She reprimanded herself for leaving him alone yesterday. Just because he was physically fit didn't mean he was able to take care of himself. From the way he'd talked, there was no way of knowing how deep his memory gaps went. He could have forgotten basics that put him in danger. Things like light the burner when you turn on the gas. Don't stick a metal object in an electrical outlet. The list was endless, and Lauren considered almost every one of them on the long drive to the ranch.

She parked in front of the big house, half-afraid of what she would find inside. Van Rooten had said Jonathan wasn't there, but she sensed he was nearby. The fears she had built to near-volcanic proportions subsided as she approached the veranda. Jonathan was okay. She knew it.

When no one answered the door, she went inside. The living room looked just as she'd left it the day before. Her footsteps echoed through the empty house as she searched the bedrooms. Jonathan's bed was unmade and the closet was full. If he'd left, he hadn't packed.

The fear that something terrible had happened to him, the fear she thought she'd conquered, began building again as she hurried to the final room. Memories of him saying how he felt about her, the way he'd looked early in the morning with his tousled hair and bare chest, came flooding back while she stood in the center of the kitchen and glanced at the unwashed coffee mugs in the sink.

The faint sound of a door being pushed open alerted her a split second before Jonathan appeared at the back door. He stood there as if nothing was amiss.

"You looking for me?" he asked, his face expressionless.

Lauren clutched the counter behind her to keep from falling. "Oh, Jon, where have you been?"

"After you called me yesterday I decided it was stupid just to sit here and wait for trouble, so I went up to the old bunkhouse."

Wanting to run into his arms, she instead slowly walked toward him. "That was smart. But I was really worried for a few minutes. When you weren't here, I was afraid something terrible had happened to you."

He must have read the pain on her face because without another word he reached out and drew her into his embrace, burying his face in her hair. It was as if he was garnering strength from her presence, just as she was from his.

"Not that I'm disappointed, but what are you doing back here so soon?" he asked as he brushed a loose curl away from her temple.

She looked up into his face. His eyes were dark and she thought she saw a glimmer of mistrust when she explained, "Van Rooten said he'd been out here to check on you and didn't find you. He wondered if you'd left and demanded to see you in the morning."

"I saw him, but it didn't look like he'd come on a social call or to see if I was minding my manners." Jonathan's voice was almost too cold and casual, as if he was distancing himself from harm.

"What did you think—that he came back to kill you?"

"I don't know what to think. The sheriff was waving a pretty big gun when he sneaked around to the back door."

Lauren was puzzled. "What do you mean, sneaked?"

"I didn't hear or see a car. He didn't knock." Jonathan described the sheriff's visit.

"That's not what he told me. He said he did everything but shoot cannons to rouse you."

Jonathan shrugged his shoulders. "Wrong."

"And you were close enough to see the gun?"

"I could nearly smell it."

The image of the tables being turned on Van Rooten caused her to chuckle more with nervous relief than amusement. "So you watched him the whole time he was here, and he never had a clue."

"If he had, I believe he'd have pulled the trigger." Jonathan tugged at the corners of his mouth for a mustache that didn't exist. "The fact is, I'm a pretty popular fellow." He paused as though waiting for Lauren to consider his words. "I've already had two visitors today."

"Two?" Lauren raised an eyebrow.

"Two. I couldn't tell much about the first fella except he was, oh, say, about average." Jonathan used his hands to demonstrate. "He eased up in a gray car and nosed around for fifteen minutes or so, then left."

Lauren wondered who the man was. "It could have been a reporter hoping to get a scoop."

"Who knows?" Jonathan opened the refrigerator. Peering inside, he asked, "Would you like a beer? That's all there is to drink unless you want some water, or I could make some coffee in that fancy little machine over there."

Lauren smiled. "I wouldn't put you out. Beer will be fine."

He opened two bottles and handed one to her before straddling a kitchen chair and taking a big sip of his own drink. Then he leaned forward and crossed his arms on the ladder back of the chair. "Just why would a reporter be interested in me?"

Lauren sat down at the table next to him and rotated the bottle in her hands as she explained about his family being prominent citizens of El Paso. How those who didn't have much seemingly enjoyed reading about the failings of those better off financially. How it helped sell newspapers.

"So I'm one of those failings?" Still clutching the bottle in one hand, John leaned forward and rested his head on his crossed arms. "I can't recall them, even after looking at all those pictures you left me."

"I told you they seemed to be very nice people. You're tall like your father, and you have your mother's coloring." Lauren hesitated, then began again. "Jon, there is one thing I didn't tell you the other day."

"Like what?" he asked.

"Your mother said you and your father got angry with each other over twenty years ago and quit speaking. So, if you do happen to remember anything, it might be good to remember that he wants to help you now."

Everything was getting more complicated for John. He closed his eyes and concentrated, trying to pull up an image of his father other than the one in a photo, but his efforts were of no avail. Rubbing his hands over his face, he grew disheartened. The only things he'd recalled were a couple of flashes too short to be called memories. When he was captured and had stared up at the blinking lights on the hovering helicopter, he'd remembered seeing lights swooping down another time. He flinched, realizing those lights had been on the airstrip not a quarter of a mile away from where he was sitting right now.

And earlier today he'd experienced another unsettling vision—of Van Rooten bragging about his lawyer. Other than the sheriff being involved both times, John still hadn't sorted out what the flashes meant. Were they hallucinations brought on by cocaine?

Even that didn't make sense. After all, he'd never seen Van Rooten until the trial, so how could he remember something that never happened, hallucination or not? He felt Lauren lay a hand on his shoulder and move around behind him. Her touch was gentle and reassuring, as was her voice. "Things will work out, Jon. Your memory will come back. It just may take time."

He didn't move, but sat there savoring the feel of her fingers as they massaged his neck. As Lauren's fingers continued to caress the muscles and work their way up to his temples, John leaned back until the top of his head was resting against her soft breasts. He sighed with contentment. During the past thirty-odd hours while she'd been gone, all the muscles in his body had grown harder and more tightly wound in his effort to stay alert. He hadn't allowed himself the luxury of relaxing until now.

As Lauren soothed the furrows from Jonathan's brow and massaged from his forehead down his hairline to the top of his spine, she felt the tension and confusion leave his body. She denied herself the luxury of thinking of him as a man. Instead she focused her attention on the way his muscles were relaxing under her fingertips, not the way his bronzed skin looked under her hands, nor the way the dark hair curled over his ears.

After a few minutes, he appeared to be asleep, his head almost cradled between her breasts. She wondered when he had last slept well. Probably before Saul had been shot.

When her hands ceased moving, he slowly sat up and rolled his head around as if to get the last of the kinks out. "That felt good."

"I hope it relaxed you a little." It had done everything except relax her. Stepping back to avoid the potential fire, she took her beer bottle and poured the rest of the drink in the sink.

The kitchen was growing dimmer as night began to fall, and the waning light brought back memories of another evening. She recalled the night before last—now an eternity ago—when she and Jonathan had stood here together and prepared a meal. Had it only been two days since she'd almost made love to him on the floor of the living room?

And earlier today, when she'd thought something had happened to him, she'd regretted having missed the experience.

She folded her arms over her chest and watched him. He seemed lost, unsure of what to do or what to say. It was hard to imagine the inner turmoil he must be feeling because he couldn't remember anything about himself or his family. She realized she would have to be his bridge to reality.

Now was as good a time as any to begin. "Did you find anything that seemed familiar to you while I was gone?"

"Other than the clothes fitting me, this place could belong to anybody. That polished vehicle outside doesn't mean a thing. Nothing's struck a chord with me one way or the other."

"I'd hoped the pictures, the books, the surroundings would help."

"In a way, they did. When Van Rooten was here and I was huddled out in one of the stalls, I think I remembered something. It was kind of like an impression of seeing him before, holding a gun...a rifle...my rifle, apparently—" he nodded his head toward the living room and its empty gun case "—and firing it. He has to be involved some way. The smuggling or the murder." Jonathan shrugged his shoulders. "Or both."

Lauren's face froze when she realized the significance of what he had said. If Chester were involved in smuggling, then Jon... She refused to follow that line of thought. She focused her energy instead on Jonathan. "Let's look at this positively. You remember something. If Chester was holding a rifle, it means he could have been shooting at you. That's where you got your wound."

"It could also have happened another day."

She ignored that. "No. According to what I read about amnesia, any memories you have would probably be significant. Being shot at certainly qualifies. I wouldn't be at all surprised if Chester's behind the drug smuggling and probably the murder and you just happened on it. That would explain a lot...and means Chester wants you dead." She started pacing the tile floor, answering her internal questions. "He doesn't want to charge you with any drug-related crime. If he did, Robert would start digging around and might find something the sheriff doesn't want anyone to know."

"That gives me an idea." Jonathan's eyes burned emerald bright with hope. "But..." He paused. "I'd have to leave the ranch."

"You can't, Jon. The judge would issue a bench warrant for your arrest and you'd end up back in jail. Besides, Van Rooten would have the perfect excuse to shoot if he caught up with you outside of the ranch."

"Lauren, I can't just sit here and wait for the sheriff to return to kill me, if that's what he aims to do." He caught her as she walked by, closed his large hands over her shoulders and squeezed. "Next time, he might be successful. I've got to sleep eventually."

His hands transmitted some of the desperation he was feeling, and Lauren wished she could wave a wand and fix the situation. But it wasn't that simple. "I think you should let Ted come out and stay. Two of you would be harder to catch unawares. Plus, Ted and I might be able to do for you what you can't. In fact, tomorrow I'm going to begin investigating the sheriff's finances. Besides, if he knows we're watching him, he may back off for a while or slip up."

"Ted, you said. He's your brother?"

"Yes, and—"

"I don't want anyone out here I don't know." His voice lowered until it wove its own special web around her heart. "I'd rather have *you* stay."

She didn't resist when he pulled her nearer until there were only a few inches separating their bodies. The heat radiating from his skin seeped into her pores, and with it a strong desire to get closer to its source.

He was hard to resist with his blazing eyes and inviting lips. Would it hurt to kiss him once more? Every time he touched her, kissed her, it became more difficult to say no the next time. Her wants and needs warred with her better judgment. When she'd thought he might be dead, she'd wished they had made love so she would have the memory to cherish. And the relief of seeing him alive and well reduced her defenses against him. She wanted to feel his lips on hers more than anything in the world. "I shouldn't..."

He cupped her chin in one hand and held it firmly as he lowered his head, stopping mere inches from her lips. His warm breath fanned across her cheeks. "Tell me to stop."

When she was able to speak, her voice was barely a whisper. "I don't want to." With those words she rose on tiptoe to press her lips to his.

She felt the tight restraint he'd kept on his own passion ebb from his muscles as he hauled her against him, molding her body to his in a desperate attempt to find what he was seeking. The feel of his arms wrapping around her gave her a sense of security and contentment, as if she was coming home. The utter joy that washed over her as he searched her mouth with his couldn't be wrong no matter what ethics decreed. She gave up the battle and buried her hands in his hair. Here in Jonathan McCain's embrace she felt whole.

John groaned and gave himself up totally to the desire pulsing through his veins. He knew he was taking a chance falling in love with this woman. But no matter how hard he denied his feelings, they were there—in the middle of his confusion over his identity, in the middle of his fear for his life. He couldn't get away from them no matter how hard he tried. When he needed to be concentrating on his own problems, all he could think about was her smile, the way she felt in his arms, the way she moaned softly when he kissed her.

As she sagged against him in total surrender, he took her weight in his arms and set her on the kitchen table. Immediately she pulled his head back down to hers and parted his lips with the tip of her tongue. The way she responded without inhibition was so erotic he felt like he would explode with the need to make love to her. He ran his hands up and down her denim-clad legs, relishing the heat of her body, imprinting it on his mind, knowing that soon he was going to have to call a halt to this. Even though she was a willing participant, he didn't want her to compromise her own ethics for him. He didn't want to be responsible for her feeling guilty later.

Of their own volition, his hands ignored his brain and slid farther up her legs until he was cupping her firm buttocks in his palms and settling himself between the vee of her legs. An involuntary shudder racked his body as he tore his lips away from hers and leaned his head against her hair. He knew he had to stop or there would be no turning back for either of them. He held her tightly as he took deep breaths in an effort to gain control. She, too, seemed to be struggling with her desires as she buried her head against his chest. Neither of them moved for several seconds.

The first coherent thought Lauren had was of the phone ringing. As Jonathan took a step backward, she slid from the table and took the receiver he handed her. Trying to quell the quaver in her voice, she answered, "Hello?"

"Is that you, Lauren?" Lyna hollered. "I can't hear you. The connection must be bad. Are you okay?"

Lauren cleared her throat. "Yes, Lyna, I'm fine."

"I'm glad you are, because you're fixing to get sick when I tell you some bad news."

Lauren hadn't heard much lately that wasn't bad. "What's happened?"

"I got a call from the police. Someone broke into the office this evening, must have set off the alarm. They went through your desk and files, and that's not all. Your neighbors also called the cops. Apparently, when whoever broke in didn't find what they were looking for in the office, they tried your house. Or maybe they did the house first. I'm not sure. Anyway, we've got a mess here in the office, and you've got a bigger mess at your house.''

Lauren sagged as she listened to Lyna go into more detail. ''Oh, great. I'll be back as soon as I can,'' she said, while nestling back into the embrace Jonathan offered to steady her weak knees.

''I'll be waiting. By the way, did you find Jonathan?''

''Yes. Van Rooten was crying wolf.''

''Have you got him to talk yet?'' Lyna's stage whisper was loud enough to be heard for several feet. ''Did you find out what he really knows about the killing? Robert thinks he may just be playing like he has amnesia. He says you gotta find out what Jonathan knows before you all get in trouble.'' She rambled on before Lauren could stop her. ''If anyone can get him to talk, you can. Just wag your butt at him. It works every time.''

Lauren felt Jonathan tense and withdraw as her friend rambled on.

Chapter 10

Lauren hung up the phone and turned to face Jonathan, who had backed away. She knew he had heard most of the conversation.

"Wag your butt?" he repeated, mimicking the secretary's voice.

"You have to know Lyna," Lauren said, trying to mitigate her words. "She says whatever she thinks, and sometimes she doesn't think at all before talking."

"So you think I'm lying to you about my memory?"

"No, I don't. Robert may have expressed some skepticism earlier, as well he should have, but he doesn't doubt you at all now." She reached out to touch him, but he sidestepped her hand.

As John eavesdropped on the conversation, his concern over Lauren's house and office had turned to anger when he realized she was using him to get information for her boss—the big Sierra attorney. The man who, according to the paper, generally got his clients off. As the thought formulated, John recalled the rest of his flashback. He closed his eyes, remembering that Van Rooten had said something about being protected by a lawyer. Was the sheriff in cahoots with Robert Jordan? Or Lauren? When John opened his eyes, she was watching him.

She gently chewed at her bottom lip before saying, "Robert and Deputy Soliz are supposed to be checking out the break-in of my house and the office."

"Like the fox guarding the henhouse." What else was he to think about her boss and the Sierra law enforcement?

Lauren shot him a look that said she thought the remark was uncalled-for, then began pacing the room while she talked, but not necessarily to him, John realized.

"I wonder why Chester's not there helping. He may be up to something…though I would think he'd be smart enough not to break into the office or my house…someone might see him. But he did know I was on my way out here…so the coast was clear." As Lauren thought aloud, she used her index finger to punctuate each new thought. "He's not smart enough to be masterminding this thing."

John suspected he knew who the mastermind was. "I remembered something else today other than Van Rooten holding a rifle." John watched her face for a reaction. If she was in league with the criminals, she sure was innocent looking.

A smile of relief spread across her face as she stopped and spun around from her pacing. "Oh, wonderful. What was it?"

It would have been easy to allow himself to believe she was honestly glad his memory was returning. He didn't understand himself how he recalled something about Chester. He'd only been in the twentieth century a few days. "It was just a flash, but I'm pretty sure his accomplice in this operation is some bigwig." John paused, bracing himself for Lauren's reaction. "An attorney."

"An attorney?" Lauren's expression turned to one of

shock, then she grabbed him by the arm. "Did he mention a name?"

"I lost the image before I remembered the name." He wasn't sure how to judge her reaction. Was she startled because he remembered something or because his memory involved a crooked attorney? Someone she might know? His gaze held hers while he willed his eyes to be emotionless.

Finally, Lauren backed away from him and crossed her arms, studying him all the while. "I think I know what you're thinking. That it could be Robert?" Her voice dropped to a whisper. "Or me."

He felt his face betray his uncertainty and figured she'd been able to read it because she jumped to another point. "Well, cowboy, you were taking a big chance telling me your memory is returning if you think I'm involved." He watched as her normally soft eyes flashed with barely controlled, blazing fury. "I might be here to finish what Van Rooten couldn't."

He stepped toward her, an eyebrow cocked. "I have to be honest and say that thought's crossed my mind."

She whirled around and started toward the front door. "I think I'd better leave."

Although he felt justified in not fully trusting her, he also felt like a heel. Then he felt angry. "What makes it so different for me to doubt you than for you to doubt me?"

"You're the one with the landing strip," she accused.

"You're the attorney," he countered.

She stopped at the steps of the porch, but kept her back to him until he touched her shoulder and gently turned her to face him. Tears glinted in her eyes, but her accusatory glare never faltered.

"I'm sorry, but look at this from my point of view. Someone is trying to kill me and I can't even remember enough to protect myself. To me, everyone is suspect. And you have to admit, where you're concerned there have been a lot of coincidences." His heart refused to believe it, but circumstances pointed to the possibility that Lauren was involved. "You showed up in the cave and claimed to have been shot at."

"You heard the shots." Her steely voice was barely more than a whisper.

"They could have been staged." He felt her tense, but she remained quiet as he continued, "What are the odds that my 'sister' would hire your partner out of all the attorneys in Texas? In fact, you could have made up this family that I'm conveniently estranged from. I can't even check the story out because I wouldn't know if they were telling me the truth. I'm at your absolute mercy whether I like it or not."

Lauren shrugged out of his grasp while John continued talking. "You offered to drive me back to this ranch. That might have just been a way to check things out so you could set me up for the sheriff. Van Rooten sure was quick about letting you know he couldn't find me. And you didn't waste any time getting yourself back out here."

Her eyes flashed fire and hurt, not guilt. "That doesn't make me a dirty lawyer or a drug smuggler."

"No, but you accused me of the same thing a couple of days ago without much more evidence."

As Lauren sped back to Sierra, the miles passed in a blur. Her traveling companion, the radio, offered no solace from the discord between her and Jonathan. The deejays sounded shallow, the music cacophonous and the news depressing. Never before had she felt that her life was right in sync with the rest of the big, bad world. No, she'd always been Little Miss Pollyanna, the things-will-turn-out-okay type that drove just about everyone else crazy. Even law school had failed to extinguish her optimistic attitude.

Well, no more. The cynicism she had escaped was settling in. All because of one man. Maybe it was because she was thirty and couldn't keep shuffling men to the sidelines forever. But she didn't really believe that. Here she'd met the fantasy of her life, a man who had set her on fire from the first minute. If it had been just lust, she could handle that as she usually did—by running away from it. But it was more than that. This was a man she wanted to protect rather than just expecting him to protect her. No, what she felt was no biological clock.

She tapped her nails against the steering wheel as she fought back the anger at his distrust of her. Intellectually, she should condemn him for having ever trusted her to begin with. He was right—she looked guilty. But her emotions were overruling her brain and it hurt like the devil. Now, on top of Jonathan's suspicions, she had one more thing to confront. Her house had been broken into.

She had read enough about break-ins and had a client who'd suffered through one to know that most people equated it with rape—a violation of their person. And the closer to Sierra she got, the more anxious she became, and the more she forced her encounter with Jonathan to the back of her mind so she could deal with what had happened to her office and home.

When she pulled up in front of her house and saw the lights blazing, she took a deep breath. She wouldn't rant or rave or cry, because she detested hysterical females. Certain she had herself under control, she opened the door and stepped out of her car. Before she even had a chance to reach the front door, Lyna hurried out to meet her.

"I've been pacing the floor waiting for you. I was over at the office for a while. The deputy took some pictures, but Robert said we need to wait and go through everything tomorrow before straightening up, so I rushed over here because you're going to need some help. Robert's at the sheriff's office filling out some forms, and he said if you need anything, call him." Lyna talked nonstop as she and Lauren entered the house.

Lauren hardly listened after she got to the middle of her

living room and surveyed the mess. It looked like a horrible Halloween prank had been played on her. Nothing was broken, but cushions were tossed about, contents of drawers littered the floor and the pictures hung askew.

She hurried to the kitchen, knowing what the person had been looking for—the photograph. Sure enough, the minute she rounded the dining alcove, she stopped, knowing the packet containing the canyon photo had been found. Most of the cookbooks were dumped on the floor, but the one where she'd hidden the photo lay open on the counter.

"Well, whoever it was found what they wanted," she said. Halfheartedly, she pushed at one of the cookbooks with her toe. She wasn't sure whether her heavy heart was more the result of the break-in or because of the lingering effects of her disagreement with Jonathan.

"What was it?" Lyna asked. "The first thing I thought about was your jewelry, but decided right off that breaking into your house and breaking into the office didn't equal jewelry."

"No, but what they got is potentially more valuable than jewelry." Lauren told Lyna about the photo that might reveal who the real murderer was.

Although there was no silence so short that Lyna couldn't fill it, she also knew when to keep her mouth shut.

Lauren said, "All the thief got was a print. The negative is at a lab in El Paso."

"Then you're still in danger if the scoundrel knows you got a picture of him. I don't think you ought to stay here by yourself. Someone could be on a stakeout watching you as we talk." Lyna pointed to the large front window and its half-open vertical blinds. "They can see through that window if they're in the correct position. A rifle could be aimed at you right now." She hurried over and snapped the blinds closed, then rubbed her hands together as though she'd taken care of the burglar. "There. That's better."

"Lyna, you watch too much television." But Lauren felt

better, too, remembering that a rifle had been trained on her only eight days earlier.

There was a quick rap at the door a split second before Robert stepped over the threshold and strolled into the kitchen. "Hello, ladies." As he scanned the room and its disarray, a frown gathered on his brow, bringing his bushy gray eyebrows closer together. He reached into his shirt pocket and withdrew an antacid. Popping it into his mouth, he said, "Not much of a housekeeper, are you?"

Lauren, appreciating his effort to lighten the mood, agreed. "It looks that way, doesn't it?"

"I was just telling Lauren that she needs to stay with me tonight," Lyna said. "What do you think, Robert?"

"I concur," he answered. "You can't do anything here until the crime lab has a go at this place. They'll want to search for fingerprints, so don't straighten up anything else."

Lauren smiled at the thought of the crime lab in Sierra. It consisted of the sheriff and his refrigerator—where he stored more sodas and candy than evidence. There had been a rumor he was going to buy a new microscope because the old one had fallen off the table and broken. She knew that with any important crime the evidence was sent elsewhere.

She didn't want the sheriff in her house without her watching his every move. The fact of the matter was, she figured Chester had something to do with this little break-in. That was something she *didn't* intend to mention in front of Lyna. All she needed was the chatty secretary spreading her suspicions around town and Chester would know Lauren was on to him.

"The sheriff's department is a little shorthanded right now because Chester's had to go out of town on personal business. One of the deputies will be here first thing in the morning. Probably Soliz." The silent message Lauren read in Robert's blue eyes told her as much as his words. He had suspected Chester the same as she had. That he didn't say any more implied that this was information he preferred to keep from Lyna.

"That's strange," Lauren murmured. "Chester said he wanted to see Jonathan in the morning."

"Vera said Chester had some business come up sudden like, and that he stormed out of his office, saying he wasn't sure how long he'd be gone. Said he'd be in touch."

Lauren intended to ask Vera just what time Chester had left—before or after the burglary.

"See?" Lyna said, oblivious to the unspoken communications. "There's no reason for you to stay here. You can come with me and we'll have a good ol' slumber party to help take your mind off this mess. Then in the morning, you can meet Deputy Soliz."

Lauren sighed as she remembered what day it was. "I've got a court date tomorrow morning."

"You can get there as easily from my house as yours."

Finally she agreed to go over to Lyna's, but it certainly didn't take her mind off the mess. On the contrary, after listening to Lyna's theories, in which she accused half the townspeople of being the guilty culprits, Lauren suggested they call it a night so she would have time to go over her notes for tomorrow.

Crawling into the high Victorian bed in Lyna's guest room, Lauren flipped through the file she'd brought with her and tried to order her thoughts. It was no use. Try as she might, she couldn't focus on tomorrow's hearing. Thank goodness it was going to be easy to prove her client had been in El Paso at the time his wife claimed he had violated a restraining order. Two weeks ago, she'd have had no problem keeping her mind on her work.

But now her life had been jarred out of complacency, all because of Jonathan McCain. She was hurt by Jonathan's withdrawal, especially after she'd almost compromised her ethics by making love to him. She felt like a first-class fool.

And to top it off, her home, her sanctuary, had been violated.

The Monday-morning blues were worse than usual for Lauren as she and Lyna waited in the office while the deputy dusted for fingerprints, then attempted to reorganize the office before she had to leave for the courtroom. Just as everything was back in half-decent shape, Lauren heard someone yelling from the outer office.

"Anyone here?" It was a man's voice, one she didn't recognize.

Lyna smoothed her hair and hurried to the front to take care of the visitor as Lauren finished shelving the last of the books behind her desk.

Less than a minute later, Lyna buzzed Lauren. "Ms. Hamilton, a Mr. Cliff Atkinson is here to see you or Mr. Jordan on some urgent business. Can you see him?"

Lauren nearly gasped when she heard the name Atkinson. The name Jonathan had uttered in the cave had a body to go with it. Now maybe there would be some answers. She swallowed. "Yes, of course. Send him right in." Her carefully modulated tone masked her eagerness to meet the man.

A stocky man of medium height, his tan houndstooth-check jacket hanging open, stepped inside Lauren's open doorway and extended his hand as he walked toward her desk. "Ms. Hamilton, I'm Clifford Atkinson. Since Jordan's not here, I need to speak with you about Jonathan McCain."

"Have a seat, Mr. Atkinson." She stood and shook his hand and waited for him to sit in the chair opposite her desk.

He hiked up a beige trouser leg and sat down, crossing an ankle over a knee. "I'm a friend of Jonathan's. The wife and I joined her folks for a holiday cruise, so I didn't know about his predicament until I got back this weekend."

"And?" Lauren prompted, somewhat amazed, or

amused perhaps, by her visitor's appearance. She'd never met a more monochromatic person. His hazel eyes, sandy-blond hair and tanned complexion blended right in with his beige clothing.

"I thought he might want some help, but when I went out to his ranch, he wasn't there. I need to see him in the worst way, but he's not answering his phone, either. I'm already committed to something today, but I'd like to see him tomorrow afternoon. Can you arrange it?" Cliff asked, fingering the sock on his crossed ankle.

Lauren found it hard to conceal her excitement. This bland-looking man had information about Jonathan's recent past, information that might help Jon deal with his confusion. She wanted to hurry Atkinson out to the ranch, but that wouldn't be wise even if she, also, didn't have a prior commitment. "I'll need to check with him before I agree."

"That's fine."

"Would you like to wait while I try to make arrangements?"

After ushering the man out to visit with Lyna, Lauren wondered how she'd be able to wait until tomorrow to see Jon.

In her excitement, she'd forgotten his distrust, but when she remembered, it was as startling as a cold shower. Her exhilaration cooled, Lauren hesitated, but it was her duty to call him regardless of how he felt about her.

She dialed the phone, hoping he would answer. She fought the fear that something had happened to him again. Maybe he hadn't answered when Cliff had called because he thought it was Lauren and didn't want to talk to her. She would know when—if—she heard his voice, all the time praying a little time had erased his distrust.

"Hello?" Jonathan's voice drifted over the phone line.

"Jon, I was worried about you. Are you okay?"

John sighed, relieved to hear Lauren's voice. It seemed to fill the large living room with a warm hominess that even the glowing fire and the mug of hot cocoa on the table by his chair couldn't do. Ever since she'd left, he'd felt guilty for hurting her feelings. After thinking things over, he knew without a doubt she couldn't be the attorney helping Van Rooten. She was too ethical. Hell, she wouldn't even go to bed with John and he knew she had wanted to. Maybe he'd picked the fight to put distance between them in order to protect her.

Finally, he remembered she'd asked how he was doing. "I'm fine. Bored, but I've found some ledgers and bills. They don't make any sense to me, but you may want to look at them when you get a chance to come back out." He hoped it would be soon.

"Would tomorrow be okay?" Her voice was pleasant but professional. The kind of voice he imagined she used to talk to her clients.

"Sure."

"Great. A man claiming to know you is here, saying he needs to meet with you."

John felt a momentary tweak of disappointment that this was a business call. He'd hoped she was missing him as much as he was missing her. He wanted her to really care how he was doing. Then the gist of what she was saying caught his attention. Maybe this man she was talking about knew something that could help him. Or hurt him, he realized.

Lauren continued, "He wouldn't say why, but he says he thinks he can be of help to you. He was driving a gray car so he must be the same man you saw at your ranch. Now, Jon, his name is significant—Cliff Atkinson."

John sat down hard in the large leather chair opposite the fireplace and stared at the fire. Atkinson. Too coincidental. Atkinson was dead. And if he wasn't, what was he doing here, now?

"Jon, do you know this man?"

He cleared his throat and leaned back. "I must. I recognize the name. Did he tell you anything else?"

"Just that he thought he could help you."

"Then I guess I'd better meet with him." The sooner he got information from Atkinson, the sooner he'd figure out what had happened to him. Maybe Atkinson was in the same time dilemma he was.

"I think I should accompany him to your place. If he knows anything, I want to hear it."

"I'd like for you to come." John needed her with him. She could be a buffer between him and this man. Besides, it would give him an opportunity to apologize.

"I guess we'll see you then, sometime after lunch tomorrow."

"Fine. And Lauren, I'm sorry. I never really thought you were in with Van Rooten. I'm just fishing for something to make me feel in control."

"That's okay, Jon. I understand." Her voice still lacked its usual warmth.

"Tell me about the break-ins." He didn't know what her place looked like, but he visualized soft femininity. A knot of anger formed in his throat as he thought of someone violating Lauren's home.

"Oh, boy. My house and the office were royal messes, but at least nothing was destroyed."

"Do you have any idea who did it? Or why?" He wished he was with her, to comfort her.

"We don't know who did it, but whoever it was got a copy of the photos I took the day we were in the canyon."

"If what we suspect is true, then it was Van Rooten, and he must think you're able to identify him." That would fit right in with the sheriff searching for him with a gun cocked and ready.

"That's what I thought, too, and so did Robert. But Chester may not have been around to do it. Robert said he's out of town."

Yeah, I'll bet. That just lent more credence to the theory that Jordan and Van Rooten were working together, but John dared not bring up his suspicion because he knew that would renew his and Lauren's argument. "Lauren, be careful. I don't want you to get hurt."

"Thanks, Jon. I can take care of myself, but I will watch over my shoulder." He heard her sigh. "Listen, I have a lot to do, so if I'm going to be coming to see you tomorrow, I've got to get busy. You take care, okay?"

John felt worse after she hung up than he had before she'd called. He cradled the mug of cocoa in his hands and studied the fire. The yellow-and-orange flames licked at the piñon logs, sending sparks curling up the chimney just as they had the night he'd held her in his arms. The only person in this world that he cared about might be in danger, and it was all because of him—whoever he was.

A Texas Ranger transported in time. A lawman trapped in the body of Jonathan McCain. A possible drug smuggler. An accused murderer. And no telling what else.

Chapter 11

The following day, John leaned against a post on the long covered porch and watched the dust kick up behind Lauren's car as it approached the ranch house. This feisty woman who'd snared his heart drove too fast. She also had more spunk than any woman he'd ever known, and he liked it.

Before the thick cloud of dust around the white car settled, Lauren had jumped out and faced him from the opposite side of the vehicle. Images of a spunky rider faded as he noticed how she was dressed. A dark business suit made her appear cool and sophisticated. Her hair was pulled back and small pearls clung to her ears. He wondered if she'd forgiven him for doubting her. He hadn't been able to tell over the phone, and now the dark glasses she wore shielded her expression.

The passenger door opened in slow motion, and a man John didn't recognize unfolded himself from the low-slung car. Cliff Atkinson was who Lauren had said would be with her. The man didn't look anything like the Atkinson who'd been shot by the firing squad in San Elizario. A connection had to exist, though, because it was just too much of a coincidence.

Using all the acting skills he could muster to cover his memory loss, John greeted his guests. "Come on in."

Lauren stepped onto the porch and slipped her shades up on top of her head, revealing the unfathomable depths of her blue eyes. She was still hurt, still angry. In understanding, John swallowed his disappointment as he opened the door. He'd hoped she had accepted his apology. "Hello, Lauren."

A polite, hesitant smile flickered on her lips in response, and then a hint of exotic flowers rose from her hair as she brushed past him on her way inside. The scent brought back memories of her wanton reaction to his kisses, and he closed his fingers around the doorknob to keep from reaching out to her.

"How you doing, jailbird?" Cliff interrupted John's thoughts with a hearty slap on his back as he followed Lauren into the house.

"Just fine since I'm not there anymore," John answered, gesturing toward the living room. "Have a seat."

Lauren crossed the room and perched on the edge of a big leather armchair before taking out a notepad. John knew she had chosen that chair to avoid being forced to sit beside him on the sofa. Her face was still cool, businesslike, but not unfriendly. Oblivious to the drama between Lauren and John, Cliff plopped down in the matching chair and promptly hiked an ankle over his knee.

John sat opposite them, where he could watch every nuance that crossed both Lauren's and Cliff's faces. Trying not to show his anticipation, he rested one arm on the back of the sofa and willed himself to relax. He'd find out soon enough what the man knew.

Cliff cleared his throat, looking from John to Lauren.

"Ms. Hamilton, I really need to talk to Jonathan alone. Would you mind?"

Lauren's shoulders stiffened at the request. "I'm here to protect Jonathan, Mr. Atkinson. I don't think it would be wise for me to leave."

"Hey, I don't mean to offend you. You can watch us through the window there if that'd make you feel better." He motioned to the French windows that looked onto the long veranda.

John watched Lauren as she considered Cliff's suggestion. Her brow furrowed in a frown and her pink lips pursed. He knew she didn't want to leave him alone with the man. But for some reason, whoever this Atkinson was, he wanted to talk privately. The thought that Atkinson didn't trust Lauren knotted John's stomach, reminding him of his own distrust.

Whatever the reason for the request, he needed to know what was going on. He caught Lauren's uncertain gaze. "Ten minutes?" he asked, keeping his voice even, trying to reassure her.

He could tell she struggled with her instincts before she finally agreed. "Okay. And I'm taking you up on your offer, Mr. Atkinson. I'll be on the porch. By the window."

The staccato sound of her heels clicking on the wooden floor emphasized her displeasure when she crossed the room. As she opened the door, she turned around and studied the two men, gauging them, as if trying to figure out what they planned to do. John wished he could determine if the expression on her face really reflected fear for his well-being or if she was having doubts about his character again.

If he had known her less well, he might not have noticed the anxious way her hand clutched at the doorknob or her eyes narrowed before she closed the door. John sank back in relief. She was scared—for him.

Cliff broke into a laugh. "She's quite a character.

Wouldn't tell me diddly-squat about you on the way out, but she sure did try to pick *my* brain about you." Leaning forward, he rested his elbows on his thighs. "Can we trust her?"

John shifted uneasily. Though he had doubted Lauren—with just cause, he had to remind himself—it still made him uncomfortable to realize someone else shared those concerns. "What do you mean?"

"Have you told her or her partner, that Jordan character, the truth?" Cliff asked. "You know, about who you are."

"No. I wasn't sure if I should." He hadn't told anyone that he was John McCain. "I didn't figure she would believe me." No one would believe he was supposed to be living in 1877!

"You might be right, but since I'm here now, I can back up your story. The agency is sorry things got out of hand before we caught up with you, but you were supposed to alert someone if there were any problems."

Alert who, and how? Were he and this man talking at cross-purposes? "I didn't have a way." Hell, Cardis wasn't going to let him walk into the telegraph office and wire for help.

"Really got tangled up, huh?" Cliff ran his finger around the collar of his shirt, then flicked open the top button. "Now I can breathe. When my wife and I got back from our holiday, I learned you'd been accused of murder. I hightailed it out here to see if I could help you, but you'd already disappeared. I couldn't believe your attorneys got you out on bail so quickly. Anyway, I came out here to find you Sunday, and you weren't around."

So Lauren's suspicions were right. Cliff was the man who'd paid him a visit. "I saw you snooping around."

Cliff frowned. "Then why the hell didn't you come out and talk to me? Time's a-passin', man!"

John was relieved that Cliff knew who he was, but didn't like hearing about time. "I was too far away. Besides, I was expecting Van Rooten and didn't have a weapon other than this kitchen knife.'' He slid the long blade out of his boot. Through the window, he saw Lauren's mouth drop open in horror. He held up a palm of his hand and shook his head to let her know everything was okay.

Cliff twisted his head toward the window and lowered his voice. "So is she the one?"

"The one?" John was confused. What was Cliff talking about?

Cliff's eyes narrowed. "You got a screw loose or something? Is she Van Rooten's contact? What do you think I meant?"

John didn't have to think now before he answered. "No, she's not connected to him in any way."

"What about Jordan? I couldn't find any dirt on him. Do you know anything about him yet?"

John had thought Atkinson knew he was John McCain, not Jonathan. But there was no bridge to the past here. Cliff was set squarely in the present, and he expected Jonathan to have some information. "I don't know anything about Jordan other than he showed up to defend me."

"You care to expand on that?" Cliff asked.

"Seems he's a friend of my folks. My sister hired him. But that's a different story. Let's get on with this." John didn't want to get sidetracked right now. He hoped this man sitting before him would say something to spark a memory.

"Okay. We know Van Rooten's dealing. We pretty well know who his suppliers are, but we don't know who fronts the dope money for him. Otherwise, we'd have made mincemeat of his ass some time ago. We know it's an attorney in this area. If it's not the D.A. like we'd thought, then who is our man—or woman?"

"I wish to hell I knew, Cliff." What he didn't know was how much longer he could carry on this facade. He couldn't answer Cliff's questions about Van Rooten. Now, if Cliff would ask something about Cardis and San Elizario, he might be able to oblige.

"We can't do a thing about Van Rooten. He's our only link."

John still couldn't figure out how Cliff fit into the picture, but at least they shared a disdain for Van Rooten. "What should I do now?" he asked.

"I don't think you should risk contacting any of our suppliers in Mexico. Things might get sticky in the circumstances."

John was stunned. Suppliers? Lauren had said the drugs came from Mexico. Was that what Atkinson was talking about? Sweat immediately broke out on John's forehead. She'd suspected he'd been involved in drug smuggling and now this Cliff was confirming it. But he couldn't let the man know how badly the news upset him.

Swiping at his face with the back of his hand, John realized he had to deal with one thing at a time. It didn't matter what time period he was from, he still valued his life and knew the sheriff presented a real danger. And maybe Cliff did, too. He swallowed and forced a tough tone into his voice. "Van Rooten has tried to kill me more than once."

"You knew the rules when you came into this. I want the records. Have you got them stashed here?"

Even though he didn't know what records Cliff was talking about, he realized that was why his house had been searched earlier. Someone else had been hunting for records, too. Van Rooten had every legal reason to search his house. But now Cliff wanted the same records. John couldn't trust anyone, including Cliff Atkinson.

Cliff continued, "Don't think we don't appreciate you putting your life on the line to warn us when the stuff is here so we can pick it up before it hits the streets. But without the evidence of money transfers, all we've got is your word. I've waited a year to put the sheriff and his pals behind bars, and we're so close I can feel it.''

John sank lower into the sofa with relief. Unless he was mistaken, Cliff was in law enforcement and that might mean he, too, was involved in a legal capacity, because Atkinson didn't seem to want to arrest him. Though John still didn't understand, he was willing to take a chance. He explained about the sheriff searching his house. "When I got back and started looking around, all I found was a partial ledger." He sure hoped it was the one Cliff was looking for. John would have a lot of explaining to do if it wasn't.

"Let me see it," Cliff said.

John went to his desk and pulled a book out of the bottom drawer. He'd studied it, hoping to find answers, but all it had done was provoke questions.

Cliff scanned the few pages with entries, then thumbed through the rest of the book. "Damn! Someone has torn out the last few pages." He stood and began to pace the floor. "Those pages are probably what we need. Without some hard evidence our hands are tied."

Convinced now that Cliff was clean, John was willing to involve Lauren. While thinking he and Cliff were somehow associated with the sheriff, John would have gone to his grave before telling him about her. "Lauren has some photographs. They won't show anything about drugs, but maybe they will show who was shooting at her."

Cliff stopped and faced him. "Huh? Who was shooting at her?"

"She can explain."

Cliff glanced toward the window. "Then you think we can tell her about us?"

John wasn't sure what "us" was, but he'd deal with that when it came up. "I'd trust her with my life." He had already done so when he'd allowed her to walk out of the cave.

"Then let's get her back in here so we can either clear some of this stuff up or make the water a little muddier."

John stood and stretched before he strode to the door and threw it open. "Lauren, would you come back in now?"

She immediately quit pacing the porch and appeared in the doorway, but she still didn't look happy with the way things were going. She did manage a halfhearted smile that was more of a question than a greeting.

John tilted his head toward Atkinson. "This guy needs to hear your canyon story, then he's going to explain some things." Cliff didn't realize it, but he was going to be explaining things to John at the same time.

"Good. I'm glad somebody knows something." She swished past him and headed toward the man who was now standing in front of the unlit fireplace.

Cliff's voice interrupted John's assessment of her sashaying across the room. "Ms. Hamilton, Jon says you've been shot at. Would you fill me in?"

Lauren sat back on the sofa and folded her arms across the buttons of her navy blue suit jacket. She'd had all the secrecy and bull she was going to stand for. The two men were acting as if they had something to hide. While she'd stood cooling her heels on the veranda, they had talked plenty. Apparently Jonathan remembered more in Cliff's presence than he did in hers. She knew her anger was fueled by hurt, hurt that Jonathan still didn't trust her. "I'd like to know who you are first."

"Since Jon assures me you're okay…" He pulled his wallet out of his inside jacket pocket and showed Lauren his identification. "I'm an agent with the Drug Enforcement Administration."

Lauren took the wallet and looked at the badge, then slowly turned her gaze to Jonathan, who was standing in the center of the room, his thumbs hooked casually in his jeans pockets. He didn't appear shocked or concerned, but the knowledge that the DEA was investigating him made her heart sink. How could she have been so wrong?

Cliff said, "Yesterday, I wasn't ready to tell you who I was, but a little nosin' around proved you are just what you say you are—a small-town lawyer."

"And what's that supposed to mean?" She wasn't sure if she was more offended by his remark about small-town lawyers or because he'd investigated her.

"Don't take offense—we never accept anyone at face value. Now, will you tell me what happened to you?" Cliff asked.

Lauren began her story, but afraid to incriminate Jonathan further, she paused and looked over at him when she got to the part about him grabbing her in the cave. He nodded almost imperceptibly, encouraging her to continue before he walked over and sat on the other end of the sofa.

When Lauren finished, Cliff said, "Now, I'm gonna give you some sensitive information, Ms. Hamilton, information we're not ready to make public."

Lauren nodded her understanding.

Cliff, with his hands in his pockets, paced back and forth in front of the fireplace as though he were searching for a place to begin. "Jon here works for the agency, too, but he's undercover."

"What?" She had considered almost every possibility, but never this. Relief flooded through her veins. If he was undercover, then he wasn't guilty of smuggling. She glanced at him and was surprised to see confusion written all over his face. Then she remembered he wouldn't know about this part of his past.

"Maybe I should start at the top. Jon and I were in the army together. We both worked in intelligence. He got out of the service and went into business in Mexico City. I went to work for the DEA. A few years ago, we got a tip about a big drug dealer in South America who was smuggling drugs through Mexico inside artifacts like the ones Jonathan's company exported. We were hunting for someone to do a little work for us. Jon was the perfect guy to work undercover for us. And him being fluent in Spanish helped a lot. Since then, we've used his services again and again." Cliff looked at Jon. "You can jump in any old time."

"No, you're doing fine," Jonathan said.

"Okay, but hey, man, stop me if you have something to add." Cliff sat back down and in the process hunched forward and propped his elbows on his knees, then began tapping his steepled fingers together. "In the past couple of years, Jon had a few close calls down there and got tired of the whole mess. He wanted out. Figuring he had a reputation to cover, he formed a dummy corporation and bought this ranch. He planned to sit back and take life easy. That didn't last as long as a drop of water in the desert. Lots of stuff was going on here in the Pecos region. Jon's past caught up with him, and it wasn't but a short time before he was approached by the local sheriff."

Finding out who Jonathan McCain really was and what he was doing on a ranch with no cattle made Lauren so excited she couldn't remain silent any longer.

"So much for peace and relaxation. I guess Chester had an offer that couldn't be resisted."

"You bet right. If Jon would allow planes to land, then the sheriff would see fit not to alert the proper authorities about Jon's prior 'drug dealings' out of the country. Jon contacted us and we asked him to take up the sheriff's deal. We figured we'd have this end cleaned up in a few months."

As Cliff Atkinson talked, Lauren became angry. The agency hadn't let Jonathan walk away. It had set him up and then had gone off and left him. They had let him get shot, wander through the desert and then cool his heels in jail for days. "Don't you usually protect your men in the field?"

"They're pretty much on their own. If we're too close, a connection's made and the cover's blown."

"How was Saul involved?" Lauren asked, wondering about the man who had been killed. "Friend or foe?"

"Foe," Cliff answered, his voice harsh.

She felt the sofa cushions give when Jonathan propped his arms on his knees and buried his head in his hands, as if the memory of the killing caused him pain.

Cliff stopped his pacing and asked, "Is there a bathroom I could use? Shouldn't have drunk so much coffee this morning."

Jonathan looked up. "Down the hall and to the left."

Silence filled the room after Cliff left. Lauren was unsure where she and Jonathan stood. It must have been a shock for him to find out he was undercover. "What do you think?" she asked him.

He ran his tongue over his lips. "Right now I'm a happy son of a gun to know I'm not a criminal, but I wish to hell I knew what did happen."

"Your memory will come back. I know it." She had to believe that. Jonathan wasn't just her partner's client, he was everything she'd ever dreamed about in a man. She'd desired a hero, wanted the derring-do of danger, but when Jonathan had brought her face-to-face with both, she'd crumbled, hurting him in the process. Words seemed so ineffectual against her earlier actions, but they were her only tool. "I'm sorry I didn't trust you. I never thought you killed Saul, but the circumstantial evidence for drug smuggling was there."

"I know." Jonathan stared off into the distance. "You don't owe me an apology. You couldn't ignore what it looked like I was doing, even though I took a bit of offense."

"Does Cliff know you can't remember what happened?" She knew Jonathan was still withholding something from her, too. She felt it every time they broached the subject of his memory loss. Maybe now that someone from his immediate past was here, Jonathan could latch on to something to give him stability and trust.

Trust.

It was such a nebulous word, easily bantered about between people. But trust had a depth that she'd often avoided, afraid she would drown in it. Then Jonathan had lured her beyond the shallows and she'd almost plunged in heart first, until her head pulled her back to false safety. Instead of relief, she'd encountered an overwhelming sadness. For both of them.

"No. I wanted to hear what he had to say first," Jonathan said.

"I think you need to tell him."

"Tell me what?" Cliff strolled back into the room and settled into the big easy chair before reaching into his pocket and withdrawing a pack of cigarettes. "Mind if I smoke?"

"Go ahead." Jonathan shrugged his shoulders as though he wondered why Cliff asked.

"Don't understand all that antismokin' stuff myself." Cliff hitched up one hip and pulled a lighter out of his pocket, cupped his hands around the flame and drew on the cigarette until a wisp of smoke circulated in the air. "Ahh—" he smiled and closed his eyes in pleasure "—a man should be allowed to enjoy his vices. Now, I need to hear everything you know up to this point, Jon."

"Well..." Jonathan leaned back and ran a finger under the collar of his chambray shirt, as though the open neck was suddenly tight. "I'm not sure I can tell you much."

Lauren sensed his dilemma and tried to intercede without giving him away. "Mr. Atkinson, I can't tell you how thankful we are that you showed up. You have no idea how badly we need you to help answer some unresolved questions."

"What she means is, I don't recollect anything about

what you told me or about the murder or anything. Lauren thinks I've got amnesia."

"Amnesia," Cliff blurted out, nearly dropping his cigarette as he stood. "Good God A'mighty. Whaddaya mean?"

"I didn't tell you everything about my being shot at," Lauren interjected. She then told Cliff about Jonathan's confusion in the cave and how his memory hadn't cleared up. "Anyway, I think the head injury caused the amnesia."

"I was wondering what the hell was wrong earlier," Cliff said, his pale hazel eyes turned toward Jonathan. "You acted like you were sizing me up when I came in."

"I was," Jonathan said.

"Seen a doctor?" Cliff asked, settling back on the edge of the chair.

"Just the one who came to visit me in jail. I didn't let on to him that anything was wrong."

Lauren explained, "I went out to the university and got some information. Actually, I was afraid for anyone to know Jonathan doesn't remember anything, so I got on the Internet. Several physicians responded, saying time and being in familiar surroundings were what an amnesiac needs."

"Sounds reasonable," Cliff said. "But if it continues much longer, we'll call in a department shrink. The immediate danger is the sheriff. Since you didn't point a finger at him, he must know or at least suspect about your amnesia. It probably saved your life. That also means he's got to get rid of you before you get your head on straight again."

"I know that. That's why I wasn't in the house Sunday to greet you." Jonathan's voice reflected an odd combination of exasperation and weariness.

"Actually," Lauren interjected, wanting to offer him a thread of hope, "Robert and I think we can get the murder charge against Jonathan reconsidered on my testimony and the photo, but that won't prove the sheriff did it.''

Cliff nodded his head in agreement. ''Nope, but I'm glad you didn't show all your cards at once. As long as the spotlight is shining on my buddy here, we can watch the folks skulking in the shadows.''

''Regardless of evidence, I'm fairly certain that Chester killed Saul,'' Lauren said. ''He's the one to watch.''

''But why would he if Saul was in on the smuggling, too? And from what you said, Cliff, there's someone else working with him,'' Jonathan stated. He looked at Lauren as though to say ''Let's not start this suspicion game again.''

''What do you know about your partner, Ms. Hamilton?'' Cliff asked.

Again Lauren had to control her rising hackles, even though Cliff had asked a perfectly legitimate question. ''I've known Robert Jordan and his wife, Eloise, for a long time. They're completely trustworthy. I'm sure you searched Robert's background and didn't find a speck of scandal.''

''No more than we found on you. But he's older and has had more chances to slip up and then try to hide it.'' Cliff raised an admonishing finger. ''We only looked one layer deep, and if there's cause, we'll peel back more until his bones are showin'.''

''I don't care how many layers you look under, Mr. Jordan is not involved with anything illegal, unethical or even sneaky.''

''I admire your confidence in your partner. I feel the same way about Jon here, though he can be a real jerk,'' Cliff said.

''I couldn't work with Robert if I doubted his integrity.'' While pleased with Cliff's offhand compliment of Jonathan, Lauren was unsettled by the man's suspicion of her partner. She cared little that the agent's job was to look at everyone askance, for she knew how warmhearted and kind

Robert Jordan was and how deeply concerned he was for the community. She'd seen the way he and his wife worked in their church, in youth activities, in making the town of Sierra wholesome.

Cliff said, "I'm not trying to get a rise out of you, but I've got to try to help Jon. You seem to want him cleared, too. So I'll buy that Jordan's on God's right-hand side. After this is over I give you permission to make me pay for the error of my ways. Okay?"

Lauren studied Cliff's earnest face. How on earth could this man irritate her one minute and charm her like a big teddy bear the next? "Okay," she agreed.

"So," Jonathan said, getting back to business, "until I remember something definite, we don't have much to go on."

"I got an idea." Cliff began chuckling. "A common belief is that the first hit knocks out the memory and the second whack restores it. So how about if I knock you on the head, Jon?"

John didn't think the suggestion was all that funny, but Lauren seemed to find humor in it because she gave Cliff a big grin. John felt a stab of jealousy that she would find Atkinson funny. "I might hit back." The matter was serious—at least to him.

He was overcome with relief that he wasn't a common drug smuggler, but this new information from Atkinson created almost as many problems as it solved. It didn't change the fact that someone wanted him dead, and it still didn't solve the dilemma of his identity. Despite what Cliff said, John still felt like a ranger, but here was one more person saying he was Jonathan McCain!

"If you won't let me hit you, how about you tell us what you do remember?" Cliff suggested.

John repeated the events from the flashbacks he'd had, hoping that repetition would trigger more information. But it didn't.

Cliff leaned back. "Well, let's look at it like this, Jonathan. You remembering the sheriff fired a rifle doesn't prove anything, since you don't know who or what he was shooting at, or when he was shooting, for that matter. The two of you might have gone huntin' together before." Cliff raised an eyebrow. "Also, you gotta remember who's been charged."

Lauren intervened. "There's always my testimony."

John started when he felt her hand close over his and give it a squeeze. She might have doubted him and he might have doubted her, but when confronted with someone else's doubts, she stood by him.

Her words were softer when she said for the second time since she'd come back in the room, "Your memory will return."

John wanted to believe that would solve the problem. He *had* to believe her or he would go crazy. He nodded and leaned against the back of the sofa, trying to control his growing frustration. He wanted something to happen. He'd had all of the sitting around he could stand.

Lauren sat poised on the edge of her seat, as if she, too, was about to explode, while Cliff stared off into space with a glazed look on his face.

Finally, Lauren asked, "Okay, what does your agency plan to do now?"

Cliff absentmindedly stubbed out his cigarette. "I hear you have some photos."

"Only one that is of any consequence, but the image in it was too small to show anything. The negative is at a lab being enhanced."

He stood and adjusted his pants. "When do you think you can have that photo back here?"

"My brother's on business in El Paso right now. I'll have to make a call, but I'm sure Ted won't mind picking it up and delivering it here in the morning."

"Good. Then try to schedule a meeting with the judge

and D.A. for tomorrow afternoon.'' He started toward the door. ''Do you guys mind if I have a look around outside?''

When both Lauren and John stood, Cliff shook his head. ''No need to come with me. I just want to do a little snoopin'.''

After the door closed behind him, John slowly turned to face Lauren. He'd already apologized and she'd accepted, but the warm look he associated with her wasn't back on her face. He wanted her to throw her arms around him and show him he was forgiven. Yet he knew he could also make the first move.

As he thrust his hand in his pocket to keep from reaching out, a sinking feeling filled his gut. Why was he, Captain John McCain, living the life of another McCain in another century? Until he found the answer he had to try and stay away from Lauren. He couldn't offer her anything but confusion.

Chapter 12

"Here you are, sis." Ted threw a large manila envelope on top of Lauren's desk. "I had two blowups made in case something happens to this one."

"Thanks for cutting your trip short to bring these back to me. I always knew brothers were good for something." She ignored his snort. After learning that Jonathan worked for the DEA, Lauren had wanted to move as fast as she could. She was anxious to see the picture but was also afraid that she'd sent her brother on a wild-goose chase. She lifted the flap and peered inside the envelope. Closing it, she looked up at Ted and their eyes locked in understanding.

"You nailed him, Lauren," he told her, his voice soft and emotionless. Ted walked over to the window, lifted a slat with a bent finger and stared across the street.

Yes, she had, but it did little to make her happy. It hurt to know that someone she'd known for a long time had crossed the line of the law. "Do you feel as bad as I do about it?"

"Yep. Chester's had a hard time the last few years, but, hell, that's no excuse. He could have killed you."

"Yes, he could have." Her perspective restored, Lauren buzzed the secretary. "Lyna, would you call Cliff Atkinson and ask him to come to the office? He's staying at the Sierra Hotel. Then you and Robert might want to come in here for a few minutes." She'd call Jonathan just as soon as they had talked to the judge.

Lauren slumped in her chair and swiveled it to face the windows so she could look out across the street toward the mountains. The elation she felt at being able to help Jonathan was tempered with sadness. She was sick to her stomach. Suspecting Chester had been one thing, but actually knowing he'd shot at her was another. "Have you told Dad?" she asked Ted as she twirled the chair back around.

A crooked grin graced her brother's face. "You gotta be kidding. He's gonna be madder than ten kinds of hell that you didn't let him know what was going on at the beginning. That job's yours, big sister."

"Thanks a lot. I'll call him tonight." That would give her dad time to blow and bluster before she saw him face-to-face.

Robert stuck his head in the door. "Lyna said you sounded excited about something."

Lauren nodded and stood up. "The picture's here." She didn't have to say any more. Robert knew what she was talking about.

"Let's see it," he said.

She withdrew the still somewhat indistinct and grainy photograph from the folder, turned it around and laid it on the desk. "This is a picture of the man who shot at me in the canyon a couple of weeks ago." Robert and Lyna hunched over the photo and studied the figure of a Caucasian male carrying a rifle. The man was dressed in a khaki uniform.

"It's Chester," Lyna gasped. "Oh, my Lord, I don't know what to say."

"That's the first time you've ever been at a loss for words," Robert commented.

Clutching her briefcase tightly, Lauren paced the cavernous hallway in the courthouse Wednesday morning. Robert had contacted Judge Estrada the afternoon before to make arrangements for a hearing, and now that it was time, she was nervous. Jonathan's future depended upon her ability to convince the judge that he had been falsely accused. Robert was already in the judge's chambers, but she was waiting for their client. She glanced at her watch. The appointment was only ten minutes away and Cliff hadn't arrived with Jonathan yet.

She'd called Jon the evening before. He'd sounded relieved and eager to get the whole thing behind him. They had talked for several minutes, but the conversation had been mostly business. There just hadn't been time since Cliff's bombshell to sort through where they stood on a personal level.

Cliff had gone out to the ranch and had spent the night there. Lauren felt relieved that Jon hadn't been left alone again.

She sighed, started toward the stairway, changed her mind and walked over to a window and looked down at the parking lot for the umpteenth time. The lot was half-full of people needing to register their vehicles, pay their property taxes or something equally mundane. Sierra wasn't a high-crime area. She caught herself tapping her nails against her briefcase, then looked at her watch again. Where were they?

Estrada wouldn't be eager to release Jonathan in any case, but if he were late, the judge would take it as a personal affront. Lauren looked up expectantly when she heard the echo of footsteps on the marble floor but was disappointed to see it was Alex Stewart. Alex was never late, even though he'd had to drive eighty miles from his office in Fort Bend.

"Hello, Lauren." Smiling, Alex stopped only a few feet away and looked her up and down in open admiration. "You look wonderful. How've you been?"

"Fine," she answered, feeling a little discomfited, wishing the man would hurry up and marry Gwen Keefer, his longtime fiancée. "And you?"

"Great. Just gearing up for the spring primaries. Say—" he gestured toward the judge's chamber "—what's this I hear? Estrada told me there might be some more evidence in the McCain case, but he didn't elaborate, except to say the DEA was claiming Jonathan worked for them."

"We'll explain in a few minutes." She looked down the hallway again, hoping to spot Cliff and Jonathan.

"My, my, but you're being secretive."

"No, I'm not, Alex. You're going to be told everything as soon as we're in Estrada's chambers."

Before he could reply, Lauren heard voices and footsteps along the corridor and looked up to see Jonathan strolling down the wide hallway as if he didn't have a care in the world. He was flanked by a U.S. marshal and Cliff.

Lauren's breath caught as she stepped away from Alex. She had only seen Jonathan in prison overalls, jeans and casual shirts, but now he wore an obviously expensive Italian suit, tailored not only to fit, but to enhance every line of his body. He was stunning. His dark hair fell over the back of his collar, giving him a devil-may-care look.

She tried to swallow the catch in her throat but couldn't. The sight of him dressed this way caused her to realize how little she knew about the real Jonathan McCain. Though Cliff had told her that Jonathan had been a successful businessman in Mexico City, the reality of it hadn't sunk in—until now. Now she realized that he didn't need her. In a few minutes, the judge and Robert would discuss the details that would make Jonathan a free man. Free to leave the ranch. Free to go back to his life. Free to leave her.

She had believed Jonathan cared for her, but that was then. This was now. He had his own resources. He had Cliff to talk with. And soon, maybe, he'd have his memory.

About the time the three men reached her and Alex, Robert stepped into the hall and said, "You folks about ready?"

"I believe so," Jonathan said, smiling at Lauren. He stopped at the open doorway and gestured for her to enter before him. She tried to pretend she wasn't affected by his presence.

"Thank you." The warmth spreading through her body because of Jonathan's smile was chilled by the scowl she saw on Alex's face. She checked her own response, aware that Alex could see his reelection being affected by what was about to be unveiled.

"You bet we are," Cliff said, seconding Jonathan. "Let's get this show on the road."

"You can bring in some more chairs if you like," the judge said, motioning to the three chairs across from his desk.

"No, this is fine." Alex stepped forward. "Lauren, why don't you and Robert be seated? And Mr. McCain, since this involves you, take this chair."

After a few disclaimers by Robert and Jonathan, Alex's suggestion was followed. Lauren wanted to gag at Alex's fake gallantry. He was obviously threatened with this impromptu hearing for Jonathan, and he needed to impress Estrada.

Cliff and the U.S. marshal leaned against the back wall, while Alex took a stance to the side of Estrada's desk, slightly behind Lauren.

Placing his elbows on the top of his starkly bare desk and interlocking his fingers, Judge Estrada leaned forward and began the hearing. "I understand from Robert that Mr. McCain works for the DEA and you have some new information." He looked directly at Lauren, his eyes as black as freshly mined coal.

"Yes, sir. I do." Refusing to let his visage intimidate her, she slowly withdrew the photograph from her briefcase and held it as she explained about being shot at and meeting Jonathan in the cave. "Sir, this is an enlargement of the photograph I took in the canyon on the day the sheriff said he was hiding from Jonathan McCain. Unarmed, he said. Notice the date on the lower right-hand side." Lauren pointed it out. "And while the image of the rifle is small, it looks like it could be the same make as the one used to kill Saul Rodriquez." Lauren didn't go into any more details because she knew Robert had already filled the judge in.

Leaving his glasses on, but lifting them from his nose so he could see beneath the lenses, the judge studied the photo. Grunting, he then handed it to Alex, who had come to stand at the end of the desk. The judge said, "This puts a different light on the initial testimony, but I don't intend to be too hasty about dismissing the charges against Mr. McCain."

While Lauren listened to Estrada, she watched Alex's jaw begin twitching as he stared at the photo. She speculated that he, too, was upset that someone they had all known and trusted for so many years had lied. In fact, he was probably furious with Van Rooten for putting him in this situation, particularly with the election in the near future. She watched as he struggled for control before he casually laid the photo back on the desk and crossed his arms.

The judge turned to Alex. "Jordan told me that Van Rooten might need to be available for questions, but when my secretary called his office, she was told that he was out of town. Do you have any idea where he is?"

Alex cleared his throat. "Not really. He said something about going to visit his brother in Phoenix."

"What?" Estrada thundered. "He left town in the middle of an investigation?"

"I really don't know, sir, but if he's gone, he must have had an emergency." Alex shifted from one foot to the other.

"Your only witness disappears, and you don't know where he is? Considering this new information and barring a plausible explanation from the sheriff, you do realize that your case isn't worth the paper it's written on."

"Yes, sir."

"I'm glad for that, counselor." Estrada had obviously lost what little patience he had. "I suggest that you get him back here within forty-eight hours with an explanation, or I'm dropping the charges against the defendant. Do you understand?"

"Yes, sir."

"Forty-eight hours."

Alex nodded.

"Well, get out of here and find him." Estrada waved him out of the room.

Lauren felt kind of sorry for Alex as he left the room. She was sure he saw his political future dissolving.

Before the door closed behind Alex, Robert said, "Judge, there's another consideration. Since I'm fairly certain the sheriff is a danger to my client—no disrespect to the marshal's abilities—Jonathan needs twenty-four-hour protection."

The judge grunted and pursed his lips while he considered the issue. "How about holding him over in jail? Van Rooten's not there."

Lauren saw Jonathan's shoulders tense beneath his custom-made suit. Anxious to intervene on his behalf, she said, "We don't know that the sheriff was the only officer involved. Jail might be dangerous."

Estrada raised an eyebrow in acknowledgment and nodded his agreement.

"And," Cliff interjected, "the ranch is too remote and hard to watch for him to go back there."

"Does anyone have a better idea?" Estrada asked.

Lauren remembered the pain on Alicia McCain's face when she'd talked about her son. Jonathan's family would be more than happy to have him come home for the first time in over twenty years. "What about his parents' house in El Paso?"

"Take care of the arrangements and I'll sign the papers." As a signal that the meeting was over, Judge Estrada stood and walked around his desk to shake hands with Jonathan.

Lauren hung back as the men began to move out of the chamber into the hall. She was apprehensive about the future, though they had accomplished what they'd wanted. Jonathan would probably be free in a couple of days. Should she make the first move and let him know she wanted to stay in touch...to allow what was developing between them to grow...to make love to him? What did a person say in a situation like this?

When Jonathan reached the door, he seemed to realize she wasn't with the others. He turned and scanned the room until he noticed her standing near the window, then he strolled over to join her.

"Thanks for everything you've done." He shoved a hand in his pocket as if he, too, didn't know what to say.

"You're more than welcome." She looked up into his jade eyes as the chamber door shut behind Robert and the judge. For a few precious minutes she and Jonathan were alone. There was so much she wanted to say, but there wasn't time. "I think you'll be safe at your parents'."

Neither of them said anything for a couple of seconds, then they both started to speak at once. He stopped. "You first."

"No. Go ahead. What were you going to say?"

"Cliff and the marshal are probably waiting for me."

Lauren tried to hide her disappointment, but was unable to force a smile.

She'd hoped he was going to say he would see her in a couple of days. "Yes, I'm sure they are."

He took his hand out of his pocket and stepped closer. "I guess this is goodbye, then."

So it was over, just as she'd feared. Her voice was low and husky when she managed to whisper, "I'll miss you."

She saw him move, then felt the pressure of his hands on her shoulders before he pulled her to him. He wrapped her in a tight embrace and buried his face in her hair. She tried to focus on the way his hard body felt against her, the scent of his cologne, the sound of his heart under her cheek so she would have the memories when he was gone. A tear slid down her cheek and onto the fabric of his suit. She was so wrapped up in her own despair she almost missed the meaning of his next words.

"I'll see you as soon as I'm a free man," he said. "Then we can pick up where we had to stop."

Before she could respond, she heard someone at the door.

Lauren and Jonathan both tensed and stepped away from each other as Cliff stuck his head in and said, "Jonathan, let's get a move on it. We need to get you to El Paso and settled in before dark."

"I'll be there in just a minute." When the door closed, he turned to Lauren, raised his hand and wiped the moisture from her cheek with the back of his finger. "Why the tears? You accomplished your objective. It looks like the charges against me will be dismissed."

She nodded and tried to smile. He was being so matter-of-fact. Didn't he understand that he was more than Robert's client? She cared about him as a man. Before she could put her mixed-up feelings into words, he pulled her into his arms and covered her lips with his.

His searing kiss was swift and desperate before he set

her away from him. "I don't want to leave. We need to talk, but I've got to go. They're waiting. I'll call you soon." He started for the door.

The kiss erased some of her doubts and his words left her with hope. Maybe things would work out between them if nothing bad happened. "Take care. You aren't out of danger, yet."

Pausing with his hand on the doorknob, he said, "I'll watch my back. You be careful, too."

Early the next day, John wandered from room to room in his so-called parents' house, undecided about what to make of the massive Georgian structure. Maybe his feeling of unrest was because he couldn't get his mind off Lauren. Their parting the afternoon before had left him troubled. When she'd said she would miss him, he had been unable to prevent himself from pulling her into his arms. He'd needed reassurance that when all of this was over, he would see her again. He'd thought she felt the same way, although her tears were those of someone who was afraid they were saying goodbye forever.

He continued ambling through the first-floor rooms, deciding that the light and intimacy of the small sunroom snuggled at the back of the house was more to his taste than the ornate front rooms. He paused in the doorway and cleared his throat to attract the attention of a slender, stately woman dressed in a silk house robe. She'd done everything possible to make him comfortable when he'd arrived last night. Still, he felt like an intruder.

"Oh, Jonathan, I'm so glad you're up early." Alicia McCain gestured toward a sideboard that held a coffeepot and an assortment of fruit and breads. "Please help yourself and join me so we can talk." Her warm chocolate eyes seemed to take measure of him as her fingers crushed the napkin into a tight little band. "I know you must feel uncomfortable about being here. That nice young attorney told us what happened—and about your amnesia."

"She told me a few things about myself, too. Namely, I haven't been much of a son." He didn't dispute the amnesia. It gave him a crutch until he found out what was going on. He poured a cup of coffee and sat down at the small, wrought-iron table with the woman who was supposed to be his mother. He had realized last night in the brief time they had all spent together that she and her husband were fine people—just the kind he would want for parents if he could choose. What he didn't understand was why Jonathan McCain had refused to have anything to do with them.

"Oh, Jonathan, let's let bygones be bygones." Her voice shook as she spoke. She compressed her lips as she fought to retain her composure. "Helena said you were handsome just like your father, and proud, too." Her voice sharpened. "Both of you are too proud for your own good."

Seemingly of its own accord, his hand slid across the table and covered one of her frail ones in comfort as she fought back tears. He didn't want this nice woman to suffer anymore for what her son had done.

She covered his hand with her free one and squeezed. "It's so good to have you home."

"I'd like to say it's good to be home, but..." he looked around the room "...I'd be saying something meaningless because I don't remember this as home. But I do want to thank you for having me."

"I understand. That Mr. Atkinson thinks your head wound caused your amnesia. Maybe being home will help restore your memory. How long do you think you'll be here?"

"No more than three days. Of course, the sheriff could show up today, and I'd have to go back to Sierra."

"I suspect Mr. Atkinson is correct in assuming that Mr. Van Rooten is deep in Mexico by now." Alicia sighed. "I hope he's found so he'll be locked up and you can be completely vindicated. And safe.''

John nodded toward the front of the house, where an officer was sitting in a parked car. ''The man outside is supposed to make sure I'm safe.'' He took a sip of his coffee, then smiled over the cup's rim at her.

With the optimism of a mother, Alicia said, ''I'm sure everything is going to turn out fine. Neither J.C. nor I had any doubt that you were innocent or that Robert could get this misunderstanding cleared up.'' Then she repeated, ''I'm just so glad you are here—''

''So am I, son. So am I.'' J.C. McCain's booming voice interrupted his wife. He crossed to the sideboard and poured himself a mug of coffee, then brought the entire platter of breads over to the table and plopped them in the center. ''Now, boy, you need to eat something.'' J.C. buttered a roll and asked, ''Does anything register around here?''

John looked at the man who was supposed to be his father. Despite the older man's attempt at bravado, pain and yearning shone from his eyes.

''No,'' John said, selecting a Danish not so much because he was hungry but because he thought it would please J.C. John still didn't understand what had happened between Jonathan and his parents, but surely it was time to go beyond the grudges.

Alicia asked, ''Did any of the photos I sent with Ms. Hamilton help?''

John shook his head. ''So far I haven't remembered anything about you or my past.''

''When you're finished eating I'll show you around the house and tell you about your youthful escapades,'' J.C. offered. ''Maybe that'll do it.''

John almost smiled at the older man's denial. It was the same thing he himself had felt a week ago. Then, he'd thought if he just tried hard enough, or encountered the right stimulus, everything would right itself. He'd either reawaken and it would be 1877 or something here would make sense. He'd since learned it wasn't that simple, so he'd quit expecting a miracle. Hoping for one, yes. But expecting one—no. Still, a guided tour of Jonathan's old home couldn't hurt.

After breakfast, J.C. told John about how he'd misjudged his scruffy, long-haired son when he'd had been arrested as a seventeen-year-old. He explained that his generation had been ready to believe the worst about all youngsters in the seventies. "I could've kicked myself a dozen times when you left, but, dammit, I guess I had too much pride. I'll always regret it."

"I guess I should say it's all forgotten," John said.

Both men smiled at the bad joke before they walked across the wide lawn, through the garage and storage areas before coming back to the main house. J.C. said, "Well, let's go into my den."

John followed J.C. into the walnut-paneled room. A large desk dominated the center and two walls lined with bookshelves contrasted with the light shining through the windows. Photographs of a young boy and girl were placed amid the books and old trophies. John crossed the room and picked up one of the framed pictures. He knew it was a photo of Jonathan and his sister, Helena. They were laughing as they wrestled with a dog and a water hose.

"That's another thing I regretted." When John raised a questioning eyebrow, J.C. looked down at the expensive floral carpeting and explained. "Einstein—that's what you named that dog—wasn't a thing like his namesake. Before he wallowed in every flower bed we had, I got rid of him." J.C.'s lips, compressed in a tight band, quivered slightly before he continued. "You cried."

John couldn't keep from hurting for the little boy in the photograph and the man standing before him, his eyes begging for forgiveness. Seeing no reason not to soothe the older man's wounds, John nodded as if he understood. When a weak smile showed on J.C.'s face, John set the gold frame back on the shelf and slowly walked around the room, looking at each item.

A Little League trophy—Jonathan's?—was displayed beside a baton-twirling trophy that must have been Helena's. He read a plaque on the wall; it was a man-of-the-year award J.C. had received from the El Paso Chamber of Commerce. Next to it was another plaque lined with small engraved bronze plates that recorded Jonathan McCain's prowess in track and field. Whatever his faults, J.C. had obviously been proud of his son.

The thought of a son reminded John of the one he'd left in San Antonio. The one he might never see again. His chest felt tight and he swallowed a couple of times before moving to the next wall. There, on a shelf about midway up, was an old tintype of a woman, and next to it was a faded brown photograph.

John's heart seemed to stop beating as he reached for the photo. "Who's this?" he asked, his voice steady despite his growing fear.

J.C. cleared his throat. "That's your great-great-grand-father, ol' Captain John McCain himself, and the other one is his wife."

The yellowed photograph was behind hazed glass, but there was no doubt in John's mind that it was a picture of himself. The ranger uniform, dark hair, fancy mustache, everything. This was a picture of him. And he had been dead for over a hundred years.

J.C. must have noticed his growing discomfort. "Are you all right?"

John couldn't speak. He just nodded and closed his eyes. It was too much to handle. He didn't believe in ghosts or reincarnation. As wave after wave of nausea passed through him, he fought to maintain some composure. Maybe J.C. would know what had happened to Tommy.

"He had a son. What happened to the son?"

"He grew up and came out here to West Texas to find out what happened to his dad. He was my grandfather Thomas." J.C. stared a moment, his lips parted in surprise. "Hey, you remembered something."

Chapter 13

Saturday evening Lauren stood in the center of the elegant hotel suite Alicia had insisted on booking for her. The day before had seemed to last forever. She'd watched the clock, dying to call Judge Estrada to be certain Chester Van Rooten still hadn't shown up in Sierra. Although she knew enough about Estrada's reputation to know he wouldn't renege on his timeline to clear Jonathan of charges, she also knew he carried a heavy load covering several counties and could have gotten overwhelmed with other work. Finally, the judge had called and announced that the charges against Jonathan had been dropped.

Lauren then called Jonathan and his parents to tell them the wonderful news. They had insisted she come to a small dinner party celebrating Jonathan's release. And now, twenty-four hours later, she surveyed El Paso through windows draped in white-and-beige damask. The glass ran from floor to ceiling along one entire wall that must have been twenty-five feet long. A traditional armoire and a sofa with matching chair were grouped around a coffee table in one part of the L-shaped room. But as Lauren crossed to the windows, the king-size bed tucked around the corner was what demanded her attention. It was the focal point of the room and had been positioned so that it faced the glass wall and the valley below. It was a room you wanted to share with someone you loved.

Since parting in the judge's chamber, Lauren had cherished Jonathan's promise that he would see her when he was a free man. Now that was a reality, and in less than three hours, she would meet him face-to-face. Had he had anything to do with his mother's kindness? Whether he had or not, it was wonderful to feel pampered and special, Lauren thought, as she laid out her clothes for the coming party. Uncertain how formal the dinner would be, she'd chosen a silk, vested pantsuit that draped every curve she had to advantage. And tonight she wanted an advantage.

She could concentrate on Jonathan as a man, not as her firm's client. And she had high hopes for the evening. Enjoying the feel of the deep pile carpet under her bare feet, she strolled to the bathroom and turned on the water in the large marble tub. Softly, she hummed to herself as she poured perfumed bath gel into the water and watched the bubbles swirl around in a small whirlpool. For the first time in days she could really relax and enjoy her surroundings— the warmth of the water as it slid up her thighs when she crawled into the tub, the fresh flowers in the crystal vase on the countertop and the soothing sounds of jazz playing in the background.

Life was good, she thought, leaning against the back of the tub and imagining Jonathan's green eyes free of the tension that had haunted them since she'd known him. Maybe his laugh would be easier, his hesitancy gone. Her father had kidded her earlier that morning, saying she reminded him of when she was a squeally teenager too excited to eat. It was true. She'd never be able to eat tonight with butterflies fluttering in her stomach.

An hour later she stood before a mirror in the sitting area and sized up her reflection while she twisted her long blond hair into a French roll. People had told her she looked great in pastels. She thought she looked pretty good in them, too, particularly the soft pink that swathed her body. Swallowing a sigh of anxiety and excitement, she clasped a strand of pearls around her neck. Then, ready to meet Jonathan at last, she headed out the door of her hotel suite.

Despite her white leather coat, Lauren stood shivering on the front porch of the McCain home while she waited for someone to open the massive door. She was prepared for the joy that flooded through her when the door opened and Jonathan stood before her, his eyes gleaming with pleasure, but she wasn't prepared for the rush of sexual awarness she felt when he reached out to pull her into the room. "God, you look good," he whispered into her ear as he slipped her coat off, his hands lingering on her shoulders.

She didn't even try to control the obvious excitement she felt. She wanted him to know she was glad to see him. "So do you," she whispered back. He looked gorgeous in slacks and a turtleneck that matched his dark hair, but that wasn't what she meant. It wouldn't have mattered if he had been wearing a burlap bag, he looked so wonderful. Some of the tension was gone from his face, and he smiled as if he was were genuinely happy, not just mildly amused.

"Come on in and close the door," J.C. said from somewhere behind Jonathan. "There's no way we can crank the heat up high enough to warm the outdoors." A knowing grin flickered on his face.

Jonathan closed the door behind Lauren and, clutching her elbow, guided her into the hall, just in time to be knocked sideways by two little boys barreling through the hallway, performing karate kicks. From the next room a woman yelled for them to stop.

"They're supposed to be my nephews," Jonathan explained as he helped Lauren regain her footing.

"They *are* your nephews." The woman, her hair as dark as Jonathan's, appeared in the archway. "They're too much like you were for them not to be, although you are a bit nicer now." Her voice was filled with affection as she looked from him to his companion. "And you must be—"

"Lauren Hamilton," Jonathan interrupted, laying his arm protectively around her shoulders. "And Lauren, this woman claims to be my sister."

"His sister's name happens to be Helena Clark," the woman said as a sandy-haired man joined them. "And this is my husband, Russell Clark."

Lauren laughed at Helena's deadpan act. "I'm pleased to meet you, Helena, Russell."

"The little warriors are Chase and Crey. I want to assure you they're not always like this." Helena clutched the boys to her, one on each side.

"No, unfortunately they're not." Russell shook his head. "They're usually worse."

"Oh, Dad!" The boys giggled, each of them tackling one of his legs.

"Why don't you attack your uncle Jon and let me get some rest?" The boys eyed Jonathan, the temptation of their father's suggestion gleaming in their eyes.

"I'm worn-out myself, boys. Another time, okay?" They groaned, but obeyed. "Now, let's go on in. I think your grandmother has dinner waiting," Jonathan said, clearly amused by the family before him.

The dining room was lit by red candles of all sizes cradled in holly boughs and sparkling gold ribbons. Lauren waited expectantly, hoping to be seated next to Jonathan, and she wasn't disappointed. All through the traditional Mexican meal, she could feel his leg pressed against hers. The conversation was gracious and general. No one mentioned any subject that might have caused distress, including Jonathan's ordeal. Alicia was the perfect hostess and everyone followed her lead, even Jonathan's nephews.

After dinner everyone retired to the living room for coffee. Helena and Russell had a time keeping their five- and eight-year-old sons from jumping about the room. Finally, after the boys almost succeeded in knocking over the Christmas tree, Helena had enough, and she and Russell took the boys upstairs and put them to bed in the guest room.

"It's becoming a tradition when we all have dinner here," Alicia explained, coming to sit opposite Lauren. "The boys like to spend the night because we let them watch TV in bed until they fall asleep."

J.C. griped, "She won't even let me do that."

"Grandchildren get privileges grandfathers don't." Alicia patted her husband on the knee before she turned from him and addressed Lauren once again. "Children are special, too. We appreciate so much what you did to help our son. I know he's grateful, also."

Lauren glanced at Jonathan, who was standing in front of the fireplace. His expression was controlled as usual, but he gave her a slight wink. So he wanted to play it cool, did he? She followed suit. "It's my responsibility to help all my clients—or clients of the firm, I should say." She almost smiled when he raised an eyebrow and frowned slightly at her comment.

"I was thinking maybe your interest extended a little beyond the normal client relationship," J.C. commented, his smile distorted by what Lauren assumed to be a nudge from Alicia.

Having years of experience sparring with her own father, Lauren replied matter-of-factly, "You're right. I don't normally put myself in danger. But your son is a special case." She glanced at Jonathan, who was walking toward the sofa. If he was bothered by his father's suggestion that their relationship had extended beyond professional contact, he was hiding it well. Too well.

Her liberty to reveal to his parents just how much she

cared for him rested entirely with Jonathan making the first acknowledgment. She was hoping that was what he was doing when he sat down. He was close enough to her that she felt his body heat, making it difficult for her to resist the urge to scoot nearer.

"And Lauren's a special woman." Jonathan laid his arm on the back of the sofa behind her. He didn't touch her, but the symbolism was there. He was making the statement that they were a couple.

Pleased by Jonathan's message to the McCains, yet feeling a little awkward, Lauren smiled. J.C. humphed and Alicia returned Lauren's smile. As if he were oblivious to the reactions, Jonathan never moved or changed expression. Lauren figured he was enjoying himself as his parents tried to size up the situation.

Finally, she sought to divert their attention away from the growing intimacy between Jonathan and herself. "It was very nice of you to invite me to El Paso this weekend. The suite is lovely beyond words, and so was the meal. Thank you."

"Next time, you'll have to stay with us," Alicia said.

Helena and Russell came back into the room in time to hear the end of the conversation. "Even though we filled up the bedrooms, we thought you should be here, since you played a part in making it possible for Jonathan to be back with us." Helena pulled a chair in closer to the group and sat down, while Russell headed to the kitchen for more coffee.

J.C. gripped Alicia's shoulder. "Yes, this is the first time we've had all of our family together in over twenty years. Even though Jonathan doesn't remember yet, we used to have some good times during the holidays."

Helena pointed an accusing finger at Jonathan. "I remember the day you told me there wasn't a Santa Claus. I'll never forgive you for that. Then you made me promise not to tell Mother and Daddy. You said we'd get more presents if we pretended to believe."

Jonathan groaned when the others laughed. "Was I that mean?"

She nodded. "I think you were born a cynic and took perverse delight in destroying every illusion I had—from the tooth fairy to the Easter Bunny, to the fact that in eighth grade Bobby Joe Blanchart didn't love me for my mind."

Everyone laughed as she continued, "And your elder nephew takes after you. He considers it his duty to make sure his younger brother isn't taken in by any of that 'hokey' stuff grown-ups pull."

Lauren remembered telling Ted that he was stupid when he insisted that Santa Claus wasn't their father. "I told my brother the same thing," she admitted, shaking her head. "I'd forgotten all about that."

Jonathan said, "What a thing to have in common—we were both mean to our younger siblings."

"I wasn't mean." Lauren tilted her head and looked down her nose at him. "Just superior. I thought it was my place to educate the ignorant masses—of which my brother was the only one on the ranch. So I practiced my powers of persuasion on poor Ted and any cows or horses I could get to listen."

"That's probably why you became a lawyer—all that arguing before the livestock." Jonathan grinned.

"I wouldn't poke fun if I were you, big brother," Helena started to tease, but her tone became more serious as she spoke. "You've always had a superior attitude, too. You were critical of everyone's faults, including your own. Until the last couple of days, that is. You seem different now." Her voice became lower and softer. "I hope *that* part of the old you doesn't return when you get your memory back."

Lauren tensed. She hoped the same thing. Would Jonathan still be the person she was falling in love with? He must have sensed her concern because he rested his fingertips on her shoulder. The pressure was so slight she had to concentrate to feel it through the thin fabric of her vest. But that barely perceptible touch made her long to feel his open palm against her naked skin. Would physical contact allay her growing fears?

Alicia, the perfect hostess, tried to calm everyone's concern. "I'm sure it won't. Why, a couple of days ago, Jonathan looked at an old family portrait and remembered something."

Lauren turned to face Jonathan. "What?"

John had wrestled with that question himself. He couldn't say he remembered something that he hadn't been aware of all along. Soon, maybe, he could share who he was with Lauren. Now, though, he couldn't say that he'd seen a picture of himself. "I saw a photograph of my great-great-grandfather Captain John McCain."

"Oh, is it the one I saw when I came by to get the photos?" she asked J.C.

"That's the one." J.C. nodded and explained, "The captain was one of the early Texas Rangers. Joined up in the early 1870s, when most of the rangers were single and a little wild. He was supposed to have come out here to West Texas to defend the salt flats. It was going to be his last duty before he resigned." J.C. shook his head. "Well, it was, but I don't believe it was the way he wanted."

"How's that, J.C.?" Russell stretched his feet out and rubbed his hands over his stomach. Helena gently nudged him. He grinned, but straightened up. "No, really, it's a good story. Miss Hamilton might get a kick out of it."

J.C. brightened, obviously pleased to retell the story. "Please indulge me, Lauren. I enjoy making suppositions about my ne'er-do-well great-grandpapa."

John sucked in his breath, unsettled by this unbecoming reference to himself. He might not have been indispensable, and maybe he hadn't done right by his family, but he'd provided them with a living. And he'd been planning to quit and raise Tommy proper. Then, too, Lauren already knew a little about the incident, but John decided to be quiet.

J.C., oblivious to John's reaction, stood and walked over to the fireplace and propped his foot on the ledge. Satisfied he had everyone's attention, he began. "He was part of a small contingent of Texas Rangers sent out here to El Paso to quell a rebellion. Seems an Anglo claimed rights to the salt flats, and the Mexicans took offense. A big brawl took place in San Elizario down the road a piece from here, and all the Anglos were hauled before a firing squad. Including John Thomas McCain. Somehow our ingenuous ancestor escaped, but it didn't do him much good."

"What do you mean?" John asked, trying to master his fight-or-flight response to the thought of the firing squad and the bullet grazing his head. He wanted to jump up and demand that someone explain what was going on. They were all sitting there as if J.C. was just relating a story about an irresponsible ancestor. But they couldn't know they were talking about him.

"He disappeared." J.C. sighed and straightened up. "Still don't know what happened to him. His son, Thomas—my grandfather—came here in the late 1890s trying to find some trace of him. He didn't find anything, but settled down here anyway."

John's fingers clasped Lauren's shoulder. He knew his heart was racing and his palms were sweating.

J.C. continued, "Must have died out in the desert. I located some records in the archives from the Mexican commander Cardis, which described how he followed him about a hundred miles east and never did catch him."

"How did you know he was planning to resign as a ranger?" Lauren asked. She flinched slightly, causing John to realize he had been tightening his grip on her shoulder as J.C. spoke. He uncurled his fingers and massaged her soft flesh.

"His diary and other personal effects were salvaged from the mercantile store in San Elizario. Someone sent them back to the family in San Antonio," Helena answered. "Remember, Jonathan? When you were at the house back in the summer, you surprised me by finally taking an interest in family history. Dad let me have the diary, then you borrowed it from me, saying you wanted to read it."

John tried to control the growing despair he felt. Not only were people telling him he was dead, but he'd left intimate details of his life to be read by anyone and everyone, including himself. He tried to sound only mildly interested when he answered. "I guess I need to find it and read it."

"Do you think it's still at the ranch?" Lauren asked.

"I can't think of a reason why it wouldn't be. That is, unless Chester decided he wanted to take that, too."

"Oh, I almost forgot. You'll have to get the guns yourself when you go back, but I went by the sheriff's office before coming out here and picked up your car keys and a few other things Van Rooten had confiscated from your house."

"I appreciate it. Now I can drive that fancy car parked in the garage when I remember how." John tried to chuckle, but his earlier nearly lighthearted mood was gone.

The talk turned to things that were less personal, but John couldn't force himself to pay attention. He wanted to get away from all the people so he could think. It wasn't that they weren't being nice. They were. It was the small talk that required him to answer occasionally or appear rude that was interfering, so when J.C. suggested a bridge game, John jumped at the chance to escape.

"If you're going to play bridge, you won't need us, so I think I'll see Lauren back to her hotel," John said.

Less than twenty minutes later Lauren closed the door of her suite behind Jonathan. At his parents' house, she had known he'd wanted to talk to her—alone. During the ride to the hotel, he'd been silent and restless. Something had upset him. She took off her coat and tossed it onto an overstuffed chair before she turned to him. "I was watching your face tonight when your father was talking about your great-great-grandfather. You made a connection between him and the bones buried on our ranch, didn't you?" She'd listened politely, not letting the McCains know she'd heard parts of the story before. And perhaps knew something they didn't.

He nodded and sat down on the sofa, burying his head in his hands. The lamplight from a nearby end table glinted off his dark hair.

Softly she said, "So did I, but it wasn't the time to say anything to your parents. Not until you tell me what is wrong. This was a person you never knew, Jon, but you're acting like it was a long-lost friend. Please, tell me what's going on?" She sat beside him and gently pried his hands from his head so she could see his face. He looked up at her with what could only be described as a haunted expression. She glimpsed a far-off look in his eyes before he leaned forward and studied the nondescript carpet.

"You won't believe me," he finally said.

"Let me decide." She clasped both of his hands in hers. "I know there's more involved in this than just amnesia. So tell me. What is it?"

He took a deep breath and turned to face her. "I didn't much care for that story because those bones may be mine." His voice was steady and sure. "I'm Captain John McCain!"

"What? I think I misunderstood you." Lauren couldn't believe her ears. Had Jonathan gone mad?

"No, you didn't misunderstand. I don't remember Jonathan McCain, but I seem to remember a lot about John McCain, Texas Ranger."

She had to make him see reason. "Jon, your own parents

recognize you. So does your sister. Cliff. Everyone. You're Jonathan McCain III.''

The corners of Jonathan's mouth gave the impression of a wry smile, though she knew no humor was intended. ''Not hardly.''

Lauren shook her head in confusion. ''What do you mean?''

''I seem to be a different person from Jonathan. Even Helena remarked tonight that I behave differently than I used to. And I like my...parents.'' He struggled with the word. ''Jonathan didn't.''

Lauren's grip on his hands tightened. ''Cliff said you'd mellowed, too.''

''See what I mean about being different? Then there's the whole question of Cliff. I don't understand anything about him, either, except his last name is Atkinson, which was the name of one of the men I was locked up with in San Elizario.''

Lauren stared at him. ''Jonathan, that has to be pure co-incidence. Lots of people have the same last name. Don't try to make it something it isn't.''

''Maybe, but...'' He shook his head.

''You've had memories only Jonathan could have had. Things like Van Rooten firing a rifle and alluding to a partner.''

''I can't explain it. Those were only brief flashes. I couldn't hold on to them. They weren't real.''

''Jonathan, you can't be John McCain. Time travel doesn't exist,'' she whispered, though she remembered reading that Stephen Hawkings now thought it possible. Maybe she ought to go back and read what the brilliant scientist had written.

''You asked me to tell you what was bothering me, so I did.''

''It's not that I think you're lying to me—it's that it just doesn't make sense. For example, what became of Jonathan?''

"I don't know." He held up his hands. "I don't understand, myself, but it appears that this is his body. Yet most of my memories and reactions are the captain's. I remember living in San Antonio and being sent here to protect Charles Howard and his salt. The best I can recall, it all happened just like J.C. said. The arrest, being in jail in San Elizario, the firing squad and me being able to scramble away during the little riot that took place. I jumped on a horse and took off, then it wasn't long before Cardis and lots of others came after me. The next thing I remember is when I awoke in the cave and you were there. The rest you know.''

Lauren stood, hoping the effort would clear some of the cobwebs that filled her brain. This was unbelievable, but she knew the cowboy wasn't intentionally lying to her. He was sincere. Though his explanation raised a lot of questions, it also explained some of his earlier reactions and lack of knowledge. "Jon, what do you remember about your life before you came out here to West Texas?''

"I remember one of my fingers was cut off when I was twelve." He held out his hand, all fingers intact. "I remember I hated farming and its backbreaking work. That's why I joined the rangers. And I have a son named Tommy back in San Antonio. I'd be bustin' my rump to get back if I didn't think it was futile.''

"If you have a son, then you must have a wife." Lauren felt a numbness creeping over her. He was married. If this bizarre story had any validity, the man she had finally fallen head over heels in love with thought he was married.

"No, she died before I was sent to El Paso. My sister is—was taking care of Tommy.''

Lauren breathed a sigh of relief over the fact that he hadn't deceived her. "I take it that Tommy was the Thomas J.C. said was his grandfather?''

Jonathan dragged a hand across his face and leaned back against the sofa. "Hell of a mess, huh?"

"Tell me about your wife." Though it was illogical to be jealous of a wife who had died a hundred and twenty years ago, Lauren was envious of the woman he thought had shared his life. It was neither the time nor place for her to express her doubts to him about who he thought he was. There'd be time for that later.

"She was a good mother. Uh…" Jonathan seemed to be struggling to remember. "She hated the rangers, wanted me at home to be a father. I'd told her that I was quitting soon. After she got a fever and died, I was filled with guilt, but restless as all get-out. My sister helped me out with Thomas. It looks like she raised him."

"And he must have turned out fine. Look at your family now. You should be proud." So that she could see him better, Lauren turned sideways on the sofa and tucked one leg under the other.

"Considering the circumstances, I don't think proud is an option. I skipped out, according to J.C., and never went back. Remember?" He looked at her as if willing her to deny the facts, then stood up and crossed to the wall of windows.

John pulled a cord and the draperies slowly parted, exposing a view of the city nestled in the valley below. Far-off traffic signals blinked red, yellow and green amid the thousands of twinkling white lights. The wonders of electricity were not only convenient, but they were beautiful, too.

He started to drop the cord, then realized what he had just done. There was no way he, John McCain, could have known how to make the draperies work. Did Jonathan's body remember how to do things from the present time? God! It was all too confusing.

He heard the soft tread of Lauren's footsteps as she walked up behind him. She was close enough that he could feel her body heat and smell the elusive perfume that drove him mad. There had been nights when he had awakened in a sweat and sworn her scent clung to the bed. Those were the nights he couldn't go back to sleep.

"What are we going to do?" She snuggled up to him, wrapping her arms around him.

The feel of her arms around his waist should have given him courage, but he was still afraid she would leave him when she had time to consider all he had told her. *"We?"* He stressed the word as he stared out the window.

"Yes. You don't think you're going to handle this alone, do you?"

He thought for several seconds before he answered. "I guess, in the past, I've always done everything pretty much by myself and I—"

"Jon," she interrupted, "people try to help people they care about."

He turned and took her face between his hands, holding it so she was forced to look up into his eyes. His voice was low, almost pleading in its intensity when he spoke. "And do you...care about me?"

The atmosphere around them changed as he waited for her answer. The air became heavier and charged with tension. He was asking for more than the words conveyed. He needed to know if she believed him, if she trusted him, if she loved him, if she wanted him.

The answer was there in her eyes before she whispered, "Yes, I do."

"As your client?"

Lauren stepped back and slowly raised her hands and began to take down her hair. He stared, transfixed by the metamorphosis from classic professional to seductive vixen as she ran her fingers through the blond tresses until they hung in a cascade around her shoulders. He clenched his fists to keep from touching her. That would be sensory overload—and foolish. Though he wanted her more than he remembered ever wanting anything, he wasn't good for her. She had a future full of promise. He had a past full of unanswerable questions.

But for the moment he allowed himself the luxury of devouring her with his eyes as the light played across her face and body. All evening he had ached to feel the silk she wore against the skin of his hands as he caressed her, and when she licked her lips with the tip of her pink tongue in a manner that was so provocative he felt himself instantly harden, every bit of common sense deserted him.

"You aren't even close to being my client anymore," she said, taking a step closer.

"Thank God!" He reached out, grasped her shoulders and pulled her hard against him. "I know I shouldn't be doing this, that I'm not the man for you, but I've waited so long for this."

He thought he was going to explode with the pure joy of finally having her in his arms. When he'd told her who he was, she hadn't laughed or ridiculed him, but instead had offered to help. His fears of being rejected had been unfounded. If only he could offer her something other than this one night.

She drew back and whispered his name in a voice so low and husky it seemed to come from the depths of her heart. "Jon," she purred, "I don't want to wait any longer."

Forgetting the problems that would be facing them tomorrow, he scooped her up and carried her to the bed.

Chapter 14

After gently laying her on the bed, John stood beside it and stared down at Lauren. She looked up at him with blue eyes that begged him to make love to her, not that he needed any begging. The fact was, he had to force himself to slow down. For a forty-year-old man who should know how to exercise restraint, it was difficult.

The sight of Lauren taking down her hair had instantly aroused him. Now the bulge straining against the fabric of his trousers was demanding he do something. But he wanted to take his time, to savor every second, to ensure that Lauren understood what she meant to him. Sometimes words failed him, but he could use his body to worship her.

Without taking his eyes from hers, he stepped back, tugged his black sweater over his head and, after tossing it toward a chair, slowly stepped back to the bed, bringing him closer to the woman of his dreams. Her blond hair shimmered in a halo against the pillow as the light from the window bathed her still-clothed body. But even silk couldn't hide the tantalizing curves. She was gorgeous.

When she raised one hand to beckon him closer he couldn't wait any longer. A low groan of complete surrender escaped from deep in his throat as he knelt on one knee beside her. For this one night he wouldn't think about who he was or what was going to become of him. He wouldn't think about the future or if making love to Lauren was wise. It didn't matter. All that mattered was burying himself deep inside her and forgetting everything but the sanity her lips and arms offered.

The mattress gave under his weight when he leaned forward and planted one hand in the pillow on either side of her head. Bracing himself above her, he savored the yearning he saw in her eyes. Though she hadn't said the words, he knew she felt what he did. She was experiencing the same aching desire to plunge ahead, but was wanting to make the night, perhaps their only night, memorable. No one knew what tomorrow was going to bring. If he could come through time, then he might be able to go back. And if faced with having to decide between his son and previous life and the woman under him, he didn't have a choice.

His son meant everything to him. He couldn't choose not to go back to San Antonio.

But that choice would rip him apart. Leaving Lauren after tonight would kill him. He knew that his heart would slowly harden and his soul shrivel until there was nothing left for anyone. If he were a stronger man, he would get up and leave before he hurt her further. But he wasn't strong. He wanted—no, he needed—to feel her hands on his body again. "Touch me," he whispered hoarsely.

She obeyed, placing her palms against his chest, her fingers spreading wide, giving him the contact he sought. He raised his head, arched his back and took a deep breath, memorizing the feel of her hands as they slid through the hair on his chest. When she splayed them across his back, he bent over her and kissed the tip of her nose, her eyelids, her cheeks, then ran his tongue over his lips, tasting her sweetness. There were so many sensations he wanted to cherish.

Beneath him, Lauren melted with the same emotions. Just the strength of his muscles filling her hands made her breath catch. She had dreamed of the feel of his hard body against hers since he'd first kissed her in the cave. Now, finally, nothing was keeping them apart. Nothing except a hundred and twenty years. She ignored her doubts about his sanity and concentrated instead on the need flooding through her veins as their lips finally met. His were demanding, as though he had waited as long as he could.

He deepened the kiss until tongue played with tongue, building within her a rousing fire. She whimpered when his hand slid under her top and his fingertips grazed her nipples through the lace of her bra. All of her senses centered on his slightest touch, and she writhed with pleasure as he continued to tease her breasts.

She wanted to feel the weight of his bare chest pressed against hers, so she slid her hands between them to the opening of her vest and began to unfasten the buttons one at a time. He rose up and watched her with smoldering eyes for several seconds before again lowering his mouth. His lips followed her hands as she slowly exposed her naked flesh to his ravishing kisses. When the last button was undone, he reached up to her shoulders and began tugging the top off. She arched her back as he pushed the vest down her arms and tossed it to the floor.

For a long moment their eyes met in silence. Then he began to trail one finger down Lauren's cheek, to rest in the hollow of her throat, where, she knew, he could feel her thundering pulse.

"You're beautiful, even more beautiful than my fantasies in the cave," he said, continuing his journey downward to the swell of her breasts. He ran his fingertip along the top edge of her bra, as if enjoying the sight of his darker skin against the milky whiteness of hers. Then he slid the straps down, exposing her engorged nipples to his gaze.

As he unclasped her bra and cast it aside, he said, "I've dreamed of this since I first touched you." His head dipped down and his tongue traced wet circles around her areola until Lauren ceased to think. All she knew was that she loved him beyond reason and she wanted to feel him inside of her, his body and soul one with hers. She threaded her fingers through his hair and moaned softly, "Oh, Jon, please...now."

He answered her plea by standing up. Through lids heavy with passion, Lauren watched in fascination as he stepped out of his pants and kicked them aside. Silhouetted against the window, his body was everything she imagined—lean, hard and ready.

When he joined her again, she rolled him flat on his back so she could straddle him. She wanted him to experience the same tortured pleasure he'd shown her. Slowly, ever so slowly, she scattered kisses down his throat, then trailed her tongue to the nipples hidden in dark hair. Those she licked and bit at until he swore softly and ground his pelvis against hers. How could she have fallen in love with him is such a short time? But as his hands slid under the waistband of her slacks, sliding them down her thighs and legs, allowing cool air to salve her burning skin, she decided some riddles weren't worth solving.

The hunger in his body and her own turned into a raw ache that demanded satisfaction. She gripped his shoulders tighter and quivered in anticipation as his hand stroked her inner thighs, until finally she'd had all she could bear. She leaned forward, her hair forming a curtain on either side of their faces. "Oh, yes, please, Jon," she murmured, just before he settled her body over his throbbing shaft. Then, grasping her waist in his hands, with one long stroke he thrust up into her wet core.

Her own gasp of surprise mingled with his low groan as

he settled deep within her. She stared down into eyes that claimed her as his. Whatever happened between them now, they would always be a part of each other. Neither moved for a moment as the importance of what had just occurred settled over them, then Lauren felt Jonathan's hips begin to rock slowly, and she matched his easy rhythm. The sensations building were new and fresh. Nothing had prepared her for the all-consuming demands of his lovemaking. Though she rode him, there was no doubt who was in control as he orchestrated their motions to a primeval beat.

The pleasure written on his face mirrored her own wonder. It no longer mattered who he was—John or Jonathan. They were one and the same—the center of her universe.

As he increased the pace, she clutched the headboard and threw her head back, sucking in air, trying to save herself from drowning. "No...not...yet," she mumbled. But it was too late. The orgasm tore through her body and she sobbed his name before collapsing onto his sweat-dampened chest.

He wrapped his arms tighter around her, and gasping for each breath, drove hard into her once, twice and then a third time. In her mindless state, Lauren felt all the muscles along his length harden, tremble, then relax as a groan escaped from deep in his throat.

Later, John gathered Lauren into the crook of his shoulder as he settled back onto the plump pillows he'd arranged against the headboard. It was reminiscent of the way he had held her in the cave less than a month ago. So much had changed. Then, he'd thought he would never see her again. Now she snuggled close and drew one leg up his until it rested across his thigh. The peace and wonder that swamped him were like nothing he had ever experienced. Here in this one woman was his reason for wanting to live.

He watched the lights of the city twinkling in the distance as he took another deep breath, telling himself that this was all really happening. He was here in Lauren's bed, and he had just made love to her. And she hadn't come up with one reason why they shouldn't—though he had plenty.

He reached for a bag of tobacco and matches on the nightstand and didn't find them. Then he remembered he didn't smoke. As a ranger, he'd taken an occasional chew of tobacco, but hadn't really liked the stuff. He didn't understand his sudden impulse. "Do you know if Jonathan smoked?" he asked, against Lauren's hair.

She stirred and glanced up at him. "There were ashtrays at the ranch, so probably. Why?"

"I don't know. I just had this craving and I wondered if my body was responding out of habit."

"You mean a cigarette after sex?"

"Yeah, I guess."

"What do you mean, yeah? Are you saying you're through with me?" He detected a teasing tone in her voice as she sat up and crossed her legs, turning so she could face him. Outlined against the night cityscape behind her, every curve, every graceful movement was framed by the large windows.

"Not hardly." His body immediately began to respond, though his brain said it couldn't. He was middle-aged, and it just didn't happen again this fast. But his body wasn't listening to reason. Not wanting to break the physical connection between them, he reached over and rested a hand on one of her thighs.

"I've never heard you say 'yeah' before. You've always said 'yes,'" she said.

"I must have picked it up from the conversations I've listened to during the past few weeks. Texans in the twentieth century use it a lot."

"I wonder how much of you is the present," she said, as he ran his fingers up and down the soft skin of her upper leg. "Your fingerprints are Jonathan McCain's. You obviously look like him and must sound like he did. Your family and Cliff all say you're J-o-n, not J-o-h-n."

"Jonathan's parents haven't seen him in over twenty years. They could easily be fooled."

"What about Helena and Cliff? They would recognize you."

"I don't have the answers yet. I want to get back to the ranch and search for the diary. Maybe there's something in it that will clear this up. I'd also like to go to San Elizario. Perhaps the answer is there." His hand slid lower to her inner thigh, where the satin skin was more sensitive.

"If you wish, I'll take you to the ranch tomorrow," she offered.

He wasn't sure she understood what they might discover and what it would mean to them. "I have to try to find out how I got here and if there's a way back."

"I know."

"And I'll have to return if I can. There's Tommy...."

"I know." Light reflected off of a single tear as it rolled from the corner of her eye.

John thought he was going to be unable to catch his next breath. The sight of her silently crying over him paralyzed his chest. With a knuckle, he caught the tear as it fell down her cheek. He felt like the lowest form of life as he pulled her into this arms.

After saying goodbye to the McCains the next morning, Lauren drove Jonathan toward San Elizario. By some unspoken agreement, they didn't discuss what had occurred between them last night. There wasn't much to say until they checked things out. She could tell that the closer they got to the town, the more preoccupied Jonathan became. He stared out the window at the passing buildings and cars. She suspected he was disappointed in the rambling barrios and mom-and-pop businesses. Was it anything like he thought it would be? Was he still sure he'd been here in 1877?

The buildings were a blend of functional architecture interspersed with territorial and mission styles from the 1800s. It was a typical border town, home of many poor and few affluent people. Lauren pulled the car into a narrow parking spot on the plaza near the center of town. Large trees that drew groundwater from the Rio Grande not far away shaded parts of the square. Leaves and dirt had collected along the curb, Lauren noticed when she opened the door.

Searching the area all the time he was slowly getting out of the car, Jonathan didn't say a word until he came around the back of the car and joined her. He took her hand and squeezed it. "I'm glad you're with me."

"So am I." She couldn't have let him do this alone.

Turning her to face him, he said, "About last night... Maybe it shouldn't have happened, but regardless of what we find here, I'm glad it did. There's no way I'm sorry for something that was so wonderful."

His words brought tears to her eyes again, but she couldn't let him see that. He would feel worse. Lowering her head, she nodded and whispered, "I have no regrets, either."

Hand in hand, they walked down the crumbling sidewalk past a gazebo toward a lovely old mission church. Judging from nearby vehicles, Lauren guessed it was teeming with parishioners. She didn't know when the white adobe building had been erected, but wondered if it might have been standing when Captain John McCain was brought to San Elizario as a prisoner.

The town was decorated for Christmas. Luminarias lined the roofs of some of the flat-topped buildings, and the paper bags filled with sand and candles edged many of the sidewalks. They looked sad and disheveled in the middle of the day, but at night the candle flames would glow through the translucent paper, creating magical light shows throughout the area.

Lauren snuggled closer to Jonathan's side as a cool

breeze rustled the trash and leaves along their path. They walked completely around the plaza before he said, "Nothing looks even vaguely familiar."

"I'm sorry. I know you hoped there would be something here that would explain what has happened to you."

"Let's just say I hoped something would jump out at me. Well, so much for that." With the palm of his hand on the small of her back, he guided her toward the car.

They were almost there when Lauren noticed a marker in the plaza partially hidden by its surroundings. "There's a historical marker, Jon. Let's go read it."

His arm settled around her shoulders and he drew her close to his side as they read the bronze plaque, which described a bloody episode of the Salt Wars that had taken place in the fall of 1877 at that site.

"People can justify fighting about almost anything, can't they?" Lauren mused as she thought about the struggle for control of the vast Guadalupe Salt Flats.

"Particularly if money's to be made." His dry comment hinted at more meaning than was evident. "Let's go get a cup of coffee," he suggested.

Minutes later they were sitting at a vinyl booth in a small café off the plaza. Colorful papier-mâché piñatas hung from the ceiling in preparation for *Las Posadas* and the holidays. Red-leafed poinsettias flanked the glass door.

John took a sip of his coffee and set his cup down before staring through the window blinds toward the plaque that told about the building where he and the other rangers had been held prisoner, then led before a firing squad. He should have been able to recollect the smell of gunpowder and the mass of unwashed people crowding around, but he didn't. Nor could he imagine the sound of Spanish insults and curses that must have been voiced as he was sentenced. He should have felt fear being in this place again, but instead he felt nothing.

Lauren's soft voice intruded on his thoughts. "Are you all right?"

He turned to face her and propped his elbows on the Formica tabletop. "I'm fine. I was just thinking." He took another sip of coffee. "You know, it's funny, in a twisted sort of way, about how events are similar."

When a confused look crossed Lauren's face, he continued, "Over a hundred years ago salt was a precious commodity in this hot desert. Hell, it was a necessity. No refrigeration, so something had to be a preservative. That meant money."

He felt her fingers close around his and it made him feel like everything was going to turn out fine. He wanted to tell her what had happened. He knew she still had doubts about him being John McCain—any reasonable person would—but the memories seemed so strong, he had to talk about it. Reconstruct his past, and maybe in the process, reconstruct himself.

"Back before this area became part of the United States the salt was there for the taking. No one owned it. The salt haulers would leave here with water barrels loaded on their wagons. They would go to a halfway station about forty-five miles out, where they'd rest and leave enough water for their return. Then they went to the flats, loaded up with salt and rested a couple of days before heading back. On the return journey they stopped at the halfway point, desperate for the water they'd left there. Then they headed back here."

Lauren let go of his hand and took a sip of her coffee. "Sounds like a grueling existence. I wonder why Charles Howard decided the salt was his."

"Money. When this area became part of the U.S., Howard finagled to get the ownership of the salt transferred to him, but he couldn't protect it. He and Cardis were fighting over it, so Howard requested ranger assistance. I was supposed to guard Howard. Instead, me and the others got ourselves arrested by the Mexicans.''

"How could they arrest you if this was the United States?''

John grinned at her naiveté. "In 1877, Mexicans controlled this area. No one paid any attention to sovereignty because that had already changed six times in less than two hundred years.''

"Real stable place.'' She took his hand. "What do you remember about being in jail here?''

"I only remember the first few days. There were several of us and we were held in that old mercantile store over there.'' He looked out the window. "I don't even remember being shot at. I just know it happened.''

"How do you know?''

"I can't answer that.'' The idea that he had such stark memories bothered him. That, and the similarity of the past with the present. "Anyway, the motivation for fighting over the salt wasn't that much different than fighting over drugs today.''

"I'd say there's a lot of difference in the effect on people.''

"Maybe. I'm talking about money. Charles Howard, Chester Van Rooten—both of them wanted money.'' John stood and offered her a hand. "Let's go. I'm anxious to get to that diary.''

Dusk was fast approaching when they drove up in front of the ranch house. It stood forlorn and deserted. There wasn't even a dog to run out to greet them as they climbed the steps to the door, and the cat was nowhere in sight. The shadows and the emptiness gave Lauren the creeps. She jumped when a coyote howled in the distance.

As though he understood how she was feeling, Jonathan said, "It's rather lonely out here, isn't it?''

"It's not that so much as wondering what has happened here."

After he closed the door behind them and flicked on the welcome overhead light, Lauren felt better. He pulled her back against his chest and rested his head on her hair while she gathered the courage to attack their mission.

She was confident in who she was, and she wanted the same for Jonathan, but she was afraid of what they might discover. For argument's sake, just suppose by some quirk of fate he *was* John McCain? If he could travel forward in time, could he go back? He would have to leave her if given the opportunity; she knew that. He wasn't the type of man to abandon his son. J.C. had said that John McCain never made it back, but maybe now he was being given another chance. His hands, resting on her shoulders, gave her little comfort.

"Maybe it won't take us too long to find the diary. The office was probably used often, so let's start there," he said.

Reluctant to give up the warmth she'd been gathering from him, she was nevertheless anxious to get it over with. Instead of the diary proving that John came from the past, maybe it would prove he didn't. Then there would be a chance for them.

After they searched the office, Lauren leaned against the desk, disappointed. "You looked through all this earlier, didn't you?"

"Yes, but I was looking for records, ledgers, that type of stuff—not an old diary. Let's try the living room."

"Okay," she agreed.

Fifteen minutes later, and still empty-handed, she placed her fists on her hips and asked, "Where should we look next?"

"There are books in every room of this house," he said. "You pick the room, and I'll follow you."

After they'd searched the guest rooms and master bedroom, he looked truly bewildered. "I can't believe we haven't found it."

Lauren frowned and scratched the top of her head, as if that would increase her thinking power. "Where could it be?"

"Maybe we'll find it later," he said as they wandered into the kitchen. "Right now, I'm hungry. We haven't eaten since breakfast."

"That's because we didn't eat breakfast until eleven o'clock."

"That's because we didn't get up until after nine o'clock," he countered, mimicking her tone.

"And whose fault was that?"

"Yours, you vixen." He laughed and pulled her toward him. "You kept me up too late last night."

"*I* kept *you* up?" She wrapped her arms around his waist and leaned back so she could see his eyes. Despite the problems and uncertainties he still faced, he looked happy and relaxed. And she felt at least partially responsible for that. "You were the one who couldn't get enough."

"And that's your fault, too. If you didn't have such a cute little butt we would have gotten more sleep, and we wouldn't be standing here starving now."

She laughed at his ridiculous logic. "So, are you hinting that since this situation is my fault, I should fix us something to eat?"

He forced a solemn expression and nodded. "That would be a start toward righting things. After we eat, we'll talk about what else you might do." A wicked grin creased his face as he let her go.

Their light banter reminded her of the way they had kidded each other in the cave. During the past few weeks the desperate situation Jonathan had been in had dampened both of their senses of humor. Now she felt lighthearted even though the dark cloud of Jonathan's identity hung over them. For this brief moment it was wonderful to pretend things were going to be fine.

"While you rustle us up some grub, I'm going to go wash my hands," he said, heading toward the hallway.

Lauren found some spaghetti and a jar of sauce in the pantry. She'd just put a pot of water on to boil when she heard a yell and then footsteps hurrying down the hallway. Tossing the towel she'd been holding onto the countertop, she rushed to the doorway.

She almost bumped into Jonathan as he burst into the kitchen, waving a faded brown book.

"Look what I found!" he exclaimed.

"In the bathroom?" she asked.

"Yeah." He shrugged. "Everybody needs something to read."

She tried to control the laughter threatening to erupt. They had searched the entire house except the bathroom. Who would ever have thought of looking there? Yet everyone she knew kept some type of reading material there. "Well, what does it say?"

"I haven't had a chance to look at it yet. I'll tell you what. You cook and I'll read to you." He pulled out a chair and sat down. Then, propping one arm on the kitchen table, he stretched his long legs out in front of him and crossed them at the ankles as he opened the small book.

His deep voice filled the kitchen as he read, along with the steam from the boiling water and the aroma of marinara sauce. Lauren worked quietly so she could catch each word. Sometimes his voice was clear and strong. Other times, when a passage affected him, his voice drifted so low she had to concentrate to hear.

He read about life in San Antonio with a woman he referred to as a good mother to his child, about the hardships they faced, about her death and his guilt. He read about the anguish he'd felt over his decision to take one last assignment with the rangers. He read about the San

Elizario salt haulers almost word for word the way he'd described them earlier that day. Then he flipped the book closed as if he'd had enough, and stood up to stretch.

His sigh tore at Lauren's heart, but he didn't mention his disappointment. Instead, he walked over to the stove, looked down, closed his eyes and sniffed deeply. "Is it ready yet?"

"Yes, it is." Lauren poured tea while he helped set the table. His lack of comments stood like a barrier between them, until Lauren had to say something. His brief light-hearted mood was gone. "I know reading that must have been upsetting."

He nodded and sat down opposite her.

They said very little while they ate the spaghetti. When they were finished they put the dishes in the dishwasher and wiped off the table. After the last spoon was put away, Jonathan leaned back against the counter, dried his hands on a paper towel and tossed it toward the trash can.

As if he had been thinking all during the meal, he picked up the conversation where it had ended before dinner. "I don't understand it, but I don't feel like I expected I would. It doesn't feel intimate…immediate. I can't form clear pictures of the situations I described in the diary. I should be more upset about my son. I'm concerned for him, but I feel almost disconnected, as if he were someone else's child. I know that Annie was small and fair, but I can't see her, I can't remember how she felt, how she smelled when I held her in my arms."

He put his hands on Lauren's shoulders and held her at arm's length while he talked. "So unlike you. I'll never forget how you try to stifle a giggle when you think you shouldn't laugh, or how soft your skin feels, or your scent after we make love. It won't matter if a hundred and twenty years do pass, I'll remember that like it was yesterday." He pulled her to him and wrapped his arms tightly around her.

With her cheek crushed against his chest, her ear to his pounding heart, she could feel his frustration and confusion. But she didn't know how to help him.

"Thanks for being here for me," he whispered against her hair.

It wasn't the first time he had expressed his gratitude, and she was beginning to understand how much he really needed her. How could she have thought otherwise? She tightened her arms around his waist and snuggled closer.

"It's late. Let's go to bed," he said.

Nothing had been said about her spending the night. "I've got to go to work in the morning, but—"

"Stay with me one more night. I need you." He buried his hand in her hair and tilted her face upward so she could see the despair in his eyes.

The job could wait. Weaving her arms around his neck, she lifted her lips to meet his, hoping she could heal the pain he was feeling.

"Oh, lady, my sweet lady," he murmured against her mouth before he hauled her hard against him.

Lauren awoke sometime in the middle of the night, shivered and rolled over, then stretched out an arm, searching for warmth. Jonathan's side of the bed was empty. Immediately she jerked up and looked at the clock. It was almost four. Memories of their lovemaking the night before flooded through her as she slipped on Jonathan's terry-cloth robe and went in search of him.

She found him in the living room, head buried in his hand. Beneath the yellow glare of a lamp, the diary lay closed on the end table. He looked up when he heard her. A haunted expression marred his handsome face. Crossing the room, she asked, "How long have you been up?"

"A couple of hours. I couldn't sleep."

When she knelt beside him, he immediately reached out and buried one of his hands in her hair and gripped her by the back of the neck, holding her as if his very life depended on it.

"Are you okay?" she asked.

He released a deep breath and looked at the ceiling. "I don't know if I am or not anymore."

"Was there something in the book that upset you?" She knew the answer before he spoke. Whatever he had read had changed him.

"Not really. There's nothing there I didn't already know." He looked down into her eyes, his own dark with pain. "In fact, everything I remember I could have gotten from this diary."

"What do you mean?"

"Every recollection I have about my life is here. I can't think of anything that I can't find in this." He picked up the book, his thumb rubbing the worn brown leather.

"But the diary was left in San Elizario. You remember things that happened after that."

"Only what is in these reports of Cardis's that I found tucked in the back of the diary." Jonathan thumped a couple of sheets of paper. "J.C. mentioned finding them in the archives."

"So what does this mean?"

"I don't know." He stood up and pulled her with him. "What if I'm not John McCain? What if I read this book and assumed his identity?"

Chapter 15

John could really be Jonathan. All the previous day he and Lauren had searched and found nothing to suggest there was any way for him to travel through time. As he read the diary, the possibility that it was the source of all his memories crept into his thoughts, until the reality of his being mentally disturbed took form. He wasn't sure which would be worse—knowing he was from the past and being unable to get back or finding out he had absorbed someone's identity from a damn book.

He felt the light touch as her fingers gently smoothed the wrinkles on his brow in an effort to reassure him. It was useless. Didn't she understand? He had been certain who he was even if the time wasn't right. Now he didn't even have that assurance. She was the only stable thing in his life, his only bridge to reality of any kind. And whatever he did would cause her more pain.

If he told her to leave, he knew she would be devastated. If he kept her with him, he would only be postponing the inevitable. There was no way she could love a man who had no past at all. But she hadn't turned him away when she'd thought he was from the past. She'd loved him until the demons had receded enough for him to laugh. That had felt so wonderful—the laughing and teasing.

He brought her hand up and turned his mouth against the softness. "God, lady, I don't know what I'd do without you," he whispered into her palm.

"You don't have to find out. I meant it when I said I'd be here, regardless of who you are. You're a wonderful man."

"I don't know about being so wonderful." Her pulse fluttered beneath his lips as he kissed her open hand, then trailed his warm breath to the sensitive skin on her inner wrist. Again his doubts and conscience were overridden by his love. He needed her. He needed the comfort she offered, the trust, the passion. When she moaned in response, he pulled her into his arms.

Quivering with anticipation, Lauren laced her fingers through his hair and opened her mouth, inviting his tongue inside. This time his kisses weren't gentle. It was as though he was trying to hold on to the present or to rid himself of the past when he ground her lips under his.

The onslaught caught her by surprise, causing her knees to weaken and buckle. Only his tight embrace prevented her from falling. Jonathan's hands moved over her roughly, as if he'd committed her body to memory and it was his to possess at will. She didn't care that there was little gentleness in him. She understood his need and frustration. Each brush of his fingers wrung soft moans from her throat, while his lips continued to devour her, to beg her to end his torment. When finally he raised his head and gasped for breath, she clutched at his shoulders to keep from falling.

The barely controlled power she felt under her hands would have been frightening if she hadn't known him. She knew he would never hurt her no matter how confused and angry he became.

He quickly shed his clothing and backed her down on the sofa, pulling open the robe she was wearing. She felt the nipples of her full breasts pucker when the cool air hit them. He lowered his head to suckle first one, then the other, tugging them deep into his mouth before releasing them. Bracing himself with one hand on the back of the sofa, he rose above her.

She breathed deeply of his male scent, hungrily licking at his nipples with her tongue, surprised that they were as hard as her own had felt. She spread her fingers, sliding them down the hard muscles of his chest and his flat abdomen until he caught her hand and closed it around his hardness. At her touch, he shuddered, and his voice, husky with need, whispered, "Now, lady, now."

With little foreplay, John sought sanity inside her. Perhaps buried deep within her softness he would find himself. But moments later, sated and physically spent, he still didn't feel complete. He felt closer to it, though. In Lauren's arms he felt he was more of a real man than he had at any other time, and he was reluctant to move from the warm cocoon she wrapped around him. Her soft purrs of contentment roused him from his troublesome thoughts.

He propped himself up on one elbow and peered down at her, feeling a bit loutish. "I'm sorry about that."

"About what?" Her voice was still low and husky from their lovemaking.

"I didn't mean to be so..." He searched for words. How did he go about apologizing for putting his own needs before her pleasure? "Did I hurt you?"

"Oh, not at all." She ran a finger along his jaw as she smiled up at him. "Jon, you need to understand something about me. I would have stopped you if I hadn't enjoyed it."

It was her matter-of-factness that brought a smile to his face. She had felt in control the entire time, despite his lack of it. He hugged her tightly and buried his face against her neck. He loved her. There was no other way to describe his feelings.

Love.

It sounded so simple, but the emotions were so complex.

The question of who he really was and his mental state kept him silent. At this point it wouldn't be fair to complicate things by telling her how he felt. Love meant promises and commitment. Not problems. And if he really were Jonathan McCain, he faced a whole new set of problems. From the little he had learned, he didn't even think he would like himself. Jonathan appeared to have been an egocentric bastard, even though Cliff had said a few nice things about him.

Very few.

When he released his hold slightly, Lauren wiggled out from under him and looked out the window, where the first sliver of light was beginning to streak, white and pink, across the sky. "I've got to go or I won't make it to work this morning. Do you want to come with me? You can stay at my house."

"Thanks. But I'd like to stay here for a few days and try to figure out how to turn this place into a real cattle ranch." In case he *was* Jonathan McCain, he was going to have to have an occupation. Returning to Mexico City wasn't an option—not with Lauren in Sierra. Plus the thought of a crowded city didn't appeal to him. "And there are several loose ends I need to tie up with Cliff. We still don't know who all is involved in the drug-smuggling operation. I think I'll go into town and pick up my guns one day this week. Until Van Rooten is behind bars, I'd feel safer with some ammunition."

"Do you feel confident enough to drive after the quick lesson I gave you yesterday?" she asked.

"You bet. Driving's easier than saddling a horse," he assured her.

A half hour later he walked Lauren to the car and kissed

her one last time. He hated to see her go, but he figured he was lucky that they'd had the last two nights together. Tomorrow might not be so kind to him.

"You will come to see me when you come to town?" She opened the car door and turned back to face him.

"Don't worry. You're top of my list." How could she doubt for a moment that he would come to town as soon as he could? "I'll give you a call."

He couldn't put his finger on why but he didn't feel right. He wanted to keep her with him on the ranch, where he could be certain she was safe. She had lived alone and taken care of herself for years, but the break-in at her house had made him uneasy. Then, too, this nagging in his gut could just be the side effects of falling in love. He could either get over it or get used to it, because he was definitely in love.

He took her face in his hands and kissed her forehead. "Take care."

A freak December blizzard blew in two nights later, and by late afternoon of the following day, Sierra was blanketed with snow. It had taken Lauren twice as long as usual to get home from work. After a quick shower, she looked out her living room window at the growing drifts. If the weather didn't stop him, Jonathan should be arriving for their date in less than an hour.

He'd said nothing could keep him away from her. And it hadn't. First, he'd come to town to pick up his guns from the sheriff's office and had dropped by to see her. Then yesterday, he came in for lunch, because he said he couldn't stay away. She smiled, remembering how he'd handled his Mercedes as if he'd been born in one. More and more things pointed to the fact that he was truly Jonathan and had suffered a severe case of amnesia. She could deal with that easier than believing he was from the past.

Realizing that in her excitement to leave work on time

she'd left some paperwork she needed the next morning, Lauren decided to make a quick trip back to the office before Jonathan arrived. Not that she expected to have time to work after dinner—not with him there.

In case Jonathan got to her house before she returned, Lauren called to tell him she'd be back in a few minutes. After several rings with no answer, she figured he'd already left the ranch. She tried his cellular phone, but didn't get him. Sighing, she flipped the device back into her purse, used to cellulars being less reliable than smoke signals because of the mountains and canyons.

If he'd just left, she thought, she had a good forty or forty-five minutes to make it to the office and back. She flicked off the light switch, stopped and turned it back on. Leaving the door unlocked so Jonathan could come in and wait, she kicked at the small snowdrift on her porch. When the white powder floated around her ankles, she smiled in delight, thinking about asking Jonathan to help build a snowman later.

Now, though, she picked her way over the frozen ground to her car and carefully eased out of the driveway. Because it snowed so infrequently, she and the other Sierra drivers were unprepared for the icy conditions.

She'd spent so much time on Jonathan's case that she'd gotten behind at work and needed to review a will before she met with the Jacquezes in their home the next morning. No sweat, she thought, feeling the energy bubble inside her like it had for the past few days. She was so much in love that she was too excited to sleep. Living for Jonathan's voice and yearning for his touch, she felt incomplete unless he was nearby.

After parking in her usual space at the rear of the law office, she slowly made her way to the door, and then, shivering from the cold, fumbled with the key, trying to insert it in the lock. The wind whipped up the snow as it whistled around the sides of the building, making it hard to see the tiny keyhole. Finally, she got the back door open and stepped inside. The hallway leading to the offices was illuminated. Funny, she thought, she didn't remember leaving a light on, and she had been the last person to leave the office that afternoon. She was so preoccupied with Jonathan she was getting careless.

Even as she rationalized her behavior she realized something was wrong—other than the light. It wasn't anything she could identify. The doors to Robert's and her offices were closed, just as they should have been. At the mouth of the hallway near the front, Lauren could see the reception area, with Lyna's well-organized desk spotlighted by moonbeams streaming in through the window. It all looked normal, but it didn't feel right.

Suddenly, the hair on the back of her neck prickled and she was faced with a decision. She could check things out or she could retreat. It only took a split second to decide to go get help. Just as she turned to run, a gloved hand reached out from behind the door and clamped over her mouth. "Make one little peep and you're dead," a man's muffled voice said, while he tightened an arm around her chest and nudged hard metal into her side.

Bile rose in Lauren's throat and her eyes widened. Desperate, she tried kicking at the man as he forced her outside, but she lost her footing on the slippery concrete. In a split second that felt like an eternity, she heard more than felt her head hit the porch. Even as she descended into unconsciousness, she couldn't believe it was happening. She'd lived thirty years and had never had a gun pointed at her; now, in the space of a few weeks, it had happened twice.

Somewhere between sleep and wakefulness, Lauren felt her nose itch. She was miserably cold and uncomfortable. Country music blared from a radio, making her ears and her head hurt. At least she was alive.

Opening her eyes the tiniest slit, she realized she'd been shoved into the back seat of a club-cab pickup. Her wrists were restricted behind her back. Tape, she thought, when she felt it pull the hair on her arm. A slight movement let her know that her ankles were also taped. And so was her mouth. Slowly she forced herself awake, fearful of moving or letting the man driving know she was regaining consciousness.

She was furious, but realized she had to keep that fury under control. First of all, there was absolutely nothing she could do now except wait. Whoever had kidnapped her hadn't done it to take her to a church social. He was dangerous. Trying to make sense of this, she realized it had to be tied in with Jonathan.

She hadn't recognized the muffled voice of the man who'd grabbed her, but Van Rooten had to be behind it. She tried to reason out what he'd have to gain.

Blackmail? Who and why? All the questions came back to Jonathan.

He would start looking as soon as he realized she was missing. But that didn't offer her much comfort. The wind would blow the snow, filling in their tracks, so there'd be none to follow. Yet she had no doubt that Jonathan would try to find her, until she remembered he hadn't answered his phone. As the impact of that thought registered, she swallowed a groan to keep from gasping out loud. Jonathan could already be hurt, or worse. Lauren traversed the emotions of fear and fury in a matter of minutes, settling into despair.

The man braked the pickup, throwing her off the seat and wedging her in the narrow space between the front and back seats. Landing on the hard ridged, rubber floor mat facedown, she nearly choked on the smell of dust.

"It's time to get out," the man growled.

Chester. It *was* Chester. Maybe she could reason with him.

He reached into the back seat and pulled at her shoulders.

She flinched in pain when her knee hit the hard metal edge of the doorway.

Trying to sit up, she saw the knife in Chester's hand. He was going to kill her! She drew back in fear.

"I'm not gonna cut you, Lauren, so just be still. I'm gonna cut this tape." He slid the knife between her ankles and sawed through the tape. Afraid the knife would slip and cut her, she tensed and remained still as he'd told her to.

"Now, if you won't scream your head off, I'll take the tape off your mouth." Chester stared at her, waiting for compliance. "Deal?"

Lauren nodded her head, but couldn't keep from wincing when he yanked the tape off her mouth.

"Come with me. We're gonna be here for a while."

She scooted out of the pickup and bent a little, testing her legs for strength. Disappointment filled her when she realized they were too stiff for her to kick Chester or to run. When he grabbed her arm to lead her through the dark, she pulled away from him, refusing to be any more compliant than she had to be. "Keep your hands off me."

She tried to ignore him as she hobbled forward, surprised when she realized she was at Jonathan's house. Why would the sheriff bring her to the ranch? As the answer began to crystallize, Lauren stumbled. Icy fear gripped her heart. Jonathan. He was dead. Chester had brought her out here to kill her, too. He meant to leave no witnesses.

Without a word, Chester grabbed her upper arm and jerked her upright. Again she tried to shrug off his hand, but he kept a firm grip on her. The adrenaline that had kept her going seeped out of her blood, leaving her trembling. She didn't have the energy to fight him.

She had to think, to plan, to save what little strength she had left. Her head was throbbing. While that should have been the least of her worries, it wasn't. She had to be able to think clearly. To save herself and Jonathan—if he was still alive.

Keeping one hand on her arm, Chester took his gun and, using the butt end, broke a glass pane out of the back door, reached in and unlocked it. Then he thrust Lauren inside.

Glass crunched under her shoes as she fought to remain upright. That was hard without the use of her hands and arms for balance. Lauren searched the room for any sign of Jonathan. Everything looked fine. She decided that if the sheriff had been there earlier he would have left the door unlocked. Surely he wouldn't have had to break and enter. That theory gave her some comfort. Maybe Jonathan wasn't here.

When the sheriff closed the door and turned to face her, she asked, "Why are you doing this, Chester?"

"It wasn't a planned thing, if that's what you're asking, Lauren. I thought I'd try again to find the negative of that picture I know you took. I didn't think anyone would get out on a night like this. But since you came in, I didn't have a choice." He shoved her down the hall to the living room, where he flipped on the lights, then pushed her onto the sofa.

To Lauren, it seemed that bad timing was going to be her death—first in Diablo Canyon and now here. She'd be safer if she didn't let Chester know she suspected as much as she did. "Why bring me here to Jonathan's?" She looked around the room and found no sign of a struggle, so he must have left of his own free will. "Where is he?"

"He'll be back. Just as soon as he finds out you're missing, he'll start huntin' for you." Chester paced the floor as he verbalized his escalating madness. "No, I hadn't planned it this way, but maybe it'll work out for the best, after all. You're the only ones who know about me. Yep, this gives me an opportunity to get rid of the both of ya. I figure the two of you had a lovers' quarrel and the son of a bitch killed you and I had to take him into custody."

God help them all. Chester did intend to kill Jonathan—
and her. Relief at the knowledge that Jonathan was alive
somewhere was overshadowed by how crazy Chester had
become. "It will never work, you know. No one will
beli—"

The sheriff spun around. "Yes, they will this time." His
voice was high and too loud. "They'll believe me. They've
always voted for me because I do what's best for the
county, and that means gettin' rid of the likes of McCain."

"Why? What did he do to you?"

"I learned he was a double-crosser. I needed money and
had asked the commissioners for a raise for years. Got nothing. Bad hours, but what the hell did the people in Sierra
really care about my well-being? So I had to get my pay
my own way." He seemed to be genuinely sad as he
stopped in front of her. "And, Lauren, as much as I hate
it, I can't let you mess up my plans, so I'm gonna take you
to another room while I get things ready. McCain'll be back
out here eventually."

He seized her by the arm and led her to the master bedroom, then thrust her down on the bed. The bed where only
days before she had made love to Jonathan. It seemed like
aeons ago, but a faint masculine scent still clung to the
pillows where her face was buried.

When Chester grabbed her legs to retape them, Lauren
kicked out. But her efforts against the larger, well-trained
lawman were futile. Deftly he rolled her over and bound
her ankles, then turned to leave. On his way out the door,
he paused for a moment, then yanked a blanket off a nearby
chair and threw it over her.

The howl of coyotes in the distance pierced the night air
and an occasional creak sounded from somewhere far away
in the house. Lauren pulled herself up on the bed and
twisted her hands, trying to work the tape loose. Realizing
it would be easier if she could get her hands in front of her
body, she tried to slip her bottom through her arms. She'd

seen it done in movies, but found she couldn't manage it. So she resorted to using her nails to feel where the end of the tape started, and when she found the ridge, she went to work. The sheriff had done a sloppy job of taping her, so there was some slack in her bonds.

She had to escape and find Jonathan. Their love was too new for them to lose one another now.

John pushed the doorbell of Lauren's house and waited for her to answer. Tonight, he planned on buying her the biggest steak in Sierra, then coming back here and making love until they couldn't move. He'd given up on doing the right thing and staying away from her until he got his memory back. That might take forever, and he couldn't wait that long. He couldn't stay away from her. He loved and needed her too much.

When she didn't answer, he rapped on the door and stamped his feet to keep warm. Still she didn't answer. He tried the doorknob. It wasn't locked, so he stepped inside. "Lauren?" he called out.

The evening before, she'd warned him that she might be a few minutes late, but it wasn't likely that her door would be unlocked and her lights would be on if she'd been at her office all day. He quickly looked through all the rooms, then found the phone. Maybe she was still at work. But there was no answer there.

Deciding that she must be on her way home, he sat down on the sofa and propped his feet up to wait. He'd give her ten minutes.

Fighting back a growing sense of uneasiness, he looked at the pictures on the wall. He understood Lauren's love for photography. She was good at it.

He glanced at his watch every two minutes, until finally he couldn't stand it any longer. He'd go looking for her. Maybe she'd had an accident in the snow.

Spotting her car parked behind the law office, he pulled

in beside it and hurried to the back door. When the knob turned in his hands, he became aggravated. Lauren ought to know to lock the door even if she hadn't planned to stay in the office two minutes. Van Rooten hadn't shown up, so they were still in danger.

"Lauren?" he called out. The overhead light was on in the hallway, so she must have been there at some point. He hurried to her office and threw open the door, half-afraid of what he was going to find. "Lauren?

"Something's not right," he muttered when he saw the chaos, but no Lauren. Her desk was a mess, and file drawers hung partially open. This was definitely more than a case of staying late at work and forgetting the time. Something had happened to her.

A frown furrowed his brow as he thumbed through his wallet, searching for Robert Jordan's card with his home phone number on it.

Drumming his fingers on the desktop, John waited for Robert to answer, then explained his concerns.

Robert said, "I'll be right over. You call in the law."

"Yeah, sure." If Chester couldn't be trusted, John doubted the deputies could either. He hung up the phone and looked around Lauren's office for signs of a struggle. He checked every room, every closet before he walked back down the hallway to the door, but he found nothing amiss. Her car. Maybe he'd find something in her car. When he yanked the car door open, the overhead light cast a glow on Lauren's purse sitting on the floorboard.

John felt his throat tightening when he saw that there were no keys in the ignition. She'd have needed them to get into the office. He straightened up and looked around. Soft flakes of snow drifted downward in the glow of a streetlight, but the beauty was lost on John. He dropped his gaze to the ground and retraced his steps to the back door of the law offices. Just as he reached the porch, Robert drove up, his car's headlamps banishing the shadows behind the building.

John noticed a hole in the snow. Kneeling down, he felt around and closed his fingers on cold metal. As Robert approached him, John held out his hand to show Robert what he'd found.

Lauren's keys.

"It doesn't look good, does it?" Robert said.

John felt his features harden. If Lauren was hurt, the son of a bitch who'd done it would pay.

"I called her dad before I came." Robert rubbed his hands together. "I expect he and Ted will be here within the half hour."

"I'm not waiting that long," John said, going back inside. "I'm calling Cliff, then I'm heading back out to the ranch." John wasn't going to be without a rifle this time. His handgun was in the glove compartment, but he intended to be prepared.

Half an hour later, he was on his way to the ranch. Deputy Soliz had shown up at the law office about the same time Cliff had, so John left the preliminary investigation in their hands. In the meantime, he didn't want to have to listen to them speculate.

He recalled looking through Lauren's house, remembering how it reminded him of the woman he loved. Other than a damp towel thrown carelessly on the bed, everything had been in place. He glanced down at the dashboard clock. Eight o'clock. Where the hell was she?

Lauren had finally gotten a good grip of the tape binding her hands and was slowly unwinding it when she heard Chester curse from the hallway. Quickly she lay back down to hide her hands. He opened the door, allowing a blade of light to cut across the room. She huddled under the blanket, hoping he wouldn't yank it back and see what she'd done. She didn't have to work hard to act terrified.

"You've been out here visitin' before, Lauren. What did you find out about McCain?"

"Not much." She knew the sheriff was wondering what Jonathan might remember and possibly have told someone.

Chester let out a nervous laugh. "Hasn't got his memory back, huh? I knew that the minute the border patrol brought him in. Gotta get him before that memory comes back. I didn't plan on it being here, though. He'll be back and I'll be waiting for him. He won't know what hit him."

"Chester, don't make it worse. Let me go."

He stared down at her. "Sorry. I really truly am. But a man's gotta do what a man's gotta do. And it's gonna look like McCain killed you, after which I killed him, trying to protect you. Can't risk takin' him into custody again. He might talk." With that, he closed the door.

Lauren frantically worked on the tape. She had to get loose soon. Maybe she could get out the window, warn Jonathan. Where had he hidden his rifles? Maybe she could get one. In the meantime, she concentrated on the tape—one inch at a time. How many times had Chester wrapped it around her? Suddenly, she felt it give and she pulled her wrists apart.

She sucked in her breath and glanced toward the door. She massaged her wrists, then reached down and untaped her feet. Hearing footsteps, she lay back down just as Chester opened the door. A strip of tape dangled from his hands.

"You might get it in your head to make a little noise when lover boy gets here. Gotta see that you don't." He lumbered toward the bed.

Oh, please, Lord, Lauren prayed. *Don't let him pull back the blanket.*

She lay on her arms as though they were still taped, but clutched her hands into fists, ready to fight if she had to. But Chester didn't seem to suspect a thing as he bent down and stuck the tape over her mouth. As he walked out, Lauren, for the first time ever, was glad that Chester was a chauvinist, never suspecting a woman would have the courage or initiative to escape.

Now, she finally had a chance to warn Jon.

Chapter 16

John turned off the highway, but hadn't traveled fifty yards when he braked and got out of the car. Leaving the headlamps on, he looked at the faint ruts not quite covered by the blowing snow. It appeared to him as if another set of tracks were laid on top of the ones made earlier by his car. He got back in and drove another hundred yards with his car door open to see if the tracks continued. They did, and no one lived down this road except him.

Why would anyone come to visit him in a snowstorm? Lauren and Cliff were the only ones who would have a reason. Their cars were in Sierra, so that ruled them out. John suspected he had an unwelcome visitor at the ranch waiting for his return. And he hoped Lauren was with him.

John backed out and drove down the highway to a rise, then picked up his cellular phone and dialed 911. After telling the authorities about the situation at the ranch, John started toward his place once again.

His fingers clutched the steering wheel as he drove the car around a curve. He had to reach Lauren before it was too late. Easing up slightly on the gas, he threaded the car between boulders that lined the road's parallel, snow-filled ruts.

He found it hard to understand why anyone would have kidnapped Lauren unless she'd accidentally walked in on someone and caught him doing something illegal. Had Chester come back to town? Or perhaps the sheriff's drug contact had taken Lauren. John would know soon.

Crossing a cattle guard, he knew he had to go the rest of the way without his headlamps. If anyone was at his ranch, the person would see the car lights, and John didn't intend to help the bastard any more than he had to. At least the moon was up and illuminated the snow-covered road enough so he could follow it.

Finally, a mile from the house, he edged off the road to make room for Cliff and any backup to get around. They would understand that he had stopped and walked the rest of the way so no one would hear the car motor.

John pulled his .38-caliber, snub-nosed revolver out of the glove compartment and checked the chamber. Absorbing what warmth he could from the vehicle before he opened the door, he shoved the gun into the back of his waistband and readjusted his leather jacket. He threw open the door, pulled the collar up around his ears and took off. He had a full mile to cover in the storm, but rather than cursing it or the darkness, he was grateful, knowing it would provide cover.

He just hoped he would get there in time. He couldn't bear the thought that something had happened to Lauren—again—because of him.

He hurried through the white skeletons of mesquite and shin oak until he was about a quarter mile from his ranch house. Then he stopped to take stock. Only a small, lonely light framed by a living room window said that the place wasn't deserted. He'd left that light on himself. Still, John sensed someone was there. The cold chills radiating over his flesh weren't just due to the snow clinging to his clothes.

Hunching his back against the north wind, John searched for signs of a vehicle, but the blowing snow had covered the tracks he'd spotted eight miles back.

Within a hundred yards of the house, caution overruled his eagerness and John stopped to listen. Not that he expected to hear anything, because the sound of the wind rustling the vegetation would camouflage almost any other noise.

Squinting so he could see better in the pale light, he looked for movements around the buildings, but other than occasional gusts of snow, nothing moved. Wanting to find out if Lauren was indeed there, he picked his way through the brush until he was only a few yards from the side of the house. Still there was no sign of life.

Suddenly John spotted what he'd been looking for. The metal barn's sliding doors were closed. When he'd pulled his car out, he had left a gap for the cat to get in from the cold. Now the door was shut tight. He didn't know if he should start there and risk being seen before Cliff arrived or wait.

He hated waiting.

Lauren eased to the side of the bed and worked her wrists and ankles to get the cramps out. Sitting there, she listened through the darkness for Chester. She knew not hearing him didn't mean he wasn't just on the other side of the door. If she could get to the straight-backed chair Jonathan kept in the corner, she could prop it under the knob. That might give her the time she needed to get out the window before Chester came in.

Lauren inched around the wall, groaning silently when the floor creaked. She waited for what seemed like interminable minutes before she took another step. Finally, she touched the chair. Now, the trick was to carry it to the door without making a sound. She'd just reached the door when it flew open.

"What do you think you're doing?" Chester shouted at her. Face red and eyes angry, he threw the chair aside when she tried to hurl it at him and grabbed her by the arms. "I'll teach you a lesson. This is all your fault, you know. If you hadn't been wandering around where you had no business being in the first place, neither one of us would be in this mess."

He shook her until Lauren thought her neck was going to break. When she felt his hold lessen, she yanked her arms away and backed up against the bed of her small prison. "Have you gone crazy?" She'd never seen him like this.

"Why do you have to call it crazy when all I wanted was a decent living?" He took a slow, deliberate step toward her, his face marred by the feral gleam in his eyes. "Don't you see that your meddlin's left me no choice?"

Terror continued building with the realization that he was indeed crazed if not crazy. "Get away from me, Chester."

"It's too late, Lauren. You've already shown me you're not going to make it easy on yourself." He closed the remaining few inches separating them until he was so near she felt his breath. "Now, I can't take a chance on your giving me away."

When he reached out and grabbed for her, she screamed and fought him with all her strength. His fingers found their away around her throat, and Lauren knew she had to will herself to relax. If she didn't fight him, maybe he wouldn't notice she was trying to change positions. She wilted and a second later kicked her knee into his groin and yanked backward at the same time, falling onto the bed.

Chester screamed in pain and coughed as he bent over, giving her the second she needed. She scrambled to her feet and stumbled to the door, dodging his feeble attempt to stop her. In the hallway, she regained her footing and sped down the hallway. She didn't know how badly she'd hurt the sheriff, but hoped it would slow him down long enough for her to get away.

She burst from the house, straight into a pair of strong arms and an immovable chest. She couldn't see who it was so she kicked and scratched at her captor. She had come this far and no one was going to prevent her escape—not even this big lug who was repeating her name over and over.

"Lauren, it's me." Jonathan's voice had a sense of urgency. "Let's get the hell out of here."

Finally, reason soaked through her adrenaline and fury enough for her to register the fact that Jonathan held her in one arm and a gun in the other. The relief was so overwhelming she wanted to collapse, but she knew Chester would be right behind her. Jonathan was right: they had to move in a hurry. If she could get her legs to cooperate.

She felt him tense a split second before he shoved her behind him, placing his body between her and the light that spilled from the open doorway, illuminating everything in its path for several yards.

Lauren peeked around his side. Chester stood on the step, pointing a gun at Jonathan. His mouth was twisted in hatred. Holding the gun with both hands, he waved it, saying, "You still don't remember anything, do you, McCain? Well, it looks like you're gonna die that way." The click of the trigger being cocked sounded like a cannon in the crisp night air.

"Don't do anything stupid, Van Rooten." Jonathan's voice was clipped. "Others are right behind me. You won't walk out of here alive."

"You always were a bullshitter. We had a good thing going, McCain. Money. Power. But, no, you double-crossing..." Chester's voice became more hysterical with every word. He tried to steady the gun, but it dipped wildly, pointing from one corner of the yard to the other.

"Run, Lauren," Jonathan whispered, taking a step away from her and pushing her toward the cover of darkness.

Still stunned, Lauren stumbled on the slick terrain, not sure she understood. Was Jonathan telling the truth about others coming or was he bluffing? Could she run without him?

John wished Cliff and the others would hurry up and arrive. His impulsive decision to catch Lauren as she stormed from the house had been stupid. He should have let her run past while he waited for Van Rooten alone. Now, he only hoped his need to reassure her didn't prove deadly.

At least he knew Lauren was okay. *If* she ran. He could see she was indecisive. "Run, dammit," he hollered, keeping his gun trained on Chester as he dived in the opposite direction.

"I told Saul you were dangerous, that we had to get rid of you. But he wouldn't listen," Chester screamed as he began firing.

"Run, Lauren, run," John yelled, rolling on the ground. He took quick aim before pulling off one shot, just as he felt a sharp pain at the side of his head. But he saw the impact of his bullet. Chester flew backward, the gun falling from his hand. Sliding down the side of the house, the sheriff clutched at his arm, blood flowing between his fingers.

John lay back on the ground, not knowing if he'd run up against a rock or another bullet. Breathing heavily, he shook his head, trying to clear up his disorientation.

For that split second, time seemed to freeze. It was deathly quiet.

Then through a fog he heard Lauren's voice. "Jon, are you okay?" she asked, kneeling beside him.

"Yeah," he answered, still clutching his revolver. He licked at his lips, meeting the salty taste of blood. When he heard the sound of running footsteps, he struggled to sit up.

"You guys all right?" Cliff called out, before bursting from the brush into the yard.

"In a manner of speaking." John lowered the pistol and slumped back down on the cold, wet ground.

An hour later, Jonathan sat on the sofa trying to get warm. He felt drained, physically and emotionally. His head ached, not just from the bump but from the rush of thoughts bombarding his brain. He remembered everything—from his childhood to Saul's murder.

But now he had to concentrate on what was going on around him. At least the cleanup was basically done—inventory, pictures, arrests. And as for honor among thieves, Van Rooten had told who his contact was—a lawyer in Ysleta, one the DEA had never suspected. Cliff had already called the El Paso office with the information, to make certain the guy didn't skip across the border before morning.

Chester was going to live. Jonathan hadn't wanted to kill him, but he was pleased the bastard had suffered double damage. Lauren had wreaked her havoc, and then Jonathan had rearranged the man's right shoulder. He'd already been whisked away to a hospital for treatment.

"Damn waste of taxpayers' money if you ask me," Cliff had said.

Alone with Lauren at last, Jonathan looked at her in admiration as she washed the blood from the side of his face. He experienced a sense of déjà vu. But at least this time he could see her. She was a real trooper. "You know, I believe you'd have escaped on your own if I hadn't shown up."

"No, he would've caught me. If I'd kept my wits about me and run like you said, we might have made it without your being hurt. But maybe not. Chester would have still been loose with the gun. No telling who would have been hurt. I'm just glad he was a bad shot.''

''I am, too. But we were in the dark and he was silhouetted like a... Ouch.''

''Sorry. But I think I've about got the bleeding stopped. At least enough to get you to the hospital and have a doctor look at it.''

''I don't need a doctor. All I did was hit my head on a rock.'' But that rock had changed everything for him. He didn't know how to tell Lauren what had happened without just doing it. ''Lauren,'' he said, ''my memory's back.''

He saw a flash of joy in her eyes, quickly replaced with uncertainty. Withdrawing the bloody cloth and staring at him, she tentatively asked, ''And?''

''I remember Chester always strutting around, bragging about how smart he was and how the money was going to buy him power.''

''Which means you're—''

''Jonathan McCain,'' he interrupted, wanting to say it first. ''I haven't worked through everything, but I know that much.''

''The head injuries, then, caused this.'' He felt her shiver before she asked, ''But what would have ever made you think you were your great-great-grandfather?''

''I think I have that figured out. I'd been reading Grandpa John's diary just before I went out to the airstrip that night. When I saw Chester raise the rifle, I dived out of the way. He managed to nick me. Apparently, Saul tried to tackle me and got in the way of Chester's second bullet.'' Jonathan leaned against the back of the sofa, hoping to ease his aching head. He could faintly hear Ted and Cliff talking in the kitchen over a cup of coffee.

''What about the name Atkinson? It was mentioned in the diary, and then there's Cliff....'' Lauren shrugged her shoulders.

''It must have been a coincidence. Perhaps in my mind

I got the two people mixed up and that led to some of my confusion. After I was shot, I knew I had to contact Atkinson and then I remembered, because I had just read it, that Atkinson had been shot in San Elizario.''

She squeezed his hand. ''I hate what happened, but everything is turning out fine. It sounds like a melodrama, but the bad guys got caught by the good guys, and you know who you are.''

''Yeah.'' He closed his eyes, not so sure things had turned out fine. There was a lot she didn't know about Jonathan McCain, and when she found out, she wasn't going to be too pleased that she was involved with him. But now his head hurt so badly he didn't want to face all of that. Not until he could think more clearly.

The relief he'd felt at finding Lauren safe was slowly turning to dismay as he realized who he was and what type of life he had led. The nature of his undercover work had required that he associate with lowlifes. Fed up with the deceit and danger, he'd wanted to get away. That was why he'd bought this ranch. He'd wanted a chance for a new life, but it hadn't happened. He'd been sucked right back in.

Jonathan McCain hadn't exactly lived an exemplary life. In fact, Cliff had been right—he was a real jerk. From the time he'd walked out of his parents' lives, he hadn't felt any particular need to be nice. He'd had enough money to get by with, doing pretty much what he wanted. With the exception of Cliff, he'd never formed close ties. He wasn't good at relationships. What's worse, he'd been rather proud of it. No, he wasn't anybody worth Lauren Hamilton's love.

Lauren closed her eyes and shifted around, trying to get comfortable in the green vinyl chair outside the emergency room. She'd finally convinced Jonathan that a trip to the hospital was necessary, and she was just waiting for him to come out of an examination room. Her own bump on the head had been superficial and the medicine the doctor had given her had already lessened the pain. Still, her energy was sapped. In retrospect everything that had happened seemed surrealistic, something she'd discount if it hadn't been for the blood. The blood had focused her attention.

Jonathan's blood.

And, yes, Chester's. Was he truly demented, or had it been the age-old story of greed and desire for position that had warped his perspective? She shivered, thinking how close he'd come to making her lose everything.

Yet, she realized, in a convoluted way she had Chester to thank for her getting to know Jonathan. If Jonathan hadn't been in that cave, hadn't been running, if Chester hadn't shot at her, she might never have met her cowboy. Oh, life was so complicated.

Smiling to herself, she leaned back. Complicated or not, Jonathan was okay.

Hearing low voices, Lauren raised her head and yawned. The white glare of the emergency room lights cast an eerie glow behind Jonathan as he shook hands with the doctor, then crossed the hall to join her. She stood.

"How are you feeling?" she asked. The white bandage taped to his temple wasn't as large as she'd expected.

"Almost as good as new. Another superficial wound, the doc said." A wry grin played on his lips. "Looks like I'll have a matched set of scars, one on each side of the head." He fingered his hairline, where the scar left by Chester's bullet was beginning to fade, as he looked up and down the hall.

"I sent everyone home," she explained. "It's after midnight and they were all exhausted."

"It's been a long day. For both of us. All of this has been too much, too fast." His voice was flat, nearly emotionless.

Lauren had a sense of foreboding. Since Jonathan had regained his memory, he'd been distant. Quiet. He'd already said more here in the hallway than he had during the drive back to Sierra. She wasn't sure if it was because he'd been tired and in pain, or because he'd been rehashing his life. Maybe he regretted their relationship now that he remembered things about himself. Maybe there was another woman in Jonathan McCain's life.

"Let's get out of here," he said. "I'll drop you by your house."

"I'll drive," Lauren suggested.

"No, I'm fine."

Both of them were close to collapse, Lauren knew, so the ten-minute drive seemed longer. Jonathan had again retreated into his own world. It was late and she wanted to ask him to stay with her. She needed to feel the security and intimacy of his arms around her tonight. After he pulled into her drive, he left the motor idling, so she asked, "Why don't you come in? I'll make you a sandwich. Besides, it's late and you aren't in any shape to drive back to the ranch tonight."

He was silent for a couple of seconds as he stared out the window. "I think I'd better get on back."

"Jonathan, don't do this." She reached out to touch his arm. He didn't pull away, but he didn't offer any encouragement, either. Whether he realized it or not, Lauren knew Jonathan needed her. "Don't shut me out. I love you."

"You don't understand." He turned to face her, but the shadows hid his expression. "I'm not the man you think I am."

"Yes, you are. Despite your amnesia, all along you were still you. The same mannerisms, ways, thought processes."

"No. You don't know me. You don't know how I've lived." He touched her cheek gently. "It hasn't all been pretty. Because of me, your life was jeopardized."

"My being shot at and kidnapped were just a matter of coincidence."

"Yeah, a coincidence that wouldn't have happened if I hadn't come into the picture."

"That's not true."

Jonathan looked away from her and leaned back against the seat. "That's not the only reason, Lauren."

Lauren felt a sudden chill. "What do you mean?"

"I don't know if we ought to see each other anymore." His voice was cool and matter-of-fact.

"Is there someone else?"

He looked at her. "What do you mean?"

"I mean is there another woman, someone you didn't remember until tonight?"

"There have been women, but no one special." His voice reflected sorrow.

Her chill was replaced by a sudden rush of anger. "Then you're saying that I mean nothing to you?"

"On the contrary. Look, Lauren, don't make this any harder," he said. "I've got to sort things out, and I just don't think..." His words trailed off as he shrugged his shoulders and turned his head away from her.

She jumped out of the car, hurling her fury at him. "I can't believe this. The mighty undercover guy would risk his all to catch smugglers, but when it comes to something personal—to me and you—you're afraid to even take a chance! You're right. I *don't* know you."

Chapter 17

It was the last morning of the year, cool and clear. Crisp, some people would say. It was perfect weather for the revelers who'd be bringing in the New Year that night, but Jonathan wasn't in a mood to celebrate anything. He didn't even plan to watch any of the specials on television. He'd put up with all the false gaiety he could at Christmas. His parents had done everything possible to make him happy, but the ache in his heart had refused to go away.

He looked out the window at the ranch he'd thought held such promise. A shin oak swayed in a lazy motion as the gentle wind rippled through it. The weatherman had said it would reach the high sixties tomorrow. Jonathan didn't care one way or the other.

He dropped the curtain and returned to pacing the floor of his living room until he thought he'd go stir-crazy. Slipping on a jacket and his black felt hat, he decided he had to get out of the confines of the house. He saw Lauren in it everywhere. Cuddled up on the sofa to avoid his bed, pacing the floor protecting him from Cliff, in the kitchen making coffee. Laughing with him, encouraging him and embracing him. Rushing out the door with terror on her face. Maybe a brisk walk would erase her from his mind, if only for a few moments. It would grant him a welcome reprieve from his guilt and loneliness.

The barns and deserted corrals stood like useless sentinels on a barren ranch. Fitting, he thought, feeling rather empty himself. Jonathan wandered through the buildings, remembering how Lauren had walked side by side with him as he tried to make sense of his life. All she'd ever done was try to help him. All he'd done was set her up for harm and disappointment.

He gave careful consideration to his past, not liking much of anything. What he'd considered independence had actually been a detachment from life. He was thoroughly disgusted that he'd wasted so many years being separated from his family. His father had apologized for believing his son guilty of drug possession, but apparently anything short of a flogging hadn't been retribution enough for the old Jonathan. The best thing that resulted from being shot and getting hit on the head with a rock was having the chip on his shoulder knocked off. And meeting Lauren. Through his own self-righteousness, he'd hurt everyone, including her.

Oblivious to the cold breeze stinging his face, he meandered among tufts of brown grass that crunched beneath his boots until he reached a knoll that overlooked the vastness of the Chihuahuan desert.

Closing his eyes, he visualized Lauren on horseback, looking up at him that day in the canyon after she'd vowed to protect him. He opened his eyes, half expecting to see her and the sorrel in the arroyo a few hundred yards away, but the only movement came from rustling blades of grass and the gray clouds floating in the dull sky.

Sure, he could have lied to Lauren and enjoyed some time with her. But he'd been afraid he'd have fallen into his old habits. Any time someone had gotten a little too close to him, he'd cut them off. Zap. The end. He'd never even felt twinges of guilt. He did now, though. More than twinges. His guilt was with him every moment. He didn't want Lauren to be hurt, yet here he was, hurting her. He was so proud of her spunkiness. Hell, if he went to see her now, she might knee him worse than she had Chester.

As much as he ached from needing her, Jonathan tried to convince himself that Lauren was better off without him. Before she'd even met him, he'd endangered her life. And then after he got to know her and love her, he'd hurt her even more.

But deep in his gut, he knew that wasn't the reason he'd said goodbye. He was a coward, afraid to take a chance, like she'd said. He was afraid that when she discovered who he really was, she wouldn't love him and he couldn't bear the thought of the pain. It was better to be aloof than to be hurt.

His restlessness unabated, he went back inside and thumbed through the books lining the shelves. He pulled out a slender volume that Helena had encouraged him to read. He'd only taken it to appease her, since it looked too much like a fairy tale to suit him. Maybe, though, his sister was trying to tell him something, so he began reading.

Half an hour later he slammed the small volume shut. He smiled, deciding for the first time in twenty-two years that he could take a chance.

All he needed was a favor from Lauren's brother Ted.

It was New Year's Eve. Lauren sat at her desk, alone. The office had been closed since noon, but after being home a couple of hours, she couldn't stand it. So she'd come back. Work was her refuge.

Angry that Jonathan hadn't listened to reason, Lauren had returned to work immediately after the kidnapping—over the objections of almost everyone. Trying to put him out of her mind was impossible, but she knew Jon needed time to sort through all he had discovered about himself. Ted and her father had tried to placate her over the holidays. Robert and Lyna were giving her a wide berth.

Lauren was furious, she was hurt. She'd been through two weeks of hell.

She would have sworn it was impossible for a day to be so long, but recently she'd been too agitated to do anything right, and now, at three o'clock, she was reworking a motion for the third time. She heard the outside door open, but because she half expected Robert to stop by, she ignored it until she felt someone watching her.

She looked up to see a pair of boots spread in a wide stance in the doorway of her office. Slowly, her eyes lifted to see long legs clad in denim, a black hat dangling from a hand and a leather jacket that failed to conceal a hard, lean male body. Dark hair teased Jonathan's collar and green eyes sparkled in his tanned face. He looked like he'd spent a lot of time outdoors during the past two weeks. She felt her pulse increase just looking at him.

"I had to see you." His voice was low and a little uncertain. "How're you doing?"

"I ought to lie and say fine, but I'm not." She wanted to take his shoulders in her hands and shake some sense into him. No, she wanted to run to his arms, but she wasn't making that mistake again. It was his move now.

"I'm not, either. I've come so we can talk this out. We've got some unfinished business that needs tending to. Would you come with me?"

"Where?"

"It's a surprise, but I'm hoping you'll like it. Just get your coat and come on." His eyes pleaded with her. "Please."

"Okay." She'd go with him to the ends of the earth if that's what he wanted.

Outside, the bright sun beat down, warming everything

with radiant heat despite the cool temperature. It was a beautiful afternoon, one that made a person want to spend it outdoors rather than in an office. Regardless of where they were going, she was glad Jonathan had rescued her from the doldrums.

Taking her elbow, he guided her to a dark green vehicle parked in front of the office and unlocked the passenger door.

"This is Ted's pickup," Lauren said, climbing in the truck.

"Yeah, sure is. He loaned it to me." Jonathan slid behind the wheel and buckled his seat belt. "We're going to need it where we're going."

She was intrigued. Where would he be taking her and why? He looked happy and carefree, as if a weight had been lifted from his shoulders. The haunted warrior look was gone, she noticed, as he pulled onto the highway and headed south.

Several minutes passed before he said anything. Then his words were direct and to the point. "Did you mean it when you said you loved me?"

Because he had ignored her declaration when she'd said it, she wanted to deny it now. She was tempted for a moment to be petty, but the look on his face when he glanced her way made her change her mind. She was beyond playing games. "Yes. I meant it."

His hands tightened briefly on the steering wheel, then he smiled and reached across the seat and took her hand. His fingers were warm as they closed around hers. "I was counting on it."

"What do you mean?" She looked at him, at his strong profile, at the narrow red wound searing his temple, at the easy way he sat in the seat. "Does it have something to do with the surprise?"

"Yeah. But before you learn what it is, you need to know something about me." Then he began talking as he stared ahead at the passing grassland. His voice was low and steady. "I was in the import-export business in Mexico. I was making a living, doing pretty well, when some guys in business across the street wanted to join forces with me. Said we'd share some of the overhead. Good for all of us. Sure, I thought. Why not?" He glanced at Lauren.

"A year or so went by before I found out why. They were smuggling drugs in my inventory, under my name." He told her of his inner struggles, his fears, and how he finally decided that setting them up would get the revenge he sought. "I wish I could say I did it just to catch the bad guys, but I didn't. I liked the excitement. And so for ten years, with the help of the DEA, I lived a double life."

Lauren listened intently, never commenting, not wanting to interrupt Jonathan. He knew what he needed to tell her.

"Last year I realized there was no double life at all. I had no personal life to speak of, and I decided I wanted out. Sold my business for a pretty good chunk of money that's gradually being transferred to the U.S." He turned off the highway and drove over a narrow trail that snaked through a pasture.

"It was a little harder to extricate myself than I thought. Just one more sting, I decided. Then I was through."

Lauren wondered if Jonathan knew how much he was like his ancestor.

"The past couple of weeks I've realized how much I've missed by cutting myself off from my family. Being around them has been fun. I've enjoyed playing with my nephews."

The more he talked, the more Lauren knew why she loved him. "You're a good man, just like I said. You needed time to learn who *you* really are—and to separate yourself from John McCain."

"I want to visit the grave you told me about. Tomorrow, maybe, but not today. Other things are more important. I'm not working for the DEA anymore. I'm going to become a bona fide rancher.'' Jonathan eased the pickup to a stop at the mouth of Diablo Canyon. ''This is as far as we drive. You ready for a ride?''

Lauren looked around and saw two saddled horses, heads down and grazing. She was delighted. ''You bet,'' she answered, nearly certain the surprise was a where, not a what.

''I was sure relieved to see you had on jeans.'' He tightened the cinch on one of the saddles. ''But I was planning on taking you by your place if you weren't dressed right.''

''I don't usually wear them to work, but with the office closed for the holiday...'' Her voice trailed off as she realized an explanation was unnecessary. ''How did you get Doc and Taco?''

''You have a very helpful brother.'' Jonathan gave her a Cheshire grin as he swung into the saddle and led off at a lope.

She owed her brother one, Lauren thought as she quickly followed Jonathan. They slowed and picked their way down a winding trail through the dry winter grass into the dark canyon bottom. The sun had long ago slipped below the towering walls, and now she had to strain to see. Not that she needed to. She knew where they were headed: the cave.

When they got to the base of the cliff, Jonathan helped her dismount, his hands lingering at her waist. Lauren sensed his impatience as they quickly hobbled the horses and left them in a patch of brown Bermuda grass near the creek.

She started up the steep bank, lost her footing and slid back down into Jonathan's arms.

He laughed. ''You need any help getting up?''

''No. I can make it on my own.'' She thought of how quickly she'd scaled it when Chester was behind her with a gun. Reaching the top, she waited for Jonathan to join her.

He skirted the thorny limbs of a squat, crooked bush that grew on the ledge in front of the cave entrance.

"Do you know what kind of plant that is?" she asked.

"No."

"It's a paloverde. According to an Indian legend, anyone who sleeps beneath its branches will have good dreams."

He frowned as though he was considering her words. "Legends are often based in truth. After all, I had a wonderful dream here."

He helped her inside, where she was surprised to see lantern light playing against the rock wall and a mound of sleeping bags and supplies piled in the center. Lyna would die of a romantic overdose when she found out about this. Lauren was more than a little overwhelmed herself. There had been occasions when she'd suspected Jonathan was a romantic, but this was above and beyond candlelight dinners or bouquets of roses.

"I met a beautiful lady in my dream," he said.

Lauren didn't know how to respond. A lump formed in her throat and she felt moisture gathering in her eyes as she turned to see the last trace of twilight disappear from the cave mouth.

"Let's see if we can start off on a better foot this time." Jonathan pulled her back against his hard body just as he had done before. She could feel his belt buckle next to her spine, but this time his arms were gentle as he leaned down and whispered against her hair. "What's your name, lady?"

"Lauren—Lauren Hamilton." She turned in the confines of his embrace so she could see him. The golden light from the lantern played across his features. "And yours, cowboy?"

"Jonathan—Jonathan McCain." He stroked her hair away from her face, and as she looked up at him, his eyes filled her with warmth.

"It's nice to meet you at last," she said.

His arms tightened. "Lauren, I'm sorry...I'm truly sorry

I hurt you, but I had to think this through. You were right. I was afraid. I was afraid that when you got to know me better you wouldn't be able to love me.''

"You didn't give me a chance.''

"I know, but I'm the type of man dads chase away with shotguns. I'm more than a little rough on the edges. I've been vengeful, set on material things and more than a little selfish.'' He took a deep breath. "And I didn't like letting people get close to me. But with your help, I can change.''

"I don't think you need my help, because you've already changed. Everything you've said has told me that.'' He'd been soulfully honest and remorseful. But amid all his confessions, he'd also revealed himself to be a capable man who had kept his sensitive nature well under control. But there was no need for that now.

He reached out and stroked the hair away from her face. "I may not always be able to share my thoughts with you like I should, but I can damn sure try. But more than anything, I'll love you as much as any man could possibly love a woman. What I'm saying is, would you marry me?''

In her wildest dreams, she'd never imagined such a beautiful proposal. She was speechless. At no time had they discussed the possibility of a real future together. That had only been a fantasy on her part. Now he was offering her that opportunity.

When she didn't respond immediately, he said, "We can make it work.'' His hands gently cupped her face as he kissed her forehead, her cheeks, the tip of her nose. His fingers combed through her hair with the smoothness of a symphony.

The complexities of this man amazed her. He could be hard and soft, brusque and gentle, confident and fearful. "Jon,'' she murmured, "what changed your mind?''

"While I wrestled with myself the last couple of days, I learned a lot I didn't like. I guess I've never known how to love. My sister gave me a book to read this past summer.

Said it might do me some good. Well, I got around to reading it and she was right. It's called *The Little Prince.*''

"I've read the story,'' Lauren said. "I've always loved it.''

"Then you know what I mean when I say you've tamed me, Lauren. I was trying to reason, to use my brain. But it's with the heart, not the brain, that one can see rightly. My heart needs you.''

"Then the answer is a thousand times yes, Jonathan McCain. I'd love to be your wife.''

The flame in the lantern flickered, taking with it all the tension in the cave. She could feel the heat of Jonathan's breath on her hair, filling her with peace. So this was what it felt like to love and be loved. Somehow, Lauren knew the old ranger had just given his approval.

* * * * *